S. HARVEY

One Man's Inheritance

One Man's Inheritance

JOHN ATTENBOROUGH

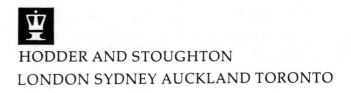

HODDER AND STOUGHTON
LONDON SYDNEY AUCKLAND TORONTO

British Library Cataloguing in Publication Data

Attenborough, John
  One man's inheritance
  I. Title
  823'.9'1F   PR6051.T/

  ISBN 0-340-23870-4

Author's Note

IN THE LITTLE Kingdom, as the County of Kent is sometimes called, you will find no village called Ockenham. But hidden among the farms and fields, unnoticed by the London motorists scurrying to the coast, are many villages which might claim to be Ockenham, and many great houses where the Mortimer-Wottons would still feel at home and among friends.

While the characters in this novel are strictly fictitious and bear no resemblance to any living persons, they are in a strange way my most familiar friends, for they have permitted me to share their world.

J.A.

Contents

Book One

A Gentleman is Born

How happy is he born and taught,
That serveth not another's will!
Whose armour is his honest thought,
And simple truth his utmost skill.

SIR HENRY WOTTON (1568–1639)

Hogben's Farm

Water Meadows

to Chartham

Little Ockenham

Main Road

The Dower House

Trout Stream

Cart Track

The Lake

Dark's Place

Ha-Ha
Lawns

Post

Kitchen
Garden

Great
House

High ground

Hill Stream

Ockenham Woods

1

IN 1902 AT the age of fourteen Gwynedd Morgan entered the service of the Mortimer-Wottons at the Great House. The embossed writing paper in the library spelt out the address – Ockenham Manor, Ockenham, near Canterbury, Kent; and soon after Gwynedd arrived she was taught by Mrs. Mortimer-Wotton always to write it in full at the top right-hand corner of the Sunday letter she was expected to post each week to her father and mother at 3, Prospect Villas, Deal. This was part of her training. Actually, everybody in the village of Ockenham referred to the Wottons' ancestral home as the Great House – or just simply as the House. Indeed, if a letter had been despatched to Mrs. Mortimer-Wotton with no address at all, it would still have been delivered to Ockenham Manor by Ben Wilson, the local postman, as surely as night follows day.

The new and strange world that Gwynedd entered seemed far removed from that of her mining family, although her home in Prospect Villas was less than twenty miles away. It was really the old doctor in Deal who engineered her change in station. The Morgans could not afford to rent a larger house away from the complex of semi-detached colliery cottages into one of which their overlarge family was crowded. And with Gwynedd leaving school with excellent reports, she was the one to seek new pastures. The Morgans were not easily persuaded – the family and chapel loyalties of the Welsh being as strong in Kent as they are in their native valleys. But the doctor reassured them. His colleague, Dr. Gardiner of Ockenham, had told him that Mrs. Mortimer-Wotton was personally known to him and half the county as a kind and responsible person and the Morgans could be certain that no harm would come to their eldest daughter.

So, early in August at the end of the school term, Gwynedd was

13

installed in a small bedroom at the Great House, close to the cook's room. Her first duties were to help Mrs. Constant in the kitchen: but she soon found herself responsible for cleaning upstairs – and more especially Mrs. Mortimer-Wotton's lovely bedroom which looked out to the garden and across the ha-ha to the lake and parkland beyond. Gradually she learnt about the family that owned Ockenham Manor – partly from the gossip in the kitchen, but chiefly from the lady of the house. Inevitably she became part of the family.

Constance Mortimer-Wotton had been a widow since 1879, when her husband had been killed in an ambush in South Africa, unsuccessfully trying to save the life of the young Prince Imperial, the last hope of the Bonapartes and the only son of Napoléon III and the Empress Eugénie. Mrs. Mortimer-Wotton never talked about her husband now. It was as if that gallant, useless skirmish in Zululand had concluded a chapter in her life which was never to be re-opened. But evidence abounded all over the house that her five years' marriage to Henry had been a happy chapter. There was, for example, the picture on the right-hand side of Mrs. Mortimer-Wotton's dressing table – the one in the silver frame which Gwynedd cleaned assiduously once a week. There she saw a very handsome officer wearing the uniform of the East Kent Yeomanry and below it the ribbon of a medal posthumously awarded. Again, there was a photograph in one of the drawers, apparently taken at a friend's villa in the South of France and inscribed, "Connie and Harry, Monte Carlo, 1876." In the library Harry's presence could be seen and felt all over the place: in two cricketing groups for instance, one in the Eton eleven: another, somewhat older, showing Harry resplendent in a striped blazer and a boater worn at a rakish angle: or again, by a water colour sketch of a horse signed H.M-W set against the easily recognisable background of Ockenham park: and even by a variety of silver cups which left little doubt that Henry Mortimer-Wotton had been artist and athlete as well as a soldier of the Queen. In every sense he fitted the picture. He was not the first of his line to be killed in battle in the flower of his youth, as the inscriptions in Ockenham Church bore witness.

14

As his living memorial there were his two sons – 'Mr. Charles' and 'Mr. Francis', as Gwynedd Morgan learned to call them. Both had inevitably followed their father to Eton. When Gwynedd arrived at the Great House, both were still unmarried and living at home when they were not enjoying the hospitality of their friends. Unvoiced though it was, there was little doubt as to Constance Mortimer-Wotton's feeling for the two sons whom she had brought up. Charles, the older boy and now aged twenty-six, was considered to be basically good but uninteresting. Francis, two years younger, was bad but exciting. Constance could think quite dispassionately about her children and her responsibility for them. She understood the form exactly. One was reliable and rather serious, the other was not – or that was how her analytical mind reasoned.

Many mothers among the County families of East Kent wondered hopefully whether their daughters might not attract the elder son's attention. After all, one could hardly do better in Edwardian England than marry the heir to the three thousand acres which went with the Great House at Ockenham. And Charles had the most charming way with him. Perhaps his patent dislike for cricket and horses did not quite fit the pattern. More Wotton than Mortimer, it was said. More of the poetic artistic strain that stemmed from the Wottons than the fighting qualities of the Lords of the Marches. Still, the position he inherited was big enough to dispense with titles or qualifications, commanding as it did almost unique status among the landed gentry of the County. If Charles's chief interest seemed to be climbing in Switzerland, which was regarded as a dangerous pastime and basically anti-social, this could be a passing and youthful phase. To match-making mothers at the turn of the century, Charles was the man to watch.

The same could hardly be said of his brother Francis. Blessed with his father's good looks and with more than his share of athletic ability emphasised by a match-winning schoolboy century at Lords, he was 'living it up' in no uncertain way. He followed the horses in the most expensive Edwardian style. He gambled for over-high stakes both at Ascot and the Bachelors' Club: and in all this seemed to enjoy the devil's own luck. His name was often in the gossip columns. There had been a party at Kettners, they said – much champagne and chorus girls – the noise of which had shaken Society, not to mention a certain royal personage who was there that evening. And when, for a handsome bet, Francis had abandoned one of the season's more prestigious dances in order to lap Grosvenor Square in pants and vest, the talk of the town had worked overtime. Eligible daughters should be warned to avoid his company – at least until the oats were sown.

Edwardian society therefore registered considerable shock when in July 1905 Bertha Hollingbourne, only daughter of Sir George Hollingbourne of Ranmoor, Sheffield, announced her engagement to Francis Mortimer-Wotton, younger son of the late Major Henry Mortimer-Wotton, D.S.O. and Mrs. Mortimer-Wotton. Surely Bertha's wealthy and recently knighted father would be alive to the gossip, no less in the busy distance of Sheffield than in the emptiness of the grouse moors. Surely Bertha, large, solid and Yorkshire bred, was not the right bride for the young rip. And anyway, what on earth was Francis doing getting engaged to this big, determined girl from the Steel City? He just wasn't running true to form. Society heads wagged agreement. In the County the only person who remained perfectly calm was Constance Mortimer-Wotton. After a moment of surprise and an hour's talk with Francis, she quietly established friendly relations with the Hollingbournes and only used her diplomatic and managerial skills to persuade them to stage the wedding at St. George's, Hanover Square, and the reception at Claridges. Never for a moment did she show anything but delight that Francis had decided to settle down with Bertha. "An excellent thing to have some good Yorkshire blood in the family," she declared to her neighbours, "and splendid to have the Dower House occupied again."

The Dower House is a traditional Georgian mansion built by an eighteenth-century Wotton, situated close to the hamlet of Little Ockenham, about half a mile away from the Great House. Overlooking a tributary of the Stour which flows quietly towards Canterbury through the Wotton land, the house's tiled roof, fine windows and high rooms exemplify Georgian architecture at its best. Bertha first saw it late on a September afternoon at an hour when the setting sun enriched the mellow red brick and high-lighted in marvellous contrast the background greens of the fields and oaks and beeches. To her, the house was a jewel worthy of its setting. A bit of a change, she admitted with a wry smile, from the solid Victorian house in Sheffield where she had been brought up: but, after her mother's death, wasn't it exactly what she and her father always intended?

Her participation in the London Season, organised by Sir George Hollingbourne through his City banking friends, had pre-pared her for change, its purpose being a planned advance into the charmed world where the Mortimer-Wottons and their like rode so nonchalantly. For both father and daughter the process had been hell. An expensive hell for Sir George Hollingbourne who paid for the dresses and the dinner parties – paid in a thousand subtle ways for the services of the Honourable Mrs. Maxwell Mottingham. But Bertha's was a more personal and far from merry hell, as she was launched, a year or two later than most, into Society's dances, Society's Ascot, Society's clichés, Society's chatter and – most terrifying of all – Society's patronising amusement as expressed by hordes of idiotic girls who had never seen England north of the Thames and looked on Bertha as if she came from another world – which was, in a manner of speaking, true. Over-size girls of less character than Bertha would have withered and died in the pro-cess, as the Honourable Mrs. Mottingham, who admired the girl's courage, was honest enough to admit. But she'd had this out with the girl's father before the London Season opened: and Sir George had, in his own style, warned his daughter. "Now look here, Bertha lass," he'd said before leaving for the North, "you're going to be miserable for the next eight months, we won't fool ourselves on that. But we know where we're going, eh? Mottingham is a sensible old trout and kind at heart, I reckon. She'll see you right." As she bloody well ought to do, he added as a personal after-thought, addressing himself to the backside of the poor old nag grinding along towards St. Pancras Station.

So for Bertha, the London Season of 1905 was hell pure and simple. Hell *tout simple*, she smiled, trying out one of the French phrases from M. Grandineau's *Le petit précepteur*, a book which had once given instruction in French to the late queen. Suddenly at the Duchess of Sutherland's house in Grosvenor Square, hell changed to heaven. A young man was introduced to Bertha. Tall enough for Bertha to forget her own height. Blue eyes, fair hair, a fair moustache and he moved into the waltz with an elegant authority in the greatest possible contrast to the clumsy, slightly alcoholic, energy of the young subalterns from Wellington Barracks. Francis and Bertha danced, they sat in the conservatory, they sipped Champagne and Bertha knew in a flash that she had placed her not very delicate feet firmly in the Mortimer-Wotton world.

The Hon. Mrs. Maxwell Mottingham watched from a discreet distance. My God, that boy's got a nerve, she thought, after all the how-de-do in the papers last week. Who'd have expected him to turn up in Grosvenor Square, of all places? And in this she did no more than echo the views of her colleagues in the 'coming out' game. Sniggering fools, they could afford to smile. They weren't responsible for Bertha. But no point in wrecking the evening. These problems were part of the job she was paid to do. Next day would be time enough to have a word with the child. But next day was a day too late. She'd been anticipated by the same young man, armed with flowers most carefully chosen. By the time Mrs. Mottingham entered the morning room, Francis Mortimer-Wotton was conversing easily with Bertha and there was a warmth about Bertha's smile which made even an old hand wonder who was the hunter and who was the hunted.

Edna Mottingham salved her conscience by writing a progress report to the girl's father, mentioning that Bertha was receiving marked attention from young Francis Mortimer-Wotton of Ockenham near Canterbury. The rest followed in its pre-ordained way. Sir George saw Francis and they discussed the prospects for 'the Twelfth'. Francis introduced Bertha to his mother. A wedding was arranged and late in October 1905, Francis and Bertha came home as man and wife from their Paris honeymoon.

By the time of their return, Bertha's life with Francis was totally new, totally absorbing, totally happy. Looking back, she could hardly remember the Archbishop taking the service. ("I'm sure you'll like him, my dear: he's a very good friend of the family.") She'd been deaf to all that army of names, Cornwallis, Guilford,

18

Northbourne, Harris, Amherst, Culpepper. On, on they came, complete with their formidable wives, as the man in the red coat mouthed the names and titles with all the relish of his temporary authority. Occasionally, Mrs. Mortimer-Wotton would whisper that this was Aunt Sophie from Ickham or Uncle Matthew from Boughton Monchelsea. Nothing held any meaning for Bertha – nothing at all – until she and Francis were away to Charing Cross and a first-class carriage of the South Eastern Railway. Even then – and for another five days – she'd been bemused, sort of puzzled. Was a society marriage really going to be as slow as the train to Tonbridge? Oh yes, Francis was full of praise, told her how marvellously she'd stood up to all those guests, admired her dove grey going-away dress, raising her little travelling veil to kiss her forehead. And then, at the Angel in Tonbridge where they spent their first night together, he'd been so very gentle, so very considerate. In Paris she asked him, provoking him, how he'd learnt to speak French and know Paris so well. But Francis smiled in the most good-natured way. He continued to say the nicest things. He was invincibly correct: at lunch time in the Ritz, sipping a Blanc de Blanc: visiting the Louvre and the Luxembourg gardens: entertained by one of Francis's school friends *en poste* at the Embassy in the rue Saint Honoré.

So the first unreal days of their honeymoon continued – part of a stylised play in which Bertha felt she was just one of the cast. Francis, her Francis, didn't love her at all. Or did he? What was the game? Could it be he was after her father's money? Or was it simply his upbringing – this boarding school business, this monastic man-only Eton or something – which actually made him nervous of her? Could he only make love, real love, to girls of another type? Were these courtesies part of the society game? Well, the ball was in her court: and she'd win. She'd show him that a girl from Sheffield could set him alight – and to hell with his fine manners. She laughed to herself, a little smile of triumph, as she remembered that sixth night in Paris. It was the evening they took a box at the opera. Who knows? *La Traviata* may have provided the spark to her intention. She smiled again. At her prompting they'd ordered supper after the theatre, chicken in aspic washed down with an imperial pint of champagne – no less. She left Francis to finish the bottle and went upstairs. She undressed thoughtfully, left her long nightie on the chair by the window, waited for him – only her head showing above the sheets of the white and gold bed. He seemed to take an age to arrive – an age undressing, cleaning his teeth, brushing his moustache. But at last he was beside her. It was then she called him Frankie for the first time. "Frankie darling," she remembered herself saying, "I'm no different from the others. Look at me, feel me, give me your hands, your mouth, show me you really love me, every bit of me . . . yes, my lovely man, take me now, now . . ." and even as they lay beside each other, Bertha knew the ecstasy of victory. After that there was no more restraint, no more doubt.

The two loved each other as naturally and happily as any other lovers in Paris that night. They made love again as the sun rose over the city. And Denise the maid who came in with the breakfast smiled as she collected Madame's nightdress from the chair.

Francis, too, felt a new sense of freedom. Looking into the Ritz's gilded shaving mirror, he addressed his well-lathered face with humorous but far from cynical resignation. "So your fine friends will say you've been had for a sucker, will they? Marry an heiress and bring joy to your bank manager? Damn it, that's what they said. Pouch the money and carry on as usual. Sounded simple, eh? But they knew nothing. Good God, they'd not been confronted with this girl's eyes, grey and honest as the day. They'd never understood her speech and mind, a world away from the mock-sophistication of the London débutantes. Life's ordered better in Yorkshire. And now you're hooked, Francis old lad. Better forget the 'men only' holidays in Deauville and that rapacious Madame and her girls in the rue de Provence. Life starts again, right now." Without a care in the world, he returned to the bedroom. Standing close beside each other at the window, he and Bertha looked out across the Place Vendôme. A new day had dawned for them both.

They took a picnic in the Bois de Boulogne, not a formal lunch at the Pré Catalan: there was a corner in the wood where they made love to each other and Frankie's light suit was ruined. And then they were away from the Ritz and up to Montmartre where, for a drink and a few francs, a long-haired art student with high cheek bones and deep-set eyes made a charcoal sketch of them as they sipped their wine. He'd handed Bertha his picture. *"Pour Madame,"* he had said, *"un petit souvenir."* And then, with an exaggerated bow, he had backed away through the crowd to get another drink with the money Francis had given him.

Now back at Ockenham they were getting their new home organised and Bertha was in the driving seat. The painting and repairs were done. The Chippendale chairs, the gift of Francis's mother, were in place in the dining room. The all too formal drawing room was warm with the Isfahan carpet which Sir George had given them. And at last the carrier had arrived with the crate of paintings forwarded by M. Dunoir from Paris. Bertha had used her own money and taste to buy them. Francis was happy enough to follow her lead and really they'd been modest in price. Dunoir said there were few people wanting them for the time being – but Madame would never regret her purchase. Bertha and Francis unpacked them together. The two small canvasses that seemed to contain all the sunshine of Provence went to the morning room: the big Dieppe seafront canvas – that was for the drawing room: the fishermen on the Seine, they would look splendid above the dining room fireplace: and finally there was the little sketch which Dunoir had agreed to frame for them. They looked at it together. Bertha said, "I bet no other girl in the County has seen you look like that, Frankie."

Francis had laughed, "No other man in Kent has seen you with nothing on, my Yorkshire darling."

Strange how that student, in all that smoke and noise, had seen right through them, seen them as they now saw themselves.

Her mother-in-law had sent up some men from the big house to help with the furniture. Bertha gave them instructions as to the pictures for the reception room. Then conspiratorially she and Francis went upstairs together. They took the sketch to their bedroom. It was too intimate for display. It was for themselves. They locked the door and lay beside each other conscious of no other world but their own.

The autumn of 1905 turned to winter. Early in the new year, Bertha told Francis she was sure she was pregnant. Old Dr.

21

Gardiner, who lived the other side of Ockenham on the way to Canterbury, confirmed the news, made his calculations and suggested that Mrs. Mortimer-Wotton would like to hear the news from Bertha before it reached the village. It was a close-run thing. In no time at all, Ockenham knew a baby was expected at the Dower House. Ben Wilson got wind of it from the kitchen staff. Breaking all security regulations, he told old John Williams at the Home Farm and then for good measure, dropped in on Jack Kemsing at the Wotton Arms. News has always travelled fast in Ockenham and the Wotton Arms is a very lively communication centre, though not always one hundred per cent accurate with its information. However, it was right this time. When Mrs. Mortimer-Wotton casually informed the vicar over tea, Edward Pendlebury assumed his pleased, slightly surprised, 'How-good-of-you-to-tell-me' look. But of course he didn't deceive Constance. The moment she saw his expression she knew he'd heard the news already. And really, why should they not all know? In a strange way, the village was part of the family. Bertha and Francis were happy. The Yorkshire girl was strong and sensible. If in due course Sam Gardiner arrived late as he usually did, Nurse Bracken from the village would be in time for all eventualities – she liked being first on the scene.

And that was the way of it. In the first week of September Bertha gave birth to a baby boy. 'No trouble at all,' said Nurse Bracken. 'No trouble at all,' echoed Dr. Gardiner as he took the news to Constance at the Great House. The little boy was strong, the mother's labour had not been too difficult. Francis was with her. An ancient tree would flourish for another generation. That evening Francis dropped in to the Wotton Arms to baptise the baby as they say down there. Free drinks all round and here's to the health of Philip Mortimer-Wotton – one day old and seven pounds heavy. Long life to him and happiness. Jack Kemsing swore that the people of Ockenham drank as much Kentish ale that night as they did at the Coronation of Edward VII.

2

CONSTANCE MORTIMER-WOTTON was a good-looking woman. The classical features, the bright eyes, the warm skin were still evident. Allied now to the poise and serenity of middle age, they gave her a distinction, a sort of authority which many a younger woman envied. She enjoyed the admiration of men like Harry's old friend Colonel Duncan over at Chilham who loved to be seen in her company and do her bidding. At first, the colonel's interest in his friend's widow had been flattering, then embarrassing and finally a little ridiculous. But the dear man's attentions, Constance reflected as she stared across the rose garden of the Great House, had at least presented her with the clearest of alternatives – to remarry and start another family and another home: or to remain in charge of Ockenham until Charles and Francis were old enough to take their father's place. She had chosen the second course of her own free will and accord and – she told herself firmly – she had no regrets. As to Tom Duncan, he could now be regarded as one, perhaps the most trusted and most understanding, of the many friends who'd helped her through these last twenty-five years while the boys were growing up.

Today, at half-past nine on a cloudless June morning in 1908, Constance was sitting dressed unfussily in a white, high neckline blouse and a full length skirt – her only jewellery, the cameo brooch given her as a wedding present by Henry's mother. Her dark hair was worn in the style of the day – piled high, perfectly secured and not a trace of grey in it. She was gazing at the garden from her desk in the small room at the south-west corner of the house which, since Harry's death, had been peculiarly her own. The west window of the room looked out on the garden and the lake, and from the outside of the house would have appeared part of the grandiose Palladian façade constructed after the old house had been gutted by fire in the eighteenth century. But the front of the house was deceptive. Turn to the window facing south and one looked out on an ancient wall built in Kentish rag and now marking the boundaries of a large and beautifully tended kitchen garden. Beyond the wall were the remains of a moat which still carried water from a hill stream to the lake. And the same moat could be traced in the ha-ha separating the flower garden and croquet lawn from the meadows sloping down to the lake and the trout stream beyond. Constance was sitting in one of the two ground floor rooms which had survived the 1770 fire, the other being the library which opened out of it. Tudor, Angevin, Norman, who would name the founding date of the first house which the moat had guarded? Architects who love the symmetry of form were all too ready to dismiss the Great House as a hotchpotch, a mess. Constance only knew that each generation of the family had added some idiosyncratic touch to the structure and that she and Harry had found their greatest personal joy in this part of the house where the Wottons had lived for eight hundred years. These two rooms were the heart of the matter.

Constance's daily routine never varied. Early morning tea with a slice of thin cut bread and butter at seven o'clock. At eight prompt, a light breakfast – guests and other members of the family having the right to show up later and eat more, if they so desired. By eight-thirty she would be ready to see the head gardener, Ted Larkin: at eight forty-five Mr. Absalom the butler: and at nine o'clock Mrs. Constant, the cook. By nine-fifteen, she would have settled the multiple problems of staff and commissariat. She was then free to arrange the larger business of her day – the family, the church, the village, the guests, the visits to friends who were mostly to be found in a ten mile radius from Canterbury: the occasional train journey to London where she would stay at her sister's house in Chelsea and generally manage to include a theatre or concert in her business or shopping programme. She liked to keep up to date with the theatre and was now rather proud of the fact that she had been one of the first to spot the talent of a young actress called Sybil Thorndike on her first appearance on the London stage.

But on this particular June day, she was concerned to provide lunch for the family solicitor, Mr. Justin Leadbitter, senior partner of Dawson and Leadbitter, and an old friend who made no secret of enjoying his food and wine.

The basic plan for his entertainment was already agreed. "You suggest grilled lamb cutlets, Mrs. Constant? That will do very well, I think. Ted Larkin is digging some new potatoes and will have the first French beans ready. A claret – The Château Figeac, Absalom? Yes, provided you're sure it's not too heavy; and perhaps a half-bottle of Sauternes for the strawberries."

Justin Leadbitter and Constance enjoyed each other's company. But today's visit was exceptional. Normally Constance would call at his Castle Street offices when she happened to be in Canterbury. There they could talk about the shortcomings of Higginson's who acted as Agents for the estate and were responsible for rent collections. They might also discuss investment policy and settle various village family problems, before proceeding to a lunch at which Justin would bring her up to date with the affairs of cathedral and city. She placed great trust in Justin Leadbitter. He was still a very good solicitor, full of knowledge and human kindness. Interested in life whether it was seen against the sunshine of cricket on the St. Lawrence ground or against the gloom of a family in trouble. And discreet, discreet as a Trappist monk. Come to think of it, his tonsure, if not his appetite, would have suited the habit of a monk.

But why, Constance wondered, had he suggested a visit to Ockenham? Her question was partly answered shortly after midday when a thunderous noise from the direction of the drive announced the solicitor's arrival. Constance hurried to the front door. "Good heavens, Justin, what's this monstrous thing?"

"Oh, come, come, Connie it's a beauty, brand new, my first car, a Darracq, a real thoroughbred. Had to show it to you. Must move with the times you know. Did the twelve miles in sixty minutes. Not bad, eh? Frightened a few sheep – but never a touch." and Mr. Leadbitter, aware of many eyes at many windows, proudly and a little short of breath descended from his now silent and stationary motor carriage.

"Well," said Constance. "That's a relief. Thank God you haven't slaughtered anybody en route. Would you care for a wash – at the back of the hall, you know where it is? Then come and tell me what's really brought you and your blessed Darracq to Ockenham."

During the meal they gossiped of this and that. "Delicious, my dear, and a really excellent claret," Justin remarked loudly enough for Absalom to hear his compliment and repeat his praise to the cook. Only after coffee had been served did Justin come out with the true reason for his visit. "Money, Constance, that's what my visit's really about. If we're not careful, your family's going to find itself out of cash. Those boys of yours are deuced expensive. And we may all have to revise our ideas with this Liberal Government in power. These new ministers, especially Lloyd George and young Churchill, have got it in for us – or so it seems to me. And their new ideas may well affect our whole way of life, at any rate our spending and saving habits, over the next ten years." Justin paused to sip his coffee. Then he became more explicit. Charles and Francis were equally on his mind.

"Let's take Charles first. Thirty, isn't he? What do you say? Shouldn't he be settling down to run the estate, with or without a wife? Tell me more about him, Constance – where he is and what he's up to."

Justin detected a note of hesitation and anxiety in her usually assured voice. Yes, she'd heard from Charles only yesterday, ... er, a longish letter from Venice. Venice? Well, he'd moved on there from Switzerland with a friend from his Eton days. "He loves travelling, you know. Apparently he hopes to find out more about one of the sixteenth-century Wottons – old Sir Henry Wotton who ended up as Provost of Eton. Apart from writing a poem or two, he headed some special mission to the Doge in the days when Venice was the banking centre of Europe. But you can tell that to the Marines," Constance exploded. "If you ask me, I'd say old Sir Henry is all my eye – a sort of schoolboy excuse. Charles now tells me – can you believe it? – he's planning to stay in Italy for the next twelve months. Writes that he's moving south to Naples and Capri when the winter mists drive him out of Venice. And before you put the question, Justin – yes, his Etonian friend and travelling companion will be moving south with him. I'm sickened by the whole business and a bit shattered, but what the devil do we do? It's Charles's life, not ours. This friend of his, who has stayed here once or twice, is to my mind an odious young man. Polite enough and very knowledgeable in artistic things, and they've always interested Charles. But you know what I mean?" Mr. Leadbitter who'd been a practising solicitor for forty years knew very well indeed. This sort of thing was always cropping up these days – and in the best families too.

He was silent for a moment, then he said gently, "I'm sorry you're so worried about Charles. I think I understand. But let's turn for a moment to Francis. I met him the other day in Canterbury and he seemed very pleased with his set-up at Little Ockenham. Very much in love, I'd say. And Bertha's just the girl for him."

"Yes, indeed." Constance relaxed. "He's blissfully happy with his bride and the little boy; and, of course, he has lots of cricket and racing to keep him occupied. There's only one problem and my practical Yorkshire daughter-in-law voiced it bluntly in this very room only a few days back. 'Mother,' she said, 'Father's been asking me what Francis does all day: he means, how does he earn his living? And to be honest, I'm stumped for an answer.' "

That gave Justin the opening he needed – seemed as if they were all thinking along the same lines. In the circumstances he felt free to tell Constance, as he'd told Francis, that the boy really must get clear of the packet of debts he'd piled up in London before he married. "I fancy he may have thought originally that marrying a steel magnate's daughter would put him in the clear. But he knows now that old Hollingbourne's dowry is in the form of shares in his Company. It's being used by Bertha, as dividends come in, to make improvements at Little Ockenham. And Francis, I'm glad to say, accepts the situation. Let's face it, Constance. At Little Ockenham Yorkshire has scored a signal victory over Kent."

"That's as may be," said Constance, who was inclined to be impatient with these male cricketing analogies. "But let's get down to business and, by way of a start, see how we can get these debts off Francis's back – if only to give his marriage a fair wind and keep it on course."

Together they made their plans. Justin advised selling the family's Speyside property in the Highlands. It had been bought as an investment two generations back; but it was a sporting estate or it was nothing, and he reckoned it could only be justified if it was used. "If we sell it entire, the cash – let's put it at £50,000 – can be divided equally between the two boys." He would ensure that Francis used his share to get rid of the past. With luck, he might persuade him to give up his flat off St. James's and, maybe, drop one or two of his clubs. Mr. Leadbitter implied he could handle Francis easily enough in his present frame of mind. He might also see whether the name of Francis Mortimer-Wotton might not look well on the board of one or two local enterprises – he'd thought of one of the Faversham breweries or the Kent Insurance Company which had just merged with the Royal. But now, perhaps, they should think further. Did not the older brother's plans suggest that it would be wise to bring Francis into the management of the estate?

Anxious about Charles, Constance was easy to convince. A double insurance, Justin called it and returned to the subject of Charles. "I think, my dear, that if Charles is staying on in Italy, I should make a journey to Venice and have a talk with him to see what's on his mind. You can't do much by writing and it's never easy to change a man's nature – nor a woman's for that matter." And there was the suspicion of a twinkle in the solicitor's eye. "But supposing I feel certain Charles is not the marrying sort, shall we say – then, I would like to make it clear that he must live on his investment income and what he earns by his own efforts. The estate cannot finance him 'in absentia', whether he's climbing in the Alps or sunning himself in Capri."

The long and short of it was that six weeks later Mr. Justin Leadbitter met Charles at the Danieli in Venice. The estate in the Highlands was sold for a most satisfactory sum. The elder brother found himself in receipt of a fixed income paid into his personal account at the Banco di Napoli. And Francis, easy-going, hail-fellow-well-met, and now relieved of his London commitments, began seriously to study the running of the estate.

Bertha was delighted with these new developments. She had nothing against Charles. He'd been a very efficient best man to his younger brother. He'd written the nicest of all the letters she'd received after the birth of her baby. But for her the salient point was that Francis, her Francis, would have a job to do for the first time in his life. And their young Philip – why not admit it, Frankie? – might find himself with an inheritance that neither she nor Francis nor anyone else for that matter could have imagined two years earlier. No good wondering what had caused Charles to opt out. Just face the facts, Frankie love: and get on with the job. You've got me beside you and Philip too. He's worth a bit of an effort.

Strange how quickly and easily these changes come to be accepted. Nobody could have been more discreet than Justin Leadbitter or Constance Mortimer-Wotton in making their dispositions. There was no visible change in the behaviour of Bertha and Francis at Little Ockenham – just that the latter was more to be seen in his mother's room at the Great House, and riding more often to the outlying farms and cottages of the estate. But down in the village people took more interest in 'Mrs. Francis' and the baby. They liked asking about Philip when Bertha called at the village shops. They paused to have a look at the pram when they were making their deliveries at the Dower House.

And this was true of the servants at the Great House. Especially Gwynedd Morgan, now clearly established as Mrs. M-W's personal maid. She was often asked to take messages from her mistress to Mrs. Francis at the Dower House. Messages, and that assortment of packages such as ladies like Mrs. Mortimer-Wotton constantly conjure up for their children and grandchildren – fresh vegetables perhaps, or a picking of raspberries: a box of chocolates, or one of Mrs. Constant's sponge cakes. Sometimes, on her half day off if the weather was fine, Gwynedd would take the footpath past the lake and across the park to Little Ockenham. Mrs. Constant used to tease her, knowing that one of the cottages housed a Baptist family who took Gwynedd with them to chapel in Chartham on Sunday evenings. Serious-minded people they were, worked hard and tended to keep themselves to themselves. Strict teetotallers too. "I shouldn't wonder, Miss Gwynedd Morgan," said Mrs. Constant as she rolled some pastry for a fruit pie, "if there isn't a young man with his eye on you down there."

Gwynedd smiled her enigmatic Welsh smile and said nothing. Mrs. Constant was always planning a romance for somebody. The truth was more simple. Gwynedd loved looking after babies, dressing them and playing with them just as she'd done with her brothers and sisters back in Prospect Villas. She didn't go over there now. It took too long. It was hardly worth it except for her annual week's holiday. And really she was so involved in the daily life at Ockenham that she was losing touch with her parents, even losing her Welsh accent as her Dad had remarked on her last visit to Deal. But Master Philip was there, close at hand, with his welcoming smile. It was a great moment for the Welsh girl when she returned with the news that Philip had walked for the first time – at least six steps: and then – a little later – when he called her Gwen. "Really, Ma'am, he really did."

Constance Mortimer-Wotton was delighted to get these progress reports from her diminutive Gwynedd. She confided to Bertha that Gwynedd Morgan was proving a treasure, which was the highest praise in Constance's vocabulary.

3

CONSTANCE was beginning to recognise in Bertha a woman after her own heart. To have made Francis happy and to have brought him back to Ockenham was quite a feat. But it was not simply that she had taken Francis in hand, or that she had produced an heir. There were other qualities that the older woman admired in the Yorkshire girl. Her common sense in running her home and winning the respect of the servants during her four years residence at Little Ockenham. Her skill in learning the names and backgrounds of the familes that lived on the Mortimer-Wotton land. Her gift for making friends in the village. Above all, her ability to fit into the local social scene without surrendering an ounce of her own forthright personality.

In Edwardian England the landed gentry of Kent were no more peculiar than those of Sussex or Hampshire or Northamptonshire. Like the members of other privileged communities they tended to develop a sort of case law of their own, a set of rules which the Establishment observed and nobody else understood. Constance who had learnt the rules in her early married life was only too happy to act as a tutor to her daughter-in-law, answering her questions about the local mysteries which the County took so seriously – the time to arrive and the clothes to wear on Ladies Day in Canterbury Cricket Week; the connection between I. Zingari and the Old Stagers and the Band of Brothers; the difference between a Man of Kent and a Kentish Man; the parallel distinction to be drawn between the Buffs and the Royal West Kent Regiment; the relationship between the civic leaders and those who lived within the Cathedral precinct. It was really very simple. Some things were 'done' and others 'not done' in Canterbury. And this girl from Sheffield made sure, by doing her homework, that she didn't make a 'gaffe' that might embarrass Francis or Constance in the enclosed society of which the Cathedral city was the fulcrum.

A deep affection grew naturally between the two women. They could laugh together. One day after a tedious social call, Bertha let herself go. "Do you know what I'd like to do with some of Francis's friends, Mother? Pack 'em in a train to York, send the men over to Sheffield to sit out three days at Bramall Lane and take their wives on a tour of York. Then the wives would come to Sheffield, and full of a new experience of beauty, confirm to their mates that York's a match for Canterbury any day of the week, with treasures and history that give it as good a claim as Canterbury to be called 'the Mother of England'. Yes – and we'd stage this grand re-union between the wives and husbands in father's steel plant where they could all feel the heat of the blast furnaces and really see York-shiremen at work. What do you say?' And she laughed, sensing that Constance must also have faced similar irritations thirty years earlier. The two women were like rebel conspirators who disci-pline their tongues more easily by sharing a common secret. But the occasional joke at society's expense was for themselves – it was an 'in' joke. To the outside world Bertha was 'to the manner born' and Francis adored her.

Now she was pregnant again. Some eighteen months after the birth of their first child, she and Francis had been very depressed by an early miscarriage. But these disappointments came to many 'young marrieds' Dr. Gardiner assured them. No cause for worry. Take things quietly and next time all would be well. The doctor's prediction seemed to be coming true. Another six months and young Philip, now nearly three years old, would have a brother or sister to play with. That would be good for him too. Bertha looked forward to bringing up a big family. As for Francis, he was carefree and full of the joy of life as he kissed his wife goodbye in the first week of August, on his way to the Yorkshire moors to join her father's shoot. "I'll send you a brace of grouse," he promised Bertha. "They'll be the very first to be shot on the twelfth: and then, when I return, we'll enjoy a special celebration *à deux*."

Bertha was happy too. It was an additional joy that Francis seemed to hit it off so well with her father.

On 12th August, after a solitary breakfast, Constance went to her room as usual. She looked at the sporting calendar on her desk without pleasure, as she noted the special prominence accorded to the start of the grouse shooting. In the old days, 'the Twelfth' had been for her a red letter day – the journey to Scotland with its preparations and packings and picnics: and then, the marvellous freedom of the moors. Come hell and high water, she and Harry and their friends would get clean away from the conventions and inhibitions of their own little world. What fun it had been, what memories it conjured up. Constance pulled herself together with a jerk. This sort of thinking had no purpose at all. Better to be glad that Francis was enjoying Sir George Hollingbourne's hospitality in Yorkshire, and get on with her own job.

But the morning proved quite as 'trying' as she had anticipated. First, there'd been a visit from Mrs. Manners, married to a good-for-nothing husband, who was generally in the Wotton Arms and, as often as not out of a job. What was it this time? Amid a flood of tears Florrie Manners announced that another daughter was in trouble. Why couldn't the woman use the word pregnant? And what else could she expect from that horde of children bereft of love and discipline? They were bound to get loose in the hop-gardens and the potato fields. No local farmer would employ the husband on a regular basis and she wished to high heaven she could banish the complete Manners family from Ockenham. But none of this showed as she spoke quietly to the mother. "Now dry those tears Mrs. Manners, and let's consider what is the best thing to do. Your daughter doesn't know which young man it is, you say? And you've no idea? Well, I'll have a word with my friends at the Salvation Army and try to persuade them to look after her and the baby and, perhaps, get her some steady work well away from Ockenham. That will be the best course, I think." And she promised to be in touch with Mrs. Manners and her daughter within the fortnight.

Next, she received a regular visitor in the person of the head-mistress of the Ockenham Church of England primary school, known to all the village as 'Miss Millie'. Constance Mortimer-Wotton had a genuine regard for Millicent Taylor. It was not Millicent's fault that she'd been kept at home by that demanding old priest, her father: and it was entirely to her credit that, after his death, she'd loyally fulfilled his last wishes that she would look after the ageing and ailing Mrs. Taylor. The wonder of it was that these things had not soured her life. Now, thanks to Constance who was one of the governors of the school that Mortimer-Wotton money had built in the '70s, Millicent Taylor was firmly established as headmistress. In the last few years she had developed a gift for teaching and controlling the children as well as her two assistants, which was proving a real blessing to the village. Millicent enjoyed bringing these end of term reports to the Great House – partly because she knew Mrs. Mortimer-Wotton was interested in the progress of the children but chiefly because she needed help to meet the school's needs for the term ahead. Mrs. Mortimer-Wotton could organise new teachers, new equipment, new lavatories; and now, she could help fill in the bewildering new statistics required by the 1902 Education Act. Together, they worked steadily through the agenda and Millicent stayed on for a light lunch, as she had done at the end of every term since her appointment as headmistress.

Millicent Taylor left sharp at two o'clock with many thank-you's and the pleasurable feeling that Mrs. Mortimer-Wotton was pleased with what she was doing at the school. And Constance, up to date with village affairs, gratefully retired for a rest. It had been a trying morning especially the talk with that poor woman Mrs. Manners with her hopeless, endless family problems. But Constance had stamina. Two hours later the afternoon sun was shining across the park into her bedroom window. She thought she'd take a walk, perhaps, before tea and she rang Gwynedd Morgan. The little Welsh girl appeared with remarkable speed as if anticipating the summons as, indeed, she was. She moved across the room to put away some clothes lying on the chair by the window and suddenly stopped short in her tracks. "Madam," she blurted out. "Quickly, come quickly. What is Master Philip doing by himself in the park? There's nobody with him I can see and he's coming up the path from the lake, . . . I think he's crying."

The older woman joined Gwynedd at the window. "Good gracious, he must have given the slip to that girl Mrs. Francis has taken on to look after him in the afternoon. Just run down at once, Gwynedd, and see what's happened."

"Yes, Madam, but I know it's the girl's day off. Master Philip must have been out with his mother."

And before Constance could ask further questions Gwynedd was out of the room and hurrying through the kitchen garden. Constance returned to the window overlooking the park. The little boy was trying to go too fast. She saw him stumble, get up, shake himself, start off again. He must have heard a call from Gwynedd for he waved and shouted something to her. Even as Constance watched, the Welsh girl reached the little boy and lifted him into her arms. She was trying to soothe him, pulling out her handkerchief to wipe the tears from his eyes.

Anxiously, Constance hurried downstairs. Something's wrong, she thought, something terribly wrong. I can feel it, sense it in the air. Little boys of three don't walk in like that on hot August afternoons. In less than no time she was beside Gwynedd and the child stuttering incoherently through his sobs. "Now, Philip, stop crying and tell me what's happened." There was authority but no hardness in her voice.

"Er . . . er . . . it's Mother, Gran . . . down by the lake." The little boy's voice was trembling. "She said find you . . . and then . . . she sort of slept."

"Oh, God, dear God," murmured Constance and then all was action. "Quick, Gwynedd, get the child to the house, leave him with Mrs. Constant, find some of the men – John Williams and Larkin for preference. Tell them to come to the lake as fast as they can. If possible, bring a stretcher and blankets with them – anything on which they can carry Mrs. Francis. Quickly now," and Constance was away down the path across the park.

She found Bertha stretched on a grass bank near the old wooden seat that overlooks the length of the lake from the south. Nearby lay a pathetic collection of picnic things, guarded by Philip's beloved teddy bear. The picture could be taken in at a glance – a special afternoon treat for the little boy, just for him and for her. But what, in heaven's name, had occurred?

Constance dropped to her knees beside the girl, loosening her skirt, feeling her pulse. Yes, she was alive . . . the grey eyes opened and then very slowly closed as if the effort was too much. The poor child was in some sort of intermittent pain, moaning as each spasm

35

wracked her body. Eleven weeks pregnant and another miscarriage? No, Constance couldn't believe it. This was something
different, more serious. The girl was trying to say something.
"Frankie darling" or so it sounded. "I must . . . see . . . you . . .
again."

Constance whipped some sal-volatile from her handbag. She
was holding it to Bertha's nose when John Williams and Larkin
appeared. They'd moved with surprising speed, complete with
blankets and a strong wire mesh frame from the potting shed. "It'll
'old 'er, never fear Ma'am," said the gardener. "We'll 'ave 'er back
'ome in no time." And with their great strength he and John
Williams lifted Bertha and eased her very gently on to the blankets
covering their improvised stretcher. How marvellously gentle
these countrymen are, Constance thought, as she moved ahead of
them along the field path to the Dower House. What next? Up to
the big double bedroom . . . turn down the sheets . . . a hot water
bottle, please, cook . . . up here, John, and don't worry about your
boots on the carpet . . . Soon, Bertha was back in her own room,
but her breathing was coming with difficulty and the pain
increasing.

And now what? Constance collected her thoughts. First, the
doctor. "John, find a bicycle somewhere and get Dr. Gardiner to
the Dower House as fast as his horse and trap can bring him. Then,
on your way back through the village, tell Nurse Bracken of the
trouble we're having. Away you go, John, and thank you for all
you're doing."

The big man was already on his way as Constance turned to
Larkin. "Now, Ted, a telegram to Mr. Francis. Ask the cook for
paper and pencil . . . and I'll write something out for the post
office." A few minutes later, Ted Larkin was running to the Great
House where he reckoned to catch the postman making his second
collection of the day. Within half an hour, Ockenham post office
was tapping out a telegram.

> Mortimer-Wotton
> Care of Hollingbourne
> Astley Lodge
> Pickering Yorks

Bertha taken ill return urgently
telegraph time place arrival
Love Mother

That was all she could do till the doctor arrived. But she must, of course , stay here for the night. Better leave the little boy where he is for the moment. She could trust Gwynedd to do the sensible thing. By now she and Mrs. Constant would be feeding Philip in the kitchen or maybe reading to him from that pile of old children's books that had once belonged to his father and uncle. Philip would be safe and happy up there.

Constance turned back to the bed. Bertha was clearly in great pain, hardly conscious. But turning back the sheets and feeling the slightly distended stomach Constance could see none of the usual signs of a miscarriage. This must be some internal problem she didn't understand. It was after six . . . would the doctor never come? She started at the sound of a knock on the door . . . but it was Bertha's cook-general.

"Beg pardon, Ma'am, Mr. Larkin's back. Says telegram's on its way but e'd like a word with you."

Constance went out to the landing and saw Larkin standing at the foot of the stairs.

"It's about Master Philip, Madam. Gwynedd Morgan says she thinks it's time she put him to bed but wants 'is pyjamas and that teddy bear 'e takes everywhere."

"Quite right. I'll find his things at once but, my goodness, Ted, I think you'll have to return by the footpath. I'm sorry to give you all this extra trouble but the teddy bear is with those picnic things by the seat."

Armed with diminutive pyjamas, dressing gown, toothbrush and a book, Ted Larkin moved off on his circuitous return journey with a message that Mrs. Mortimer-Wotton would be sleeping at the Dower House and Gwynedd was to take charge of little Philip. A very sensible girl, Gwynedd, Constance reflected. How I wish there were more people like her who can think for themselves. And Constance returned to Bertha.

But not for long. Almost at once Dr. Gardiner arrived in his trap, followed within minutes by the district nurse on her bicycle.

Constance left them in the bedroom and went downstairs to reassure the cook.

Half an hour later the old doctor emerged from his examination, leaving the nurse with Bertha. His kind old face betrayed his anxiety as he spoke. "Constance, my dear, I'm afraid your daughter is very, very ill. I'll get a specialist from Canterbury at once but I doubt if he'll risk moving her to hospital which is where she ought to be."

"But . . . what's happened, what is it Sam?"

"Well, my dear, it's an unusual situation but, unless I'm wrong, it's what we call an ectopic pregnancy. That is to say, a pregnancy in one of the tubes leading to the womb. That would account for the disquieting, intermittent pain in the side. And there must have been an internal haemorrhage out in the park which would have caused her to lie down and lose consciousness. I've left Nurse Bracken the necessary instructions and I'll be back later in the evening, hopefully with a consultant from Canterbury. But we're old friends, Constance," and the doctor's voice was breaking, "Bertha may be beyond recall. I'm so sorry to say this. A doctor is often faced with tragedy. But this means so much to you, to Francis, to the boy, to all of us in Ockenham . . . all I can say is that you have done all that was humanly possible. So very sorry . . . so very sad." His voice trailed away and a few moments later Constance heard the old man driving from the house.

The Canterbury specialist reached the house with Sam Gardiner just before midnight, but all he could do was to confirm the old doctor's diagnosis and hopefully make plans for moving the sick woman to hospital. But there was no tomorrow. At two o'clock, Bertha called out and Constance heard her whisper very faintly, "Frankie, darling, I've loved you so much and . . . and . . . Frankie, thank you for loving me . . . I made you love me didn't I? Mother understands . . . she'll always be there to help you . . . and Philip." The girl from Yorkshire didn't speak again. She died just before the sun rose on another cloudless August day.

4

At Ockenham all the mechanisms attendant on death worked smoothly through their courses. Justin Leadbitter met Francis at Ashford station and told him of Bertha's death before he reached the Dower House. Telegrams were sent to Charles in Venice and Sir George Hollingbourne in Yorkshire. Obituaries duly appeared in the County papers. Notices in *The Times* and *Morning Post* informed readers that the funeral of Mrs. Francis Mortimer-Wotton would take place at two p.m. on 18th August at the Parish Church of St. Dunstan, Ockenham.

At the appointed hour, the Rev. Edward Pendlebury headed the file of family mourners through the west door of the little church by which so many of their predecessors had entered on their last journey. Accustomed though he was to these grievous occasions, he sensed at once an unusual tension in the air. It wasn't simply that the church was full to over-flowing. The people of Ockenham would naturally be present out of respect for the family. Or even out of love for Bertha, for she'd certainly made her mark amongst them. But this was something more fundamental – yes, he'd become sensitive to these things; something more emotive than respect or love or grief. Was he being fanciful? Or were the Fates, such as the Greeks had dreaded, turning against the family which had held sway over Ockenham for eight hundred years? Against the family which had appointed him, Edward Pendlebury, to this Living? Did these country folk see further and deeper than their town cousins, and feel a personal significance in Bertha's death? A foreboding of change, a new order? Or was his imagination running away with him? Take a grip on yourself, Edward Pendlebury, this is no moment for speculation, you have a job to do. And with an effort, he banished his thoughts and controlled his voice . . .

"We brought nothing into this world and it is certain that we can carry nothing out."

Apart from Charles, still absent on the Continent, Gwynedd Morgan was the only member of the Mortimer-Wotton household missing from church. She remained at the Great House, charged to look after Philip. Yet it could be said that she too was part of the congregation. As she watched the little boy playing with his bricks, tears came to her eyes and her lips were moving silently as a biblical medley of words jostled for expression. "The Lord gave and the Lord hath taken away . . . Teach me thy ways O Lord . . . May this child be found pleasing in thy sight . . . In all this may thy servant be found faithful . . ." From her childhood the Bible had been the Welsh girl's guide. Night and morning, prayer was part of her life. Who knows? She may have been the one person in Ockenham that day who had no doubt about the ultimate wisdom of God. Resolutely Gwynedd Morgan returned to the sewing on her lap.

Inevitably, it was Constance Mortimer-Wotton who restored the routine of life at the Great House. For a week Gwynedd worried about her mistress. Sometimes, the Welsh girl could positively feel the doubts in Constance's mind. Why Bertha's life – of all lives? Where could Francis find comfort, wandering aimlessly between the two houses, speaking in monosyllables? Would her elder son, due back from the Continent, be able to help her? And what of the child? Was this great family to depend for its survival on the life of one small boy?

The period of doubt seemed to end after a talk with Tom Duncan who had driven over from Chilham to express his condolences. The colonel was a funny old stick, without much humour and liable to be pompous. But on occasions like this he could be very practical. "Got to take stock of the situation, Connie. Don't decide everything at once. Follow the old army rule. Information, Intention, Method . . . you know the form. Write out the headings and think it through, what? Clears the mind, Connie . . . clears the mind wonderfully." And Tom Duncan took his leave.

Constance returned to the desk in her room. Now then, how did it go? Information – that's easy. "The Mortimer-Wotton family

40

owns three thousand acres of land. Continuing ownership may be difficult but not impossible if we can be sure about the succession."

Intention – a visitor watching Constance at her desk would have seen a new determination in her face. A soldier would have interpreted her expression correctly – "Intention, to hold Ockenham Manor at all costs with the forces at our disposal." That's not exactly what she wrote but it's certainly what she meant.

Method – the writer hesitated. This was where Tom Duncan's cut-and-dried ideas came to a shuddering halt. Better start with some questions.

Should she persuade Charles to return to Ockenham? Should she consider altering the standing of tenant farmers – a course she knew Bertha had discussed with Francis? Should she encourage Francis to re-marry? More children? Should she bring Francis and Philip back to the Great House and lease little Ockenham to some suitable tenant? How long before Philip stood ready, educated and willing to take command?

She re-read what she had written, folded the paper carefully and put it in her handbag. A good friend, Tom Duncan, and not a bad recipe for facing her dilemma. She smiled to herself. How odd that every question she framed put an obligation on herself, seemed to assume she'd be in command. Well, well – and she smiled again – it wouldn't be the first time a woman had taken over in a crisis. And with a lighter step she went to the kitchen to see that her older son's bedroom was ready for his arrival from the Continent.

A few days later, Charles reached Ockenham – getting off the boat train at Ashford where Francis met him. His mother, no less than Francis, was surprised by his appearance. Gone were the stolid, rather heavy features she had come to associate with him. In spite of the long and tedious over-land journey from Naples whither the family cable had been redirected, he seemed younger than his years. There was a new light in his eyes, his hair was longer, his dress less formal. To his mother especially he was less constrained, more *sympathique*. With a shock she understood. This elder son of hers, admittedly the stronger character of the two boys, had made his own positive decision to get clear of a burden which he found inhibiting, even insupportable. Whoever his friends, whatever his activities, he had liberated himself from his past. He had become his own master.

Constance recalled Justin Leadbitter's diagnosis a few years earlier. It had been made while Charles was still in the process of making up his mind and highly sensitive to the influence of his friends. But now she had no doubt that the old solicitor's main conclusion had been correct – Charles would never return to Ockenham. And the mother knew in her heart that for Charles it was the right decision.

As if to prove the point, Charles opened a large artist's folder which formed the main part of his luggage. Constance was fascinated by the contents. Paintings in oil, full of colour and feeling for the Calabrian scene. Sketches of Venice's churches and canals, interspersed with water colours of the fishermen and the varied craft of the lagoons. And five canvasses from Switzerland, which stood apart from the rest. In them Constance could see and feel the mountaineer as well as the artist. The occasional small climbing figures, set against the vast background of the High Alps, gave the viewer an overwhelming sense of the strength of nature and the limitations of mere man.

When, after four weeks, Charles left again for Italy, he kissed his mother goodbye, and then, looking into her face, he said very quietly, "Mother, you *do* understand, don't you?"

Constance re-entered the house knowing for a surety that her first question had been answered in the negative. Charles had found his *métier* and it would lead him many miles from Ockenham.

For a long time Francis remained stunned by Bertha's death. He could hardly grasp what had happened. Sometimes he'd go to the nursery to play with Philip. Sometimes he'd spend half the day reading *The Times*. Occasionally he'd go to London and spend the night at White's. His mother could get no sort of sense out of him beyond his assurance that he could not bear to return to the Dower House at Little Ockenham. That, at least, was one step forward. Six months later, Constance and Francis disposed of Bertha's private effects, with the exception of the pictures, bought in Paris, which were moved to the Great House. Justin Leadbitter, clever man, let the Dower House, furnished, to the Adjutant of the Buffs.

"A good tenant, my dear, and not too permanent if Francis wants to go back there."

On Justin's advice, Constance made no changes in the arrangements with the Agent for the estate though both of them knew, as Bertha had known, that he wasn't taking sufficient interest to ensure a proper rental and revenue from the farming. "Better wait, my dear. Francis may have his own ideas and I reckon that impossible feller, Lloyd George, will have his hands full for a few years. Who knows? The Liberals may lose the next election and then we can think again."

Gradually, Constance's other questions were sorted out. Philip, adaptable as all small children are and taking each day as it comes, was soon installed at the Great House with a bedroom of his own and Gwynedd sleeping next door. He seemed a sturdy little chap; big for his age, Gwynedd thought, and singularly happy with his own devices. A pity he had no companions of his own class, or was it? I don't know, I'm sure, sighed Gwynedd.

But even that problem found its natural solution. Philip was down in the kitchen quite literally to see what was cooking when Amos, one of John Williams's children, came over from the Home Farm with a message for Mrs. Constant. Young Philip was delighted to meet a boy of his own age and Amos, rising four, was equally pleased. Quite a handful he was for Mrs. Williams with a two-year-old on her hands, and now expecting again. But a nice family, trusted in the village as well as the Great House. John's country lore was just about the nearest thing to farming technology the estate possessed. He ran the Home Farm under the barest direction from the Mortimer-Wottons and without interference from the Agent whom he did not like. He was rightly trusted. He knew the seasons and the soil he tilled. And people worked happily under him, not only the waggoner but even the difficult old stockman who thought he knew everything about the Mortimer-Wotton herd of Guernseys that supplied the best milk in the district.

For Philip and Amos it was the beginning of a long friendship. As soon as they were five they started school with Miss Millie, at first accompanied to the door of the school house by Gwynedd Morgan. By the age of seven, they were riding their bicycles unescorted down the drive, racing each other or making rings round the old postman all the way to the Lodge gates. Philip. helped by Gwynedd, initially, found reading easy and didn't try very hard until he found that school is a competitive world and the others were overtaking him. As Miss Millie said, it would never do to be beaten by the younger children, by Margie Kemsing for instance from the Wotton Arms or by that bright little Evans boy from the post office. Miss Millie looked after the younger children herself, taught them manners and cleanliness as well as the elements of the three Rs. She was no respecter of persons, keeping order without fear or favourites. If admonition went unheeded, discipline was straightforward. A flexible rubber ruler used with discretion – boys on the bottom, girls on the hand – and always administered in private. For more serious crime – as when the eldest Kemsing boy hit one of the assistant mistresses in the face with an ink pellet – Miss Millie had her own method. 'Straight home, out of school at once. I'll be talking to your father.' And next morning young Kemsing returned much chastened. It was extremely painful to be at the wrong end of Jack Kemsing's belt. The parents in Ockenham knew the schoolmistress didn't send children home without good reason. Fathers and mothers alike, they trusted Millicent Taylor.

That went for Constance too. It was she rather than Francis who made the decision not to bother about private schools or tutors for Philip. And the success of an experiment, which initially raised a few County eyebrows, proved her right. Quite apart from what he learnt, Philip made a host of friends in the village. Neither he nor his companions worried about home backgrounds or class distinctions. They were children in a small world and the holidays were never lonely.

Francis remained an enigma. He acquiesced in his mother's suggestions, whether they concerned Philip or the Estate. Some thought he didn't care. Others, who knew him better, saw that in taking the line of least resistance, he was simply running true to form. But – make no mistake – Francis had his own integrity, his code of honour. On learning that, as Bertha left no will, her property and her investments in Hollingbourne's Steel Mills devolved on him, he immediately arranged for all Bertha's fortune to be held in trust for Philip. He even made over to his son's ownership the pictures Bertha had bought in Paris – only retaining for himself the sketch made in Montmartre. Meanwhile he rented a flat in Ryder Street just off St. James's, hardly returning to Ockenham except at the weekends where he could enjoy good cricket in the summer and rough shooting in the winter.

Home or away, Francis never lacked friends, most of whom shared the same tastes, wore the same school tie and enjoyed membership of the same clubs. It was their good fortune – or maybe their fate – to be born rich enough not to spend their lives earning a living. They were members of a society which did 'its own thing'. They had time to be idle, time to be eccentric, time to journey to the ends of the earth, time to be members of parliament, time to serve. Whatever talents they used or misused, they stuck by their friends. They also shared by inheritance and upbringing one other common quality. But for most of them in 1911 the test of courage still lay ahead. Francis was not untypical.

The chief exception to this generalisation about his friends was Sir George Hollingbourne. Bertha's father was a real 'rough diamond', educated in the toughest of Yorkshire homes. But he liked Francis for himself as well as for Bertha's sake. And like Bertha, he trusted him. A year before her death, he appointed Francis to the Board of one of his London companies. Francis was expected to attend a monthly Board meeting in London – it made a good excuse for renting the Ryder Street flat: and those meetings were varied with the occasional trip to Sheffield.

It was on one of these visits that Sir George Hollingbourne announced his somewhat sudden marriage to a young lady on his staff. "Not quite right, my boy, for your mother or the Honourable Mottingham: nor for some of my friends among the Master Cutlers of Sheffield, if it comes to that. But a lovely lass all the same, a real good-looker. The fact is that I can't do without her and she can't do without me." From which Francis inferred quite rightly that Hollingbourne, the old rascal, was starting another family.

But his father-in-law had something else on his mind. "Now look, Francis. This means that just for a few months, I've got to stay around, yer know. Can't do my usual American trip: and some-body's got to keep contact with those fellers in Cleveland. So what about you? I'd say you'll go down well with 'em – you've got the style. We can get you briefed – it's keeping in touch that's important in the steel game ... Have to stick together these days. I'm serious, I wouldn't make the proposition if I didn't believe in you. So sleep on it tonight, lad, and tell me the answer in the morning. Right? And now for the Verve Clicquot and I'll introduce you to the new Lady Hollingbourne."

So in 1911 Francis Mortimer-Wotton made his first visit to America. He made friends with Americans the moment he boarded the Cunarder at Liverpool. They liked his manner and admired his looks. He, for his part, was delighted with their sense of direction and purpose. The mutual attraction didn't weaken. When he reached Cleveland, Hollingbourne's business friends entertained him like royalty. The wealth, the servants ... fantastic: he began to understand the meaning of the word 'millionaire'.

It was at one of these parties in Cleveland that he met Eleanor Fletcher. She was the only daughter of one of the great steel men, a member of a German immigrant family, née Fleischer, which had made its American fortune the hard way. Francis met Eleanor at a point in her life when she was determined to enjoy the London Season: and Eleanor was the sort of girl who generally got what she wanted. Francis was easy game. It was not difficult to persuade him to organise her visit to England. Once there, she was seen everywhere with him, making a brief visit to Ockenham with which she was genuinely impressed. If people thought her a bit outspoken, they ascribed this to her American birth. What they saw was a good-looking, dark-haired, well-proportioned girl, rather above average height, with a refreshing enthusiasm for the culture which Cleveland couldn't provide. What Constance saw was a determined young woman who, like Bertha, would probably supply a bit of motive power to her easy-going son. Who could say how she would fit into the scheme of things at Ockenham? She was inclined to reserve judgment.

Francis and Eleanor were married in Cleveland on Francis's second visit to America. None of his friends knew whether he really loved her or whether he had fallen for the American girl on the rebound.

"Odd chap, Francis," they agreed. "Normally, the life and soul of a party ... the prettiest girls falling for him ... and then he suddenly goes broody and takes one of these Flanders Mares to wife. You never can tell, can you?" And they returned philosophically to their shooting and racing and cricket. They didn't think for a minute that his second marriage would keep Francis away from his friends and familiar stamping grounds.

5

FRANCIS AND ELEANOR were still on their honeymoon in America when the telegraph boy rode up the beech avenue to the Great House with a telegram for Francis.

Constance opened it.

> Regret Charles Mortimer-Wotton lost in
> avalanche with two companions stop missing
> believed dead stop British Vice-Consul and
> English community informed stop we send
> profound sympathy
> The Direction Couttet's Hotel Chamonix
> 30th June 1912

The words stared back at Constance from the dingy paper. At first her eyes registered disbelief, then a dim comprehension. The telegram fluttered to the ground like a leaf in autumn and Constance sank into her chair, stunned by the news.

She was still sitting there, staring sightless except for her memories, when Gwynedd came in to clean the room. Automatically the girl picked up the telegram, glanced at it and suddenly understood its significance. For a moment she was half-minded to leave on tip-toe when some instinct prompted her to kneel beside her mistress. "There, there now, don't cry Madam." She found herself mouthing the sort of words she'd use if Master Philip hurt himself.

"Thank you, Gwynedd, thank you dear. You mustn't worry. I'm just a silly old woman, I'll pull myself together in a moment. A cup of tea, perhaps. No, wait. I'll go to my bedroom. Please, I don't want to see anyone. Can you make sure of that? And thank you again for helping me."

Next day the papers carried the news of the disaster in Switzerland and, in the absence of Francis, Mr. Absalom dealt with all enquiries at the Great House. Meanwhile Tom Duncan and Justin Leadbitter arranged to accompany Constance to Chamonix. Neither had really expected her to take this further blow so hard. But neither appreciated the new understanding between mother and son which had followed Bertha's death.

Ever since his school days Charles had written fairly regularly to his mother when away from home. But the routine duty letters of an earlier day had in the past year given place to a much more intimate correspondence, almost as if Charles was determined to explain himself to the one person who really understood why he had turned his back on Ockenham.

Constance found herself reading his letters again and again. They were wide ranging and essentially subjective – technical problems about his painting, the relaxed joy of sailing around the Venetian lagoons with the local fishermen, his ambitions to be a great climber. One letter, written in September of the previous year, she carried in her handbag to Switzerland and showed to her two companions.

Darling Mother,

I'm writing from Couttet's Hotel in Chamonix where the great Edward Whymper is also staying. Do you remember how thrilled I was when he lectured at Eton on his ascent of the Matterhorn? All those frustrating attempts – and then, finally, success! I read and re-read his *Scrambles in the Alps*. And I get the odd feeling that we are birds of a feather – artists as well as climbers, men who have to be out on our own.

I fear he's a sick man. But to me and my friends, Kurt Ulrich and Gianni Donati, he is marvellously kind. He seems very interested in the paintings I showed him the other day. And when we told him of the dawn we'd seen from the summit of Mont Blanc, his blue eyes lit up as if he too was seeing the miracle again. Those masters at Eton would inevitably have quoted Homer's 'rosy-fingered dawn'. But Mother, honestly, it was unbelievable. The three of us saw the giants of the Alps set alight by the sunrise, one after another. We looked north to the gleaming water of Geneva and the Jura massif, east to Monte Rosa and the snows of the Oberland, west to the Dauphiné and the summit of Monte Viso and southwards to a luminous mist over the Italian plains which made Kurt and me laugh at dear old benighted Gianni. What an unforgettable moment of sheer joy!

And here's an extraordinary thing. Edward Whymper says he believes the bodies of those who lost their lives on Mont Blanc in 1870 may be found at the end of the Glacier des Bossons this year or next – forty years later. Strange how time shrinks in the face of these great mountains. Fred Payot, the famous Chamonix guide, is of the same opinion and Kurt believes we may get in on the hunt next year, Who's to say?

Meanwhile, my greetings to you and Francis, not forgetting young Philip . . .

Fourteen days later, Constance and her companions returned to England. There was little to be done at Chamonix and nothing to be said. Another avalanche had taken its toll of human life. Charles, like his father before him, was dead, untimely dead, leaving no traces of mortality. For Constance another chapter had closed.

Back at the Great House, she listlessly watched Philip playing football with Amos Williams on the croquet lawn. It sent her mind back sentimentally to Bertha – what a splendidly assured future she'd projected for Bertha and Francis. Then she returned to look at one of her eldest son's pictures hanging in her room. These fateful might-have-beens . . . these promises unfulfilled . . . these many hopes a-dying . . . Why should she be chosen to face this succession of tragedies? But hold on a minute. There . . . out in the garden . . . there's Philip laughing and running with Amos. "Look forward, woman," she apostrophised herself sharply. "Your concern is the future, not the past. Stop looking over your shoulder or you'll end up like Lot's wife."

On receiving the news of Charles's death Francis and Eleanor immediately cut short their holiday and managed to book a first-class cabin in the Lusitania. During the voyage home, Eleanor saw her husband in a new light. Until that moment he had talked of his home in Kent as if it held no problems at all. "You'll like it down at Ockenham, Ellie. I'm sure you will."

"But Francis . . ."

"O.K. darling, I promise we'll start life in London so that you can meet your friends and get the feel of England at the centre of things, enjoy the theatres, the parties . . . the lot. For a start, we'll just move down to the ancestral home for an occasional weekend."

That was a promise to Eleanor and Francis wouldn't be allowed to go back on it.

But the promise weighed more heavily on him with every sea mile nearer Liverpool. "Francis, come out with it. You're worried about Ockenham, aren't you?"

"Well, not exactly worried, m'dear: but a bit anxious about Mother I suppose. We'll have to see how the land lies when we get home, but I reckon she'll be pretty lonely at the Great House. Not because of old Charles, of course. He left the place years ago. But suppose we cart off young Philip to London . . . devilish awkward, I'd say." And Francis ordered another drink for them both.

Eleanor wouldn't be put off so easily. "Awkward for whom, Francis? Your mother? Your son? Yourself? Hi, what about me? It could be devilish awkward for your new American wife to mix it with your mother and all those retainers . . . devilish awkward to hit it off with a seven-year-old step-son. You've got somebody else to think about now, you know."

Francis saw warning lights flashing everywhere. "O.K., O.K. darling, let's wait and see," was all he said. And they moved from the promenade deck to place their bets on the number of miles the Lusitania had sailed in the last twenty-four hours.

But it *was* going to be devilish awkward all the same. Similar thoughts, similar arguments were coursing through the mind of Constance Mortimer-Wotton – and, indeed, through the mind of Gwynedd Morgan. Their thinking, however, was centred on Philip. Each knew perfectly well that the boy ought to live with his new mother. But that was easier said than done. If Eleanor and Francis were determined to live in London, how would the child cope? Not only a new mother to get used to, but a new home, new surroundings, new friends, new school . . . Yes, it would be devilish awkward . . . and two people, at least, would be miserable without the boy. Since Bertha's death Philip had become an integral part of their lives. The two women only began to measure how much he meant to each of them when Francis and Eleanor returned as man and wife from America.

Constance had arranged for Francis and Eleanor to occupy the best spare bedroom at the Great House until they could settle into their newly acquired town house in Chelsea. The room would give Eleanor a splendid view over the lake and park and there would be no need to uproot Philip from his special room next to Gwynedd Morgan. "We'll take things one step at a time Gwynedd," said Mrs. Mortimer-Wotton. "It's wise, I think, not to change Master Philip's routine until he's got used to his new mother. For the moment, I'll arrange for you to carry on as usual and then we'll see . . . But for goodness sake girl, don't look so unutterably gloomy. It's a wedding, not a funeral we're talking about."

"Yes, Ma'am, I'm sorry I'm sure," stuttered the Welsh girl hurrying from the presence. Really, she thought, there's no call to talk to me like that. I fancy Mrs. Mortimer-Wotton must be more worried than she likes to admit. And with that thought in mind she sought out Mrs. Constant in the kitchen to warn her that Mrs. M-W was a little out of sorts and might need careful handling for the next few days until the new Mrs. Francis had settled in.

Actually, the first meeting between Philip and his step-mother was not inauspicious. The little boy may have been a little nervous but Eleanor and Francis arrived with a model yacht. No need to worry about introductions or explanations. The yacht was the thing. Philip's eyes shone with excitement as he clutched the boat. He could hardly say 'thank you' before he was planning its maiden voyage across the lake.

"Come on, Father. Let's go and sail it. Oh do come on, all of you. What shall we call her? We've got hours before tea, haven't we Granny? I'll just go and find Amos – he must be there for the launch." And Philip, with the boat under his arm, ran off to find his friend.

Half an hour later Francis, Eleanor and two small boys could be seen totally absorbed in their task by the lakeside. It was a sight to charm the eye. The park still marvellously green on this late

August day, green as any stretch of pasture in the Stour valley. The great oaks and beeches standing haughtily in their majestic groups with the work-a-day Guernseys munching away or sheltering in the shade of the trees while they patiently waited the call to the evening milking. And there, in the foreground, a model yacht with two adults busily employed and two small boys hopping about in excitement. The rudder adjusted, the sail set to take the light westerly breeze a'beam: and suddenly, to the accompaniment of much waving and shouting, the little ship was away, keeping her course across the lake.

It was a brave sight indeed. And Constance, watching the scene from the rose garden in front of the house, reckoned she'd been witness to a very successful launch. She was happier still when Philip told her he'd decided to name his yacht 'America'. That's Francis at his best, she thought. It'll be no bad thing if Philip inherits his father's tact.

That evening they drank to the health of 'America' in the best burgundy decanted by Mr. Absalom earlier in the day to celebrate Eleanor's first night at Ockenham as the new 'Mrs. Francis'. But what with the social calls and local introductions that had to be made, Francis and Eleanor could spare little time for Philip in the ensuing week. Soon it was clear that until they were established in Chelsea, Philip would continue to live at the Great House where he could at least continue his schooling under Miss Millie.

But at the end of the autumn term, nothing had been done to resolve the situation. Francis was, in all conscience, hard enough to tie down when it came to making decisions. 'Live and let live' was his normal approach to any problem, to which rule he might well have added his own special gloss – 'If decisions have to be made let the women make them.'

Yet it was not solely Francis's fault that Philip continued under his grandmother's tutelage at Ockenham. The simple truth was that Eleanor was having the time of her life in London. In 1912, the Empire's capital city was a world away from Cleveland, Ohio. Buckingham Palace housed a new king recently proclaimed King-Emperor at the Imperial Durbar in Delhi. From Whitehall the country was ruled by a cabinet reckoned to be the most brilliant ever assembled by a British political party – whether you liked its views or not. There was Sir Edward Grey at the Foreign Office keeping his calm eye on machinations in the Balkans. The Franco-British naval agreement was successfully concluded – "one in the eye for Kaiser Bill," said one of Francis's friends at a party in Tite Street, momentarily forgetting his hostess's Teutonic origins. And if foreign politics were too much to stomach at the dinner table, what interesting speculations could be made about Lloyd George and the Marconi scandal! Dear Francis always seemed to know somebody who was privy to the latest form at Westminster.

Equally, his friends were *au fait* with the world of the theatre and Francis and Eleanor were frequently to be seen at first nights, some of which presented plays guaranteed to shock the more conservative elements among the critics and public. There was, for instance, that impertinent Irishman, Shaw, tilting at the Establishment in Pygmalion – Francis, to be fair to him, enjoyed the play as much as anybody in the theatre. There were great paintings and painters to be talked about – and those strange Post-Impressionists and their new exhibition to come to grips with. And *Rosenkavalier* which had just made its sensational debut.

In short, London's international society provided a full life for those with money to enjoy it. And Francis with his numerous contacts, and Eleanor with her American friends at the Embassy, were in the midst of it. But there was one art-form which Francis simply coundn't take despite Eleanor's new-found enthusiasm. The opera, possibly. Music certainly, whether it was Elgar's new E flat Symphony or Alexander's Rag-time band. But the ballet, no. "Sorry m'dear, I just can't stick it whatever your friends say. Diaghilev in Paris? No, they're all the same to me – a damned effeminate lot."

"Francis, you're being ridiculous," Eleanor protested, "and here we are with a marvellous invitation from the Hofmanns in Paris and seats for Ravel's *Daphnis and Chloe* and Stravinsky's *Petrushka*. You must come."

But for once in a way, Francis was adamant. All Eleanor's French-speaking husband would do was to escort her to Paris and leave her safely installed in a new hotel near the Arc de Triomphe. As for himself, he would fulfil a promise made to his mother and take the train to Chamonix where he would arrange to photograph the plaque erected there to Charles's memory.

So it was decided. Francis travelled on the night train to Switzerland. From Chamonix he posted to his mother a photograph of his brother's simple, unobtrusive memorial, set in the same style as the Whymper headstone standing nearby in the little cemetery at Chamonix.

In Memoriam
Charles Mortimer-Wotton
– artist and mountaineer
who loved the high hills.
1874–1912

Francis was sure she would wish to have this record for her scrap book of memories, and this, after all, provided him with a reason for leaving Paris.

He took rather more time writing to inform Eleanor that he had received a chance invitation to visit friends in Bern and Zurich and, therefore, could not be with her again until her ballet visit to Paris was completed.

He worded his letter very tactfully, with many expressions of affection and hope that Stravinsky and Ravel had come up to Ellie's expectations. But as he addressed the envelope to Eleanor's Paris hotel, he admitted some doubt in his mind as to whether she would accept his letter at its face value. He didn't like deceiving her but equally he couldn't fool himself. He knew that he simply couldn't face staying with Eleanor in Paris. Keeping away from the Ritz and the Place Vendôme was simply not the answer. The shops of Paris, the cafés, the trees, the opera – they all conjured up memories of his first marriage with a poignancy that was suddenly unbearable. Bertha's spirit was everywhere. Even in the few hours before he took the cab to the Gare de L'Est, he was painfully aware that Eleanor could never be to him what Bertha had been.

Ah well, he reflected as he posted the letter from Chamonix, she knows for a fact that I'm bored stiff by this ballet craze. And it really *is* true that I have friends in the Swiss capital. The alibi is as fool proof as anything Sherlock Holmes could think up. So keep your fingers crossed, old boy, and hope for the best.

But the visit to Switzerland took a more serious turn when he met Algy Crosthwaite at the British Embassy in Bern. Algy was an old school friend, his considerable ability masked by a lighthearted approach to life which had always appealed to Francis in the old days when they'd been playing cricket for Eton. Now, he was First Secretary at the Embassy and moving up the diplomatic scale as easily and swiftly as he'd moved to the top at school. Everybody agreed that one of these fine days he'd end up as ambassador in Paris or Washington.

But Algy Crosthwaite was anything but lighthearted that evening as he and Francis dined in the restaurant of the Three Bears. "We don't fancy the look of things, Frankie," he said. "This Central European business is getting out of hand. And there are far too many rumours going around little old Switzerland for my liking."

"Algy, don't be so frightfully heavy. What the devil d'you mean?"

"Simply this, dear boy. The Balkans are in a ferment – with Serbia, Greece, Roumania and God knows who, lining up against Bulgaria and Turkey. Troubled waters y'know: and far too many people interested in the fishing rights."

"But the Balkans are a long way from England, aren't they?"

"That's what everybody in England keeps saying. They don't understand the world is getting smaller. I don't want to spoil the evening but there's something to be said for that old Latin tag, 'Si pacem velis, para bellum'. In other words, if you're in the Territorials, polish up your buttons. And now let's enjoy the brandy while we can."

Algy was not to be drawn further. But Francis got the message loud and clear. Next day he read the *Neue Zürcher Zeitung* and the *Journal de Genève* with a new interest. He bought a number of books about Central Europe and looked at the map. By the time he was back in London he'd come to a simple decision – he'd polish up his buttons and tell his friends why.

That was one of the odd things about Francis which Eleanor never really understood. Once he made up his mind he acted with a determination that brooked no interference. Perhaps it was his Mortimer blood asserting itself. In this case, action took the form of fixing himself up in the Territorials and, quite literally, preparing himself for war. No sooner was he back from Switzerland than a new Francis began to show. By the middle of 1913, He was commanding a company in the Territorial Battalion of the Royal East Kent Regiment based on Canterbury and was often to be found at Territorial Headquarters in St. Peter's Street or dining at the officers' mess at the depot. He acquired a manual of French military terms from a pal in the War Office. "I tell you, my dear," he confided to Eleanor, "I'm going to chat up these French generals as effectively as Kitchener." And he seized every opportunity of picking up information about the European political scene.

Happily, his new enthusiasm for the military art coincided with Eleanor's first pregnancy and made his absence from the West End less noticeable. Late in October his wife gave birth to a boy in the most exclusive nursing home in the Harley Street area. It was all very simple and efficient and expensive. In due course, the smartest of nannies was wheeling the newest Mortimer-Wotton in the gardens by the Chelsea embankment and sometimes via Harrods to Kensington Gardens in order to discuss her charge and her mistress with similar well-dressed nursemaids on the same trade route.

The child was duly christened Robert Mortimer-Wotton in the parish church at Ockenham where, for a change, the London nanny looked and felt somewhat incongruous. The short sojourn and quick return to London naturally caused people in the village to wonder why the baby couldn't have been born in the Great House and to speculate on the reactions of old Mrs. Mortimer-Wotton to the continued residence of Francis and Eleanor in Chelsea. At the Great House the other servants went out of their way to be kind to Gwynedd, sensing that even the most faithful of Baptists might reasonably take umbrage at that uniformed Miss Hoity-toity with her fine London airs. But, in the country, life goes on and gossip soon finds new topics for old. Those who cared most about these things remained tight lipped with one exception.

The seven year-old Philip was audibly explicit. "When's my new mother going to bring my brother to live here?" he demanded of his father on his next visit. "Me and Amos and Margie want a baby to play with. And so does Gwynedd," he added with that percipience which adults so often find surprising in children.

"Never worry, old son," replied Francis. "Bobby will be here before very long. And he'll be much more fun when he can walk and talk."

Philip rushed off to tell Gwynedd whom he and his friends, working on the good old rhyming principle, now addressed as the Gorgon, following a story from Greek mythology by Miss Millie.

"Gorgon, dear Gorgon, it's a promise," he shouted. "Father's going to bring my brother Robert to live with us here."

"That's as may be," replied the Welsh girl, borrowing one of Mrs. M-W's favourite expressions and returning to her endless task of darning socks.

But there were no 'ifs' and 'buts' about Francis's promise to young Philip. Early in the summer of 1914, Eleanor, Francis and the baby took up residence 'for the summer' in the Great House, leaving the London nannie in her natural habitat and armed with impeccable references. In July, the Adjutant of the Buffs informed Constance that he and his wife would be giving up the tenancy of the Dower House. A week later Captain Francis Mortimer-Wotton was called to the colours. On 4th August, the United Kingdom declared war on Germany. And life at the Great House assumed new and more complicated dimensions.

6

IN THE sun-drenched summer of 1914, an outside observer might well have predicted that, in the Great House at Ockenham, Mrs. Mortimer-Wotton and her new daughter-in-law were bound to be set on a collision course.

Consider the situation. On the one side Constance: châtelaine for the past thirty-five years, sixty years old and greatly respected, assured in her command and surrounded by servants devoted to her. On the other side Eleanor: enthusiastic, forceful, American, with a strong will but little feeling for country life. Inevitably the younger woman must feel an intruder, sensitive to comparison with the earlier wife who still held the affection of these Mortimer-Wotton retainers. For all she knew, they might be making comparisons between Bertha's son and hers. A vague background fear, perhaps: something of her own imagining. But hardly surprising. How could she be expected to understand that for the servants of the Great House loyalty to her husband was a long-term commitment irrespective of the women in his life? For Eleanor time was the essence of the contract. It was not in her nature to hasten slowly.

Add to this basis for antagonism the absence of Francis who might have acted as catalyst, and the likelihood of trouble in the nursery where Gwynedd Morgan was bound to ask, "Who do I take my orders from?" – and the stage seemed set for a battle royal.

Or so the outside observer might have thought. But he would have been wrong, for he would have under-estimated the management skills of the lady of the house. Constance foresaw her daughter-in-law problem way ahead of the rest of the field and made her plans accordingly. Her first priority was naturally young Philip, now eight years old. It was, after all, his future on which her strategy must be based. He was the pawn at risk.

Inspiration came from a chance remark by Millicent Taylor on her routine visit to the Great House before the start of the summer term. Constance saw her opening and seized it. "So you're worried about Philip, Millicent?"

"Not exactly worried, Mrs. Mortimer-Wotton – But if you'll pardon the expression, he's getting rather 'bossy'. It's not just that he's big and strong for his years – after all, we're used to handling children up to fourteen at the school. But the other children of his age tend to do what he does and think what he thinks. I don't think it is good for Philip to get his way so easily. He's taking leadership for granted if you see what I mean."

"That's very well expressed, dear. Thank you for speaking so clearly. I'll have a talk with Philip's father this week and we'll decide together what's best for the boy. It's probably time for a change anyway if he has to take that ridiculous Latin for his Eton exam as his father and uncle had to do. Though what good 'hic, haec, hoc' has done them I cannot imagine."

That was the moment which prompted the decision to arrange for Philip to follow his father to Tudor Court near Basingstoke where Mr. Charles Furnival, M.A. (Oxon) guaranteed to get any boy into Eton, irrespective of the height or lowliness of his birth or intelligence.

So that's a good start, thought Constance. With Philip at boarding school for two-thirds of the year, Gwynedd's loyalties can be more easily re-directed. A few days later, when the Welsh girl entered Mrs. Mortimer-Wotton's corner room with the daily mid-morning tea, Constance made her next move.

"Gwynedd," she began "now that you are walking out with Albert Pittock, I believe you ought to have some additional help in the nursery."

"But, Madam, I'm sure I can manage by myself," the girl replied, outwardly blushing and inwardly wondering how on earth her mistress knew about Bertie. "Master Philip's no trouble these days and the baby's very good."

"Yes, but we have to look ahead, you know. And I need you too, Gwynedd. Where should I be without you? Once the war's over, I expect you'll be setting up a new home and Mr. and Mrs. Francis will be much happier if the children can be cared for by someone you have trained." And Gwynedd received a handsome rise of ten shillings a week, together with the assurance that the eldest of the Evans children from the post office would be joining her in the next few days.

Finally Constance had a talk with Eleanor. "It won't be easy, my dear, to fit into the routine here. But I promise not to get in your way. They say this stupid war will be over by Christmas and then you and Francis can decide together where you want to live. I shall be happy to move to the Dower House the moment you take on the responsibilities here. Meanwhile we'll muddle along happily, I'm sure."

Eleanor was gratified by her mother-in-law's straightforward approach. Clearly, she wanted to enjoy a happy relationship with her son's second wife. It was only as month succeeded month that the American girl realised with a shock that, while the war lasted, she would never exercise independent command unless she took some initiative on her own.

The opportunity for action came when her mother-in-law, as President of the regional V.A.D. organisation, was master-minding a local campaign for recruiting more nurses.

"Well, here's your first volunteer," said Eleanor and that was the start of a career which turned the young American into a skilled nurse, a first class driver and mechanic and brought her, after a dramatic visit to the Western Front, to a top administrative job in converting a series of country houses, including the Dower House at Little Ockenham, into convalescent homes for wounded officers and men evacuated from the Field Hospitals behind the Western Front.

Eleanor's energy and drive won her the independent command she wanted: and with it, the genuine respect of those who worked under her. Only Constance saw that these activities took her daughter-in-law away from the estate and the Great House. Who could say, thought Constance, whether that was a good or a bad thing? Certainly, it made wartime living easier for everybody.

But that was all in the future. The immediate task was more humdrum – getting young Philip equipped for Furnival's. Which meant a visit to Peter Robinson's where they duly purchased a

Norfolk jacket, the regulation school tie and Eton collars, football vests, shorts and boots, and a straw hat and Eton suit for Sundays. "A fabulous racket," Eleanor concluded as she totted up the bill. Happily the shopping expedition was combined with a visit to the Zoo and a tremendous tea at Gunters in Berkeley Square where a uniformed Francis, looking very handsome as a captain in the Buffs, joined Constance, Eleanor and Philip.

On his return to Ockenham Philip told Gwynedd all about the London expedition while he practised adjusting his studs and tie to his Eton collar. "Gorgon, if only you'd been with us," he cried. "You could have joined me on the elephant ride ... those great animals ... fantastic ... and the way they use their trunks ... oh damn this front stud."

"Now, Master Philip, swearing won't help whatever your father thinks. Stop chattering about the elephants and concentrate on keeping the tie on the rim of the collar. There, that's better. Now, on with the new jacket to see how it fits," and Gwynedd stood back to get a better view of her charge. "My word, you're quite the gentleman now, young man. They'll hardly know you down in the village." Little did she appreciate the irony of her words.

For the rest of the holidays, Philip wore his old clothes and enjoyed the old familiar things with Amos and Margie and the rest of the local children. Together, they sailed 'America' on the lake and rode their bicycles round the lanes. Together they watched the village cricket side playing in the park. Once John Williams took them in one of the farm wagons on a full day's outing to Seasalter where they bathed and picnicked from a most ample hamper jointly prepared by Mrs. Constant, Mrs. Williams and Mrs. Kemsing. When Philip was not with the other children, he was happy enough playing with his small brother or explaining where he kept his toys to the fourteen-year-old Evans girl. "I like Welsh people," he told Dorothy Evans tactfully, 'they always seem to want to help. I expect you'll soon be able to think up stories about dragons and wizards like the Gorgon does. Though, of course" he added, "she learnt about them from her father who met the monsters down a coal-mine long ago. And you were born over the post office in Ockenham so yours will be a different shape, won't they?" And Dorothy put the books and bricks away while Gwynedd smiled as she gave Bobby his last bottle before bed. Philip was really no trouble at all.

And then on the last Sunday before the new school term, came the Cathedral parade of the Territorial Battalion of The Buffs. The ancient buildings of Canterbury were glowing in the afternoon light of the September sunshine as the 4th Battalion, the Royal East Kent Regiment, wheeled into the Military Road from the Old Infantry Barracks. Down Saint Rodigund's they came in columns of fours, chests out, arms swinging, the regimental band at their head. On through the crowded streets towards the saluting base at the West Gate, where the City Mayor and the Colonel of the Buffs were stationed, surrounded by the notables of the City and County. Among them, in five reserved seats, could be seen the Ockenham party, which had made the ten-mile journey in Mrs. Mortimer-Wotton's Rolls Royce landaulette after an early lunch. Constance and Eleanor were there, of course, in their smartest dresses. So too were Philip and Amos Williams. The two boys had sat on the tip-up seats of the new car while Gwynedd had ridden beside Parkinson, the chauffeur. Now, safely in their seats, they chattered away while they waited for the heads of the columns to reach them. "Mr. Kemsing says the chap who hits the big drum has got a remarkable thirst," whispered Amos.

"Father says he'll be at the head of 'C' company, marching out in front," said Philip.

"Albert Pittock, now he's a lance corporal will be nearest us," said Gwynedd proudly, "but he'll have to keep his eyes straight to the front when they get the command 'eyes right'."

"Why will he do that, Gorgon?" demanded the two boys.

But an end to the questions. The band goes by. 'C' company is in view. No time for explanations. The children are standing up, craning their necks. So is the Welsh nurse, clutching Philip's hand with a strange, excited force. Bravely the men of Kent pass by in the pride of their uniforms. For the little party from Ockenham, no soldiers in the long column seem quite as smart as the officer commanding 'C' company and the newly promoted Albert Pittock. Surreptitiously, Gwynedd pulls out her handkerchief. "What are you crying about?" asks Philip.

"I don't rightly know, dear," comes the tremulous answer.

"Excitement I expect, or perhaps I'm wondering when Albert will be back at Little Ockenham. There may be others in the crowd, thinking like me . But have you ever seen such splendid soldiers?"

Early in 1915, the Territorial Battalion of the Buffs was transported East of Suez to replace the second regular Battalion recently returned from India. But Francis Mortimer-Wotton was not of the company.

"Sorry, Francis," the colonel had told him a few weeks earlier, "I can't help it. The War House has got your number in its little book. You're due to join our gallant allies. It's your damned proficiency in the French language that's done it. I've argued with those Staff wallahs but they're not playing ball. I suppose they're a bit shy on French speakers. The best thing you can do is to give the Buffs a decent write-up at French headquarters." And there was no more for Francis to say beyond a rather miserable goodbye to the men he had trained and worked with for the last eighteen months.

But it was not France that claimed the newly promoted liaison officer. After a short period of training at the War Office, Francis landed in Salonika late in 1915 to take up duty as chief French-speaking liaison officer under the British G.O.C. A nice chap, General Milne, who shared many mutual friendships with the Mortimer-Wottons: and a first class soldier into the bargain, with no illusions about his French superior officer

"Don't let us mince words, Francis. General Sarrail is an absolute stinker – an ambitious politico who likes to be called the only republican general in France. Joffre can't stick his guts, that's why he's in this God-forsaken hole. But Briand says he commands the loyalty of some hundred deputies, whatever that may mean. And to be fair to Sarrail, he put up a very good show at the first battle of Verdun. Militarily speaking, he'll do a good job provided he gets the chance."

With that admonition, Col. Mortimer-Wotton set off for the French headquarters. It was a new experience and, for a time, great fun. The French did themselves well. The Intelligence Staff with whom he was chiefly in touch gave him a clear picture of the complicated political scene against which every military move in Salonika had to be calculated.

And there was plenty of gossip about the general's lady – *"Tout à fait charmante, mais aussie dangereuse, cette Mme. Joséphine. Attention, mon brave."* And the French officers gave Francis a knowing look.

But Francis soon became disenchanted with life in a place which the Germans unkindly called 'the greatest allied internment camp in the world.'

To escape boredom, he agreed to make a circuitous journey to Bucharest with his French opposite number, Pierre Leduc, and in due course reported on the Roumanians to General Milne. "You won't like 'em, Sir. Officers all over the streets, plenty of make-up, dressed to the nines and for the most part only interested in women. Absolute shockers."

"C'est la guerre," remarked the general philosophically. And Francis returned to French headquarters. But not for long. General Sarrail had, from the start, received him with every mark of courtesy and Francis was not surprised when he was informed that Madame Joséphine wished to take lessons in English. But the English lessons became more frequent and the vivacious Madame Joséphine began to show a greater interest in her English tutor than in the English language. The French officers found it most diverting.

Suddenly, on a routine visit to British headquarters, Francis was told that the G.O.C. wanted to see him. "Trouble, old boy," his friends told him, "but don't worry. The general has quite a twinkle in his eye this morning."

General Milne was, indeed, in a genial mood. "What the hell have you been up to with that woman, Francis? I've had the most cryptic note from my master which more or less tells me to get you out of Salonika at top speed."

"Good God, Sir, really? Well, I'll be very happy if you accept the general's suggestion. Madame is truly *formidable.*"

"Well, it suits me too," said the general, "because I want you for a cloak-and-dagger job right up your street. I'll ring for Norton Griffiths who is in charge of Operation Fireworks and needs a mate."

It seemed the High Command had decided that the Roumanian oil wells situated in Wallachia to the north of Bucharest would fall to the Germans for a certainty as soon as the snows melted and von

Mackensen moved his seasoned veterans across the passes. They had therefore to be destroyed: and the task could not be left to our dubious allies.

"So you two have to get there first," concluded the G.O.C. "Mortimer-Wotton knows the road, having gone on a holiday with a French pal last year. And Norton Griffiths knows all about oil and pyrotechnics generally. Have a good journey – out as fast as you can and back in your own time. Good luck."

Norton Griffiths and Francis reached Wallachia in record time via Uskub and Craiova, keeping well north of Bucharest. Near Ploesti they established a hideout for the explosives, and set about their task. They jammed oil rigs and fired the installations. The damage was spectacular. In Griffiths' words Guy Fawkes couldn't have put on a bigger show. They had succeeded in achieving complete surprise, the Roumanians assuming quite reasonably that the German armies to the north-west would not move before the late spring.

But after fourteen days of fireworks, it was too hot for comfort. Griffiths decided their best chance of survival was to travel singly and the two men parted company after discarding their army truck and uniforms. In fact, they passed through Nish within a week of each other and Norton Griffiths eventually got back through Thessaly to Salonika. But the Bulgars were showing up everywhere and Francis decided to move south-west towards the old Serbo-Albanian boundary where he reckoned he could rely on the Serbs for help.

The Serbian peasants were a blood-thirsty lot, slitting the throats of Bulgarians as a national duty, regardless of reprisals, but they had a touching faith in the British and never let Francis down – feeding and clothing him and finally moving him in a farm cart towards Lake Okhrida. It was there that he was knocked out by malaria. For six weeks he was tended by an old woman who was desperately poor but seemed to regard Francis as her special responsibility for the rest of the war. When at last he was strong enough to move, it was the very devil getting away. But eventually he made his way to Durazzo, hopped a fishing boat sailing through the straights of Otranto and finally landed at Corfu to be greeted by the blessed sight of a British naval frigate in port. It was months before the British hospital at Corfu allowed him home but early in July 1918 he sailed for England, four stone lighter than his fighting weight in 1915.

All said and done, it was quite a journey. His D.S.O. was well-deserved. But Francis was one of the lucky ones. There were 5,688 casualties of the Royal East Kent Regiment recorded in the Warrior's Chapel of Canterbury Cathedral, and among them was the name of Sgt. A. Pittock, MM., killed in Mesopotamia while serving with the 5th Buffs in the assault on Kut.

Bertie remained the only man in Gwynedd's life. His photograph in a silver frame was to be seen on her dressing table for the rest of her days. As the years passed she learnt to hide her grief as her mistress had done ever since that hour, long ago, when Henry Mortimer-Wotton had also died in a distant land fighting for his country. Gwynedd never looked at another man. Henceforward, the chances of life and the death of Albert Pittock involved her in total commitment to the Mortimer-Wotton family.

7

TUDOR COURT – or Furnival's, to use the name by which the school was most widely known – had been started in 1890 as a tutorial establishment for the sons of gentlemen by the Rev. Eustace Furnival, in order to augment his meagre stipend and make fuller use of an over-large and rambling vicarage in the Chilterns. It was, however, Charles Furnival, the son of the Rev. Eustace and, like him, a King's Scholar at Eton, who moved the school to Tudor Court near Basingstoke and made it one of the best known preparatory schools in the South of England.

Theoretically, Furnival's prepared boys for all the leading public schools and for entry into the navy via Osborne. In practice, it concentrated on Eton, Charles Furnival shrewdly appreciating that Eton, with its old boys straddling politics, society and the diplomatic service, was attractive not only to its traditional supporters among the nobility and land-owners of England, but also to those newly-rich Edwardian tycoons who desperately wanted to be accepted by those at the top of the class pyramid.

The fees were correspondingly high and the waiting list long enough for Charles Furnival to select the families who sent their sons to his seventy-strong school. And, in a very real sense, he never let the parents down. There was a string of King's Scholars who received their first grounding in Latin and Greek at Furnival's and a much larger number of boys of moderate and low intelligence who, under Charles Furnival's forceful guidance, passed into Eton successfully.

Indeed, failure was unknown. As a special conceit, the boys were taught to speak in Etonian language so that the school matron was referred to as 'the Dame', terms were 'Halves', forms were 'Divisions' and a desk was a 'Burry'. They also became stoically accustomed to the frequency of corporal punishment such as the

Rev. Eustace and his son had themselves endured in their own days at Eton. The boys were quickly made aware of the scale of penalties applied. Idleness or mediocre results at work meant a visit to the study where the offender received two, three or four strokes with a light cane, the severity of the punishment depending on the age or persistence of the offender. Making trouble in the form room or noise in the dormitory could mean heavier retribution with the same implement which was delivered in quantity with the textbooks by the school's supplier in London. These were comparatively light offences and, in the course of his five years at Furnival's, neither idler nor boy of spirit escaped.

There were, however, more serious crimes such as lying, cheating and bullying when the headmaster beat the offenders with a long cane as used at Eton. Such executions were greatly feared and so rare as to be sensational.

The Draconian code, enforced at Furnival's, would certainly be called in question today, as would the authority over younger boys given by Charles Furnival to the thirteen-year-old prefects at his school – another spin-off from Etonian custom. But Charles and Francis Mortimer-Wotton and their contemporaries had come to expect such discipline as a necessary prelude to their further education. And Philip and the twelve other boys who started life at Furnival's in the autumn of 1914 accepted school life as it came to them – an unpleasant experience which made home and holidays all the more attractive.

Philip, for his part, moved steadily up the school but without particular distinction. Big for his age and of no more than average ability, he was not expected to win much honour for the school either at work or games. His size marked him, in the eyes of Charles Furnival, as a possible goal-keeper in the soccer term, a rugger forward who could use his height in the line-out and perhaps a fast bowler in the summer – if only he could get his limbs under control – which the headmaster doubted. Whatever happened, Philip would give a fair account of himself in the boxing ring, boxing being compulsory for all boys unless excused by a medical certificate. During the next four years Philip's end-of-term reports showed little variation. "Making steady progress on all fronts," "must work harder on subjects he doesn't enjoy," "congratulations on winning the junior boxing cup" and, rather more interesting, frequent references to his kindness to other boys. It was not a bad summary of the lad's character that Charles Furnival spelt out to the parents. Neither Eleanor, Constance nor Francis, to whom the reports were forwarded, had any cause for anxiety.

Charles Furnival was, however, beset by many wartime problems. The difficulties of rationing and finding domestic staff, the lack of younger men to help with the teaching, the tragic dilemma of boys whose fathers were fighting and dying on the Western Front – too much was falling on his shoulders and those of the Dame. The pressure began to affect the headmaster's health and it was with a sense of relief that he invited his nephew, Captain Jason Furnival, to help him run the school.

It proved a disastrous mistake. Jason Furnival had served with the Guards in France and, so it was said, been invalided out of the army with shell shock. But schoolboys quickly make their own assessments of a master's character and they are generally 'on target'. The boys at Furnival's soon had cause to dislike Jason's temper. They found he couldn't teach and he boasted about his cricket. They thought he gave his mousy little wife a rotten time. They particularly resented his constant reference to his war service – the more offensive because there was hardly a boy in the school whose father was not fighting overseas. They began to mock him. Philip was considered very funny when he shouted into the changing room one day, "Get a move on, you chaps. I want more spit and polish. Pick 'em up, pick 'em up or you'll find yourselves in the glass-house."

Nobody knew what the gibberish meant but the bogus Guardee accent was unmistakable and soon Smith minor was asking his friends in the third form if they'd heard Mortimer-Wotton taking off the captain – he's an absolute hoot. Brian Melchester's verses were also quoted by the more daring in the secrecy of the lavatories –

> Captain Jason
> Fetch the basin
> You cause us all to spew.
> Don't hang about

You red-faced lout
But fetch it P.D.Q.

Rudely simple or simply rude – it added up to a deep-seated and universal dislike of old Furnie's nephew. When the school re-assembled in the summer term to learn that Charles Furnival was convalescing after a slight stroke and that Captain Jason was in charge of the school, trouble was as certain as night following day.

As always, the big flare-up had small beginnings. On a summer afternoon when they should have been watching cricket, Chaudari, whose father was in the Indian Civil Service, and young Levine whose family was related to Sir Ernest Cassel, were engaged in testing the strength of a new magnifying glass by focussing the sun on some dry leaves. It was much more exciting than watching the first eleven playing against a neighbouring school, called Lincoln Lodge: but Levine's magnifying glass became somewhat over-publicised when the smoke began to rise and the cricket had to be stopped while the fire was extinguished.

Philip had been playing for the school, opening the bowling and getting three quick wickets with three terrifying deliveries before knocking out his own wicket keeper with a ball which might have been called a bumper. He was taken off for bowling dangerously ("Hell, I couldn't help it, it was the wicket, not me"), and, apart from missing a catch and letting two boundaries through his legs, took little further part in the game.

Later that evening, he was kicking a ball around the gym with two of his friends when Smith minor burst in.

"I say, Rotten (the inevitable nickname even though it didn't rhyme), the Sixth have got Chaudari and Levine in their room. They've locked the door and they're going to beat them up with gym shoes."

Philip turned to his friends. "Poor little devils, I don't like it, do you? An Indian and a Jew, both in their first year? Oh no, we stop it, I think."

"Go on, you wouldn't dare."

"Of course, I would – but I'll need a bit of help. Come on." And with cries ranging from "Where's the Sheriff of Nottingham" to "Vanguard of Liberty, ye men of Kent", Philip led the assault.

Forcing the door, he winded the head of the school with a straight left to the stomach; Melchester threw the gym shoes out of the window: and the raiders were already making a triumphant and noisy escape with the two small boys when Captain Furnival appeared.

He was in a foul temper, red in the face and shouting. "So it's you, is it Mortimer-Wotton, with your supercilious contempt for authority, eh? What are you yapping about? Sticking up for those young fire-raisers? You're challenging authority, that's what you're doing. I'll darn well show you who's in charge in this school. You'll grovel for this before I'm finished with you." And Philip was hauled off to the study.

The boys listened with bated breath, as near to the study as they dared go. The first stroke . . . "Gawd, it's the long stick and poor old Rotten in his gym shorts." Two . . . Three . . . Four . . . not a sound from Philip. "By heavens, he's got guts" . . . Five . . . Six . . . A tiny whimper. "The man's a swine, grunting too . . . the devil."

Suddenly the mouse-like figure of Mrs. Jason Furnival rushed across the hall and burst into the study. The boys heard a furious feminine voice . . . then another stroke halfway up the victim's back . . . Jason Furnival shouting, "Get out of my sight," and Philip Mortimer-Wotton staggered out of the study to the comfort of his friends.

It was too much to bear. Philip was in agony. Screaming at them not to touch him, he crept off to the bathroom to take off his shorts. Brian Melchester joined him a few moments later and inspected the marks on his friend's back and buttocks . . . "God almighty . . . You're in a hell of a mess. The bloody sadist, he'll be in trouble for this, I promise you. But I reckon you ought to see the Dame."

"Not on your bleeding life," replied Philip. "I'm going to mop up and get out. I'm damned if I'll stay here to be cuddled by women and pestered by kids to show them what my arse looks like. Let's get started."

Philip was resolved to get away from this horrible place once and for all. That meant immediate action. He rolled up the pathetic bundle of clothes and towels and tucked them in his bed – that would surprise the poor old Dame – and bound them up with the school tie for good measure. A quick change – walking shoes, open shirt, a couple of pull-overs, no identifiable insignia: and with three pound notes surreptitiously borrowed by Melchester, he made his getaway. Out through the bootroom window into the playing fields – "Close the window and nobody, Mel ... but nobody has any idea where I've gone. Understood?" And with a whispered good luck in his ear and the window bolted behind him, Philip was off into the night.

Shrewdly, he moved in the opposite direction from Basingstoke. Somehow, he'd got to make Farnham or Aldershot – every bit of ten miles, he reckoned – before the hue and cry started. On a lane near Odiham he pulled himself up, unnoticed, into a horse drawn farm wagon, and two miles outside Aldershot dropped off near a golf course where he dozed in a shelter. Stiff and aching he managed the last two miles into Aldershot as day was breaking.

Suddenly, he heard noisy footsteps and laughter behind him, soldiers for certain. They'd tell him the way to the station: surely he could trust them. He waited for them to catch up.

"Mornin' sonny," one of them greeted him. "So you want the station? Well, you'd better 'itch up with us, 'cos that's where we're off to. Bound for London, eh? And 'ave *you* got forty-eight hours leave too?" The men from the Hampshires were in high good humour.

Philip decided to take a chance. "Well, it's not exactly leave, but my father's in hospital, just back from the Middle East, and I've got permission to see him."

"Fair enough, laddie, that's your story – so we'll see you up to Waterloo. Safety in numbers, yer know. What d'you say, Nobby?"

"That's right by me, Ginger. 'E looks just like my nephew that I'm escortin' back to 'is London 'ome."

"There you are, laddie. Follow Uncle Nobby to the platform and tell us all about yourself in the train."

The men were as good as their word. They took his money for the ticket they bought him, and gave him an apple and an enormous sandwich.

Soon Philip was no more than a small boy fast asleep, out to the world and wedged amongst a company of soldiers on the London train. But just after leaving Woking he stirred and screamed in his sleep. Ginger looked at him curiously and said to his mate, "This kid's in right trouble for sure. Poor little bugger. We'll 'ave to leave 'im with somebody. Better wake 'im up gradual-like and ask a few questions.''

By Clapham Junction, they'd got the whole miserable story out of the boy, thrown a blood-stained handkerchief out of the window and replaced it with one of their own. More important, they'd formulated a plan.

"Now this is what we do, young Philip, to get you 'ome to your Pa – 'and you over to the Salvation Army. Don't worry. They're good blokes, always to be found at Waterloo on the look-out for lost souls like us. We fix it up over a nice cup o' cha. See?''

Sure enough, the two men hustled their charge, willy nilly, past the ticket barrier and into the Salvation Army canteen where a Salvation Army lassie found a more senior officer who might have been looking after lost children in London all his life. A hurried thank you from Philip – 'no names, no packdrill, matey' – and Ginger and Nobby were off into the crowd.

The Salvationist took Philip into an office, got his home address and rang Ockenham. "Can I speak to the father or mother of Philip Mortimer-Wotton?''

Constance answered. "Philip's father's in hospital and his mother's away from the house on V.A.D. duty. It's his grandmother speaking. Can I help? Run away from school, you say? And you think, officer, he should come home at once? Very severe bruising, requires nursing? I agree, explanations later. I'll arrange to meet the Waterloo train arriving Ashford at eleven-thirty. I think, officer, it'll be best if you can provide a companion: and please be sure to send your account to me personally.''

Only Gwynedd knew what was amiss. The last thing Constance did before leaving with Parkinson to meet the London train was to tell Gwynedd to have Philip's bed properly aired. Two hours later, the Rolls was back from Ashford and Philip was bathed and tucked up in bed, his lacerations dressed and Gwynedd fussing round him.

There had been two telephone calls from Basingstoke while Constance had been away and one from the police station at Canterbury. Now Constance answered a further call.

"Captain Furnival speaking from Tudor Court. Mrs.

Mortimer-Wotton, I'm very sorry to report . . ." He got no further.

Quivering with fury, Constance forced herself to control her voice. "I fear you will be sorry for much more than your reporting, Mr. Furnival. My grandson is safely home, thanks to his own courage, the kindness of some soldiers and the good offices of the Salvation Army who, let me say, know more than most people about the maltreatment of children. They will make a full report on the case, no doubt. Meanwhile, it is to be hoped that your disgusting behaviour will not damage Philip, physically or mentally, for life. The other parents will no doubt learn of your brutality from their own children and take such action as they think fit. But I can assure you now that Philip Mortimer-Wotton will not be returning to Tudor Court . . . ever." And Constance banged the receiver back into its bracket.

Next she rang the Canterbury Police apologising for any trouble that might have been caused and instructing them to inform their colleagues in Hampshire that her grandson was safely home. Finally, she told Absalom that she would accept no telephone calls from the Basingstoke area or from Tudor Court, and would he please bring her a double whisky.

That same evening Francis rang Melchester's father, from Millbank Hospital. Before the end of term, the old-boy network was in full operation. Parents arranged to move their boys to other schools. New entries came to a halt. The agencies excluded Tudor Court from their recommendations. A year later and Furnival's belonged to the past tense and Captain Furnival had emigrated. The Mortimer-Wottons were not without influence when they chose to use it.

As to Philip, he continued all his life to love soldiers and admire the Salvation Army. For Jason Furnival he maintained an unrelenting hatred as the embodiment of all that was beastly in the human race.

8

THREE WEEKS AFTER his escape from Tudor Court, Philip was still in a state of shock – or that is how it seemed to those who lived in the Great House. Physically, he was on the mend. But he continued to show all the signs of mental depression – refusing to go out and meet other people. In the old phrase, 'he would not be comforted'.

Gwynedd, who used to wake him with a cup of tea and, sometimes, a slice of bread and butter saved from the tray she took to Mrs. Mortimer-Wotton at seven o'clock each morning, was deeply concerned. The boy who in previous holidays had laughed at her efforts to get him out of bed ("I'm stronger than a Gorgon, oh little Gwynedd Morgan"), waited for her arrival, awake, bored and listless. Gwynedd knew he was sleeping badly. Again and again she found him with his bed clothes all over the place and his eyes staring aimlessly at the ceiling. And then there was the nightmare, when she'd woken to an agonised cry and discovered him sweating with terror.

All this the Welsh girl reported to her mistress. "I never liked that school, Ma'am – as bad as anything Charles Dickens ever thought up. Poor little chap, it's a shame."

"Now, Gwynedd, stop talking like that." Mrs. Mortimer-Wotton was in her most authoritative mood. "What's done cannot be undone. Somehow or other we have to get Philip thinking about the future, not the past."

Or just thinking and doing *something*, she added to herself, for really the boy was most difficult. He'd hardly touched the favourite dishes which Mrs. Constant cooked for him. He'd been downright rude to Eleanor which was more than tiresome. He refused point-blank to meet the children in the village – "I won't go near them, Gran, until I can bathe in the river at Chilham with nothing on and nobody noticing the marks on my bottom." He wouldn't have any of his school friends to stay – not even Brian Melchester who had spent a week at Ockenham the previous holidays.

A visit to his father in hospital did nothing to help. Returning from London he shook Eleanor by asking in an almost analytical tone of voice, "Is Father going to die, Mother? He looks very thin and yellow and sort of unhappy too." It was a disconcerting reaction to the first expedition away from Ockenham – let alone a frustrating experience for Eleanor who had planned the trip and for Francis who had made a considerable effort to be cheerful on one of his bad days of recurrent fever.

Apart from the books he was endlessly reading, Philip's chief consolation lay in the company of his small step-brother. Only Bobby, now aged five, succeeded in making the twelve-year-old Philip forget his troubles. Sometimes the older boy played with Bobby for hours on end. Together, they wandered into the gardens and the park: and Philip would become almost animated as he recounted to the grown-ups Bobby's comical remarks or spoke of his skill in kicking a small football round the lawn. One day Dorothy Evans surprised him teaching the little boy to read. "I could hardly keep myself from laughing out loud," she told Gwynedd, "with Master Philip looking so serious and Bobby trying so hard."

Somehow or other, the little boy induced in Philip a patience and toleration which he showed to no one else. With Bobby, at least, he was happy. And to Bobby, Philip was a hero.

Constance was still worrying about her elder grandson when Justin Leadbitter invited her to Canterbury to meet a new acquaintance. "A parson, Constance, name of Waddilove, just appointed to a canonry and so entitled to one of those delightful small houses in the Precincts. Ever heard of him? Apparently your husband knew him at Eton, but that was er . . . how shall I put it, before the poor chap lost his way in India."

"Ever heard of him? Arthur Waddilove, a poor chap losing his way in India?" Constance was astonished. "Why, Justin, what a ridiculously small horizon you solicitors have, to be sure. Everybody of Henry's generation at Eton knows something about

Arthur Waddilove – the last man to lose his way anywhere, if his schoolboy reputation is any guide.''

Her mind flew back to the days of her courtship in the early eighteen seventies when Arthur had been a sort of schoolboy-and-Oxford hero. A fine athlete – that's how he and Harry had met – he'd also won an open classical scholarship to Oxford, picked up a cricket 'blue' as well as a 'double first' and then passed first into the Indian Civil Service.

But such achievements do not in themselves create a legend. Arthur's fame rested on the rarer feat that, within five years of reaching India, he had rejected all thought of fame. He had resigned from the I.C.S., gone into some sort of Retreat run by an Indian guru and finally emerged to become a priest in the Anglican communion. For a short time, Constance seemed to recall, he'd been involved in teaching: was it a C.M.S. school near Agra? – but always he had refused advancement, insisting that his mission in life was to serve and teach and live with the under-privileged people of the sub-continent. Oh yes, there were other stories too – his friendship with Rabindranath Tagore, his visit to Gandhi's Ashram, his presence in Delhi at the time of the Montague-Chelmsford reforms. His activities were never publicised. But to those who had any link with the India of the war years the name of Arthur Waddilove held significance – to some people, as a humble man of God moving through the myriad villages of India; to shrewd civil servants at the India Office, as an Englishman who understood the thought processes of the leaders of Indian opinion; but to others, more numerous, who wanted the Raj to continue for ever in its nineteenth-century image, as a dangerous revolutionary and a disgrace to the education which he had been privileged to enjoy.

Constance was therefore highly intrigued by Justin's invitation and in the event was fascinated by the new resident in the Cathedral Precincts. Arthur Waddilove proved to be tall, every bit of six foot three inches, stooping slightly as if to enter doors and houses built for smaller men. His bright deep-set eyes dominated the company he was in – young eyes they seemed, for all his sixty-eight years. And then Constance was aware of the high cheekbones, the sallow skin and the thin hands which in spite of their thinness were so expressive of strength. Or was it experience? This man must have seen and heard and suffered so much more than his more conventional school contemporaries who had remained, as if by right of inheritance, inside the well worn corridors of power. He must have an extraordinary story to tell.

But Arthur Waddilove was not talking about himself that morning. With a deceptive suavity, he directed question after question to Constance. How was life at Ockenham? He hadn't been there since he'd played for Henry's side against the Band of Brothers in 1872 or thereabouts. And how was it with Francis? Yes, he understood just how low malaria brings a man. And the loss of Charles of which he'd heard from some mountaineers he'd met in Darjeeling: how infinitely sad. "But the future, Constance, two grandsons, you say, with a seven year gap?" Long before the meal was over, Constance found herself telling Arthur Waddilove of Philip and Bobby and Bertha's death and Francis's second wife. Justin Leadbitter, that old and skilled solicitor, sat back and marvelled at the sheer professionalism with which his friend uncovered the trouble centres in Constance's life. Never had he heard Constance talk so much about her family.

The outcome was that on the following Saturday afternoon Arthur Waddilove, taking up the vague invitation extended to him at lunch, arrived unannounced at Ockenham. "I thought I'd try out my new bicycle, Constance, and couldn't think of a better destination than the cricket ground I used to know. I swear it's as lovely as it ever was, with the changing colour of the leaves and the lengthening shadows of the September sun. And you can't say that of every corner of wartime England. If only the cricketers were back." And the tall man casually rose from the tea table in the rose garden to punt Bobby's straying football back to the croquet lawn where his hostess's two grandsons were playing some complicated game of their own.

This early September visit was the first of many that Arthur Waddilove made to Ockenham. In a remarkably short time, he managed to get acquainted with Eleanor and at her suggestion he visited Francis in hospital. Without appearing to intrude, he picked up the names and backgrounds of the different members of the household, and they were glad of his presence. In the first week in October, when he was invited by old Pendlebury to preach at the Harvest Festival service, he spoke of the certainty of the peace to come with such authority and simplicity that there was not a member of the little congregation who did not leave the church with a lighter step. Wherever he went, he radiated new hope. That was the sort of man he was.

Constance was never quite sure who first suggested that Philip would be happier with a private tutor than at a new school. Nor could she trace the process by which Eleanor persuaded Francis that Arthur Waddilove was the man for the job. Still less did she understand how her difficult grandson accepted the idea with such equanimity. But certain it was that by mid-September, and well before the sermon in Ockenham Church, Philip was boarding at the canon's little house under the protection of the great Cathedral. Nor did he evince any regret at being separated from his home or his erstwhile school friends. After a few days' residence in the Precincts, Arthur Waddilove reported to Ockenham that, on the evidence of his own eyes and those of his housekeeper, Philip was sleeping and eating as well as any healthy twelve-year-old could be expected to do.

It was the start of a golden year in Philip's life. The canon proved as unconventional as he was direct in his approach to the purpose. On his first day away from Ockenham, Arthur Waddilove dealt with the boy's unspoken question. "No need to call me Sir, or Canon, Philip. You and I will get on best if we call each other by our Christian names just as we'll call my housekeeper Emily and her beloved cat, Tabitha."

Next, he went through a number of Eton entrance papers with Philip "Got to satisfy the examiners, my son, but I tell you what. We'll get the Latin and the Maths out of the way on the rainy days. When it's fine, we'll go out and learn about England."

And so they did. Philip armed himself with a notebook with separate pages for different centuries, beginning firmly with 55 B.C. "And we'll cut out the Stone Age, it's deadly boring." One day they cycled to Deal – "We may as well see where Julius Caesar landed." And then while they fished on the pier, Arthur Waddilove discoursed on the Roman Empire, cunningly emphasising the bits that might come in useful – how the Romans came to

Gaul, what brought them over to Britain, why they were in Palestine in the time of Christ. Never more than a quarter of an hour without having a look at the lines: and one great moment when together they landed a crab at a point in the story when the Romano-British families in Kent and East Anglia were fleeing from the German invaders to join King Arthur in the Celtic west.

Another day they visited Richborough on the Stour estuary behind Sandwich, with the canon bringing the huge base to life – the men on the transports tying up at the quay after sighting the walled camp from far out in the Channel, the legions filing out of the North Gate towards Canterbury, and so to Rochester and London and Boadicea's rebellion.

Philip loved it all. His enthusiasm was reflected not only in the care with which he filled in his history notebook with notes and postcards bought on these little expeditions, but also in the three long letters Arthur made him write each week. "Letters are more interesting than essays, Philip. Just let yourself go and don't worry about the spelling. Who do you send 'em to? Oh, anybody you like – your father and mother can share one now that your father is back at the Great House. Then there's your grandmother, and Gwynedd, and Miss Millie: or your friend Melchester. You'd be surprised how people like getting letters in the post. I'll take a look at them just to see you've got the facts straight."

Round Canterbury they pottered, sometimes helping Emily with the shopping ("You check the bill, Philip"), looking at the Norman keep at the end of Castle Street ("See how the Normans guarded the river crossings? They were good soldiers"), stopping in the Cathedral at the stairs near the North transept where Thomas Becket was murdered by the drunken knights of Henry II. "A terrible deed, but less important to you and me, Philip, than the fire which happened three years later in 1174 and led to the rebuilding of the Cathedral by William of Sens and William the Englishman. Just think of the millions of men and women whom their great building has inspired." And the tall old priest and his twelve-year-old pupil gazed west down the nave, then up to the roof and east to the majesty of the choir and the High Altar. At that moment, the awe and wonder of the place took hold of the boy in some strange way so that in later life he returned to the exact point in the Cathedral where he and his tutor had once stood. It was, in its own way, an act of worship.

History came to life with Arthur Waddilove, as naturally as a flower blossoms in the sun. Standing beside the Black Prince's tomb and gazing on his armour and emblazoned doublet, Philip was standing shoulder to shoulder with the English at Poitiers, he was aware of the Prince's great love for the Fair Maid of Kent, he shared her sorrow for the Prince's death and the failure of their son Richard. Walking in the ruins of the Priory and St. Augustine's Abbey, he saw with his own eyes the crime of Henry VIII: back in the crypt he learnt of the damage caused by Dick Culmer, the Puritan. ("Beware, Philip, of materialists like the Tudors and religious fanatics like Culmer. They commit great sins under the guise of respectability and religion.")

Much of this was recorded in the long letters Philip wrote each week to his chosen correspondents. But there was one event which found no place in the letters home. Early on November 11th Philip and Arthur visited the Poor Priests Hospital, built long ago by the barefoot Franciscans. Arthur was just starting to tell Philip how St. Francis had renounced his wealth and his inheritance, when there was a great roar outside the little building. 'Armistice signed . . . Germans surrender' and the good citizens of Canterbury were rushing headlong into the streets. Arthur turned to the boy, his eyes alight. "In a minute or two we'll shout with the best of them, Philip: but first I think we'll say a prayer together." And the words of Saint Francis issued quietly from the old man's lips.

"You are holy, Lord God, you alone work wonders.
You are the Lord God, living and true.
You are patience . . . you are peace.
You are our hope, you are our faith.
Lord God, make me an instrument of your peace. Where there is hatred let me sow love, where there is injury, pardon: where there is discord, union: where there is darkness, light: where there is sadness, joy."

Then they rose from their knees, the old man and the boy, and joined the crowd outside.

Seven months later Philip Mortimer-Wotton was duly offered a place at Eton, like his father and uncle and grandfather before him. "A boy of average intelligence," the college examiners reported laconically. "But his essay on 'my home town' showed unusual powers of observation."

To celebrate the occasion, the family and Arthur Waddilove motored over to Eton during the summer holidays. Eleanor, taking her first look at the school where Francis had been educated, stood amazed at its age-old splendours. "So Philip," she thought, "and Bobby too are to be part of this place, part of its tradition. And I . . . shall always remain outside it." She sighed and turned to join the others, noticing without surprise that Philip did not seem in any way over-awed by the size of the establishment.

By appointment they took tea with Philip's housemaster, Charles Ullathorne. Arthur knew him well enough to be on first-name terms. Clearly, they had met on many previous occasions. Not for the first time, Eleanor was aware of the extent and depth of the canon's friendships.

On his return to Canterbury, Arthur Waddilove wrote the following letter to the housemaster.

My dear Charles,

This letter is about Philip Mortimer-Wotton.

As I think you are aware, my temporary employment as his tutor followed a disgraceful affair at Furnival's when the boy was unmercifully beaten for committing a minor offence which should have been regarded as a quixotic act.

It has taken time for him to recover his natural buoyancy. But he's a friendly lad and I hope that even during adolescence he will not prove too moody or difficult.

Nevertheless, I feel I should explain that Philip, for all his family background, has had a far from easy childhood. His mother, many of whose Yorkshire qualities he inherits, died when he was three. His father married again: and for perfectly understandable reasons he and the second wife saw little of Philip in the years preceding 1914.

During the war, Eleanor, the second wife, devoted her considerable energies to war work, while the father, Francis

Mortimer-Wotton, was fighting on the Salonika front until invalided out with malaria in July 1918.

As a result, the boy has been separated too long from his parents, and brought up by his grandmother and the staff at Ockenham. The latter have done their work with much understanding and the boy holds them in great affection. But now, a new problem faces him. Old Mrs. Mortimer-Wotton will shortly be moving to the Dower House with some of her most trusted servants. Francis and Eleanor will take over at Ockenham Manor.

Philip will have to adjust himself to an entirely new situation, simultaneously with his arrival at Eton. And so, incidentally, will his father and step-mother. Family relationships will not be easy.

The parents know I am writing to you about Philip but have not seen the words of this letter, so I shall be grateful if you will regard it, in the army's phrase, as 'demi-official'.

I am due to preach in Chapel next term and also give a talk about India to some of the senior boys. Perhaps we shall be able to meet then.

Meanwhile, I commend Philip to your care. I believe he has great potential for good.

> Yours sincerely,
> Arthur Waddilove.

Arthur read the letter carefully, thoughtfully folded and sealed it and took it to the post box at the Christ Church gate. He and Emily and Tabitha would miss Philip. The boy was such a delightful companion. Yes, indeed . . . and a more rewarding assignment than some of those who sought him out. But there, Saint Francis didn't choose which beggar to help. Nor could he. For some people, they just turn up and they are not always dressed in poor men's clothes. As Arthur Waddilove returned through the Precincts in the cool of the evening to the comfort of his little house, he murmured to himself as if in prayer, "I hope the boy will do well. I believe he has it in him. But I wonder . . . I wonder." And his thought was not of Philip at Eton, but of Francis and Eleanor at Ockenham.

Book Two

A Gentleman at War

Whose passions not his masters are,
Whose soul is still prepared for death;
Untied unto the world by care
Of public fame, or private breath.

SIR HENRY WOTTON (1568–1639)

9

IN 1919, the dead were duly counted and honoured. The wounded received pensions. The statesmen, arguing about ethnic frontiers at the Palace of Versailles, brought new nations to birth. The map of Africa and the island-dotted Pacific increasingly blushed with the pink of Empire.

But who can measure the grief of war – the mother who has lost her son, the girl who has lost her lover, the homes and businesses that have been disrupted? And who can comprehend the change that war has wrought in the minds of those who survive and in the people that were once familiar to them? So much has been lost, so much has been suffered. So much has changed.

Francis, returning to Ockenham after his clearance from hospital, realised with a sense of shock that he could recognise the buildings more easily than the people. The house was there and the lake and the church and the village – still familiar in outline, even if short on paint and maintenance. But those he had once loved? Bertha's Philip? Grown into a gangling, over-serious, hard-to-know schoolboy. Eleanor's baby? Now a tough little five-year-old, but at least young enough to be friendly to a stranger. His mother, Gwynedd, Edward Pendlebury, old Absalom, Mrs. Constant? All changed. All of them tired. All of them older, so much, much older. And Eleanor, his lively, exciting American bride of 1912? Here in Ockenham he was meeting another person, somebody he didn't know. He'd already been puzzled by this odd sense of separation when she was making routine visits to him in hospital. His fault, he thought: the depressing effects of malaria. But now he was grimly aware she had no use for him. She seemed hard as nails, cold. He meant nothing to her.

Tenderness and youth were gone from Eleanor. By every trial he knew it. He touched her and she made no response. He kissed her and it meant nothing. When they went to bed in the room where they had made love at weekends in the old days, she roused no desire in him. She permitted him to enter her body. But when he came, he provoked no answering passion. Duty had been done – that was that. They separated, lying away from each other on either side of the double bed. There was nothing to say, no whispered endearment, no grief.

Eleanor slept. Francis lay awake until dawn. Hour after waking hour, the same thought drummed through his head. "I, Francis Mortimer-Wotton, am in bed with a stranger, a woman who does not need me, a wife I no longer identify as the girl I married in Cleveland, Ohio, and lived with in Tite Street, Chelsea. Is it my fault or hers that the excitement of love has no meaning? Can we in time recover desire? Or do we admit that love is dead and blame this war for yet another casualty?"

Eleanor slept. But then she had faced the problem long before the return of Francis to Ockenham. She was almost surprised at being there to greet her husband. How could she forget the night at Rouen, and the young captain in the Greenjackets who gave her dinner in that crumby hotel, made her laugh until she forgot the horror of the Field Hospital, then climbed hand in hand with her to the room upstairs, fumblingly took off her nurse's starchy uniform and made love to her throughout that night? There for sure was love – spontaneous, exciting, illicit. He'd done the loveliest things to her, reminded her she was a woman, not a nurse. She'd never seen him again, never expected to do so. It could have been, for all she knew, his last happiness before death. For her it had simply been the first – and so, the best remembered – of many similar adventures.

None of the others had any great significance until she met an R.A.M.C. Colonel at Hythe. For some months the two met regularly on and off duty. He wanted her to marry him, to give up Francis as he was prepared to give up his wife.

"It's our lives, my love," he'd say as she lay expectant in his arms in a field well away from the gossip of the hospital; or, "Our future is together," as his hands caressed her body in the little pub outside Tenterden.

Sometimes she still wondered why she'd held back, for she

didn't care a hoot for conventions. Must have been part of the family make-up, she supposed; her German-American parents who had prided themselves on their ability to assess the future without emotion. And the future, she'd concluded, is not for lovers. Almost to her surprise, she'd returned to Ockenham with a passionate interest in her own pre-war child.

But what did Bobby's father mean to her? Way back in 1916, she had declared her independence of him. These casual wartime lovers, to whom she had so willingly given herself, had told her in their snatched moments of ecstasy what physical love really meant. She'd learnt something of which she may have been dimly aware even before Francis left her in 1915. Now she was sure, with all the certainty of her woman's mind and body, that she had never replaced Bertha in Francis's affection. And how could pity for a returning soldier replace the reckless passion of these war years? Far better face it. Refuse to be second best. Fight free of a marriage you contracted for all the silly reasons which once, long ago, filled the ambitious mind of a Cleveland girl in search of the glamour and culture of Europe. Make a new life your own way – but somehow, somehow, dear God, without losing Bobby.

After weeks of indecision, Francis and Eleanor had it out together. They were walking in the Ockenham Woods on the high ground to the south-west of the estate, when Francis stopped dead in his tracks. He turned to his wife and his voice, unusually clipped and authoritative, betrayed the strain he was under.

"We've got to sort ourselves out, Ellie – once and for all," he said. "If you can't stick the idea of living with me, you'd better get out. I'll fix a divorce. A tart in Brighton and a hotel bill: that's all you need. It's a perfectly simple process of law."

"Simple?" said Eleanor – she'd never known him so brutally positive. "Simple? What about Bobby? Does he go with me?"

"Oh, I suppose so. That's the way it goes, I believe."

"But you don't understand. Bobby loves Ockenham. This is his world. And Philip means everything to him. I'm not prepared to give up Bobby. And equally, I'm not prepared to wreck his life."

"So it's a case of wanting the cake and the ha'penny, eh? You want to stay on at the Great House. Is that it? And remain my wife in name? For God's sake, make up your mind. We're not children.

I don't care a damn what other people think. But this house and land are mine – and Philip's after me. If you and Bobby stay here, you remain part of the Mortimer-Wotton set-up. That's flat."

Never before had Eleanor seen her husband in this mood – angry, unyielding, autocratic as his ancestors must have been. But the effort suddenly exhausted him. She saw him sweating and fumbling for his malaria pills. Involuntarily, she took his arm and helped him down the hill towards the house – the trained V.A.D. nurse helping the walking wounded along a rough path. She got him into bed, and drew the curtains of the room to keep the sunlight from his eyes. There was even pity in her eyes as she looked in to see that he was sleeping before she retired to a separate room where a bed had been made up for her.

And that's how it remained at Ockenham. There was no divorce. But Colonel and Mrs. Mortimer-Wotton went their separate ways. It was no more than an admission by both of them that the other commitments remained.

There were, however, curious consequences. With Francis weak from recurring bouts of malaria, it was Eleanor who assumed control at the Great House.

First the move of her mother-in-law had to be arranged. No simple matter, meeting Constance's wish to live in the Dower House. In fact, a major upheaval involving furniture and prized possessions and – more awkwardly – people. Gwynedd Morgan insisted on moving with old Mrs. Mortimer-Wotton. So too did Ted Larkin, the gardener, and Mrs. Constant, the cook. Where Mrs. M-W went, they went. "They'd do what they could to oblige the Colonel and Mrs. Francis at the Great House – yes, of course. Madam," – but their first loyalty was too personal, too long established for redirection. And anyway, "What would Mrs. M-W do without them?"

What indeed? Constance was ready to hand over the running of the estate and the Great House to Francis and Eleanor, but that wasn't the end of her world. Far from it. As she confessed to Tom Duncan when he escorted her to Folkestone races that summer, "I'm sixty-five years old as you know, Tom. That's well over retiring age for a working woman! But I shall be most upset if you don't continue to take me to the races for many years to come."

And the two of them settled down happily to Mrs. Constant's game pie and the colonel's champagne. In 1920 life at sixty-five could still be fun for those with good health and money to spend.

Naturally enough, Constance's decision involved others outside the family. The old people in the village, the anxious parents, the doctor, the vicar, even the local policeman conspired as village people do, to reconstruct their lines of communication so that the network continued to centre inexorably on the Dower House where old Mrs. Mortimer-Wotton now resided. So much so, that Millicent Taylor who, on retiring from her post at the village school, had established herself in a white-washed thatched cottage in Little Ockenham, found herself visiting the Dower House, three mornings weekly, to help Constance with her correspondence.

Eleanor was not worried. She did not expect it otherwise: nor did she fancy herself in the role that the village expected her mother-in-law to play. At the Great House a second anxiety was much more pressing – the family income was running short. Somehow Francis must be made to understand.

He had been spending more and more time at his London flat. But next time he visited Ockenham, Eleanor tackled him in her own direct way. "Now sit down, Francis, and look the facts in the face. We'll start with your mother. She's not going to change her way of life, is she? And that's very expensive."

"So what?" said Francis unhelpfully, knowing that Constance was guaranteed to exceed any income she happened to receive. Hadn't she taught him and his brother to spend to their heart's content? Mother was a natural spender.

Undeterred, Eleanor continued. "I think you must have a word with Justin Leadbitter, Francis. I've told him you'll be seeing him in Canterbury before the week is out – and fix up an annuity sufficient to cover the staff and upkeep of the Dower House as well as your mother's personal needs. Old Leadbitter knows the form exactly and that way she'll have no embarrassing interest in the estate when she dies. See what I'm getting at?"

Francis saw exactly. So did the old solicitor. But when the annuity for Constance had been arranged the liquid assets of the family had also been reduced by £20,000.

"So now," said Eleanor, "where do the bees go for honey? I'm damned if my American capital is going to be used for the restoration and upkeep of this old house. My personal requirements certainly: Bobby's education, if you like. But the rest – Philip, the house, the servants, your London clubs and all your other expenses – are not being paid by me."

"Of course not. I wouldn't hear of it," replied Francis, though he was only too conscious that his personal income had been eroded by old Hollingbourne's death and the merging of his steel business which left Francis in the cold. "But what do you suggest?"

Eleanor outlined her plan. "First we put the Mortimer-Wotton land to work. Get rid of that useless Agent and put up the rents of the tenant farmers to a sensible figure. If they can't make out, we'll have to take 'em over ourselves and set up a bit of 'distance' farming – at least in the land towards Chartham where the ground's right for wheat and barley. Next we get rid of the milk round – no money in it, too many people to pay, too many slow payers, too many government regulations. Agreed?"

"I'm sure you're right." Francis was taken aback. "But what about the people concerned? The district relies on our milk, you know."

"I know, I know – the people who've served the family, man and boy, for the last thousand years. But the world is changing. And some of them, Francis, have been robbing your family for far too long. Take Absalom, for example. Have you ever checked the old toper's personal raids on the cellar? I tell you, we've got to run this place on business lines – or get rid of it."

Francis was in no state to argue – his malaria tended to recur at moments like this. Soon Eleanor was running the Mortimer-Wotton lands with the same drive and efficiency that one supposes the Fleischer family must have exercised when they first emigrated to America. And probably with the same shrewd assessment of the personal equation. She took her hurdles straight. Nobody minded much when Absalom, the old rogue, transferred his services to a family in West Kent. A living-in cook and housemaid were quickly found while Dorothy Evans was happy to remain in charge of Bobby. Though less spare time was enjoyed in the kitchen, there was much less waste. And, under Eleanor, nobody worked too hard for comfort.

Outside the house, Eleanor quickly recognised the shrewd, knowledgeable qualities of John Williams at the Home Farm, and put the gardens under his control also. He was a natural ally, for he had always disliked the Agent in Canterbury, and enjoyed getting rid of him. He also enjoyed the feeling that somebody at the Great House was more interested in the way the estate was farmed than in the rents it threw up and the shooting it provided. As for the milk round, it was nothing but a headache, especially after the death of Sam Jones in the 'flu epidemic. Not much to look at, Sam Jones, but he'd been very clever at getting cash from the people in the village, and John had been unable to find a reliable successor. Eleanor and John Williams proved a good partnership. Apart from their mutual respect, John's children showed every sign of staying on the land – a very useful nucleus for the future.

Eleanor, for her part, soon became a very well-known character in Ashford, Faversham and Canterbury, as she studied the market prices, and bargained with the corn merchants. Correspondingly she found less and less time for the County. Francis's friends remained reasonably polite, but even before the war she had never had the patience to conform to their ways and learn their esoteric jargon. Now she considered them faintly ridiculous in their determination to bring back the former days. "Definitely old-hat," she labelled them, "with a distinct odour of moth balls." She'd leave the luxury of nostalgia to Francis and those with longer memories. Eleanor belonged to a brave new world in which she intended to lay new foundations.

Fair enough! But Philip, returning from his second half at Eton, was bewildered to find his step-mother in the driving seat. Increasingly, he tended to wander down to the Dower House, theoretically when Eleanor was away for the day. "Actually," as he told Gwynedd in a schoolboy aside, "the food down here is much better than up at the house." And then to Mrs. Constant, with a diplomacy that belied his years, "Visiting day, Mrs. C., just to make sure the Gorgon keeps her pecker up."

The two women retailed the compliments to each other and agreed in a phrase common to them both, that "Mr. Philip really was a one." For them, the son of the house could do no wrong.

During the holidays Philip was much in his grandmother's company. That shrewd old lady fully understood the relationship between Francis and Eleanor. Nor was she over-concerned. "She wasn't born yesterday, for heaven's sake." Such problems had arisen many times before in the great houses of England as well as the royal palaces of Europe. Her philosophy and experience told her that time could solve everything provided nobody behaved too stupidly. Indeed, she envisaged Philip as the catalyst in the formula which would be applied in God's good time. But hasten slowly, she warned herself. This boy you are involving is still at school. Watch your step or you'll take a tumble. And the old lady, wise in her generation, proceeded on her devious feminine way.

First, Philip must not be alienated from his step-mother – so strengthen his friendship with Bobby and, perhaps, John Williams's son, Amos. Very casually she said to Philip one day – "Bobby seems to have made a good start at Summerfields. Showing promise as a cricketer, I'm told. Shows he's learnt a lot from your bowling to him in the net you and Amos fixed up for him at the side of the croquet lawn." And Philip warmed to the compliment. Constance had never known a boy of fifteen indifferent to praise.

Next, steer Philip closer to Francis now, more often than not, residing in London. So, one day when the boy was enjoying lunch with her at the Dower House, she said *à propos* of nothing – "My word, Philip, you're growing fast. I believe your father should introduce you to his tailor in Sackville Street." No more than that – but the same evening she telephoned her son – "Mother speaking, dear . . . yes, I'm well, thank you . . . had a delightful visit from Philip today . . . he seems happy at Ullathorne's . . . but he can do with a bit more self-confidence – always the same with growing boys. What about taking him to that tailor of yours, there's nothing like new clothes for making you feel good . . . What? Oh just a country suit and some new Eton tails, I should think . . . What are you saying? Costs too much? Now, really, Francis, it's Philip I'm talking about, not the state of the pound sterling . . ." And the old lady rang off, confident that she'd made her point. Francis always believed in dressing well.

94

But while his grandmother worked to repair the links in a family chain comprising Francis – Philip – Bobby – Eleanor, she had less effect on Philip's thinking than his old tutor, Arthur Waddilove.

Contact was renewed on a day when Constance had business to do in the Castle Street offices of Dawson and Leadbitter. While she was busy with her lawyer, Philip who had cadged a lift into Canterbury with his grandmother, paid a call on the canon. The Precincts, he noticed, were marvellously unchanged. It was re-assuring to see Bell Harry, the Cathedral's great central tower, still guarding the little houses below, as if the world had never been at war. And Emily and her cat as well as Arthur gave him a welcome as if he was coming home.

"What's news?" he demanded, confident that the answer would be nothing. The canon laughed. "News, Philip? Well, leaving aside the front page story that Tabitha has produced five tabby kittens and Emily's found a home for all of them, I've taken up golf."

"No, honestly?"

"It's a fact, my son: and I've got myself down by prayer and practice to an eighteen handicap. Of course, it's an old man's game, but . . . you want to try your hand? Why, that's fine by me. And if the game makes you wild, the air at Sandwich – remember our day at Richborough? – really is a tonic."

And so a holiday routine developed. On the following Wednesday – and on many Wednesdays thereafter – Philip took to the Sandwich road in Arthur's Singer two-seater. A second-hand, modest machine by comparison with Gran's bible-black Rolls and Eleanor's whizz-bang of a Lancia. "But," Philip told Gwynedd Morgan after his first ride in it, "you can find out a lot about people by the cars they use. Now this Singer, Gorgon, it's quiet and anything but showy, but it's got something." And that was a fair schoolboy's description of Arthur Waddilove as well as his car.

Once arrived at the course, the canon played eighteen holes with a fellow member of St. George's while Philip received a lesson from the professional and then worked away on the practice ground or pottered down to the sea, as the spirit moved him. He and the old man lunched together in the clubhouse – a jolly good lunch too – and then they chugged back past Wingham and Littlebourne to Canterbury whence Philip bicycled home to Ockenham. Wednesday after Wednesday, they followed the same drill.

Somehow, when travelling with Arthur, Philip felt free to talk to his heart's content. He chattered about Eton and Ockenham and Eleanor's new plans. He rambled on about his friends in the house and Mr. Ullathorne and Bobby and his grandmother and his visit to the London tailor with Francis – a very decent meal at Father's club, too, Arthur: and always back again to the changes at the Great House. The dairy round sold and new tractors ordered from America – quite a costly affair, John Williams tells me. And Arthur listened. He was a good listener.

The boy, walled in by tradition, was clearly trying to come to terms with a changing world. "Change," Arthur mused. "It looks bigger, Philip, when you see it at your front door: but change is what history's about.

What you have to understand is why change comes, then you can decide how to adjust to it. Take this new Labour party, for instance, that all your friends in the County are getting so wild about. Why is it gaining strength? Because of the disgusting greed of the Victorians which caused a large number of Englishmen to hate their bosses and demand a change in the system. Don't let anybody fool you. Those who sow hate, reap rebellion."

And then, as if to show the counterweight of tradition which Philip and his friends would have to carry or cast away in their individual lives, Arthur turned to his old love.

"Tradition, you know, has its strength, too. Look at India. Always an interplay between traditions far older than the College Chapel at Eton and something as new as broadcasting – or even as new as our Empire out there. The Raj, a hundred and fifty years old? What's that to a people whose genius has continued to absorb its invaders for more than a thousand years? None of your friends will believe me, Philip. But one day India will gobble us up as she gobbled Alexander's Greeks three hundred years before Christ or the great Moghuls, eight hundred years later who thought they were building for eternity at Lahore and Delhi and Agra. These things take time and each invader brings the benefit of change. But in the end the genius of a nation or a family – its tradition, if you like – wins through . . ." and Arthur's sentence trailed away in recollection of the Indian road he had chosen to walk.

Often, praying in his small room at night, his mind had a habit of returning to Philip – an ordinary sort of lad, people would think: good-natured, kindly, better dressed and better endowed than most, a good man to know and trust.

The outside world, aware of the poor, the starving and the lonely, would find it very odd to hear him pray: "Oh God, grant to Philip grace to comprehend the loneliness of his inheritance and strength to carry the weight of it." But those were the words that came to his lips. On the horizon of his vision the old man could descry no easy route for the boy – no passes through the mountains. He bowed his head once more. Was it a gift of God or a curse that he, Arthur Waddilove, saw so often, so clearly, the shape of things to come?

10

ETON has suffered more than most English schools from an unhappy minority of its *alumni* who have presented it to the outside world as a paradise for the bully and a breeding ground for the homosexual. But in contrast to his miserable experience at Furnival's, Philip saw none of these things in his five years at Eton. Ullathorne's house wasn't a great house if greatness was to be measured by success. But old Ullage, to use the name by which their tutor was universally known to his boys, regarded success, in work or play or music or art, only as incidental to the lives of the boys whom parents placed in his care. As a result, Ullathorne's was a happy and a popular house, and in the Twenties possessed the longest of all the waiting lists for Eton – a contingency which provided the housemaster with his chief and most constant problem.

At this ancient foundation Philip was to the manner born. Even if Furnival's hadn't made him familiar with the college jargon of 'Dame' and 'Tutor', 'Division' and 'White Ticket', 'Absence' and 'Library', he would have found himself at home in a place which had been familiar to his forebears for many generations – right back to 1624 when Sir Henry Wotton had reigned as Provost. The lay-out of School Yard and the soaring magnificence of King Henry VI's Chapel were, so to speak, part of his family history.

Mr. Ullathorne and the Dame, aware of this association, noted more prosaically that young Mortimer-Wotton's size made him clumsy, and a bit lazy, so that he tended to be the last to arrive when a member of Library shouted 'Boy!'. They also noted, as did the senior members of the house, that he was extremely good-natured, not only about being last, and thus the one to be landed with whatever chore or errand was commanded, but in his relationship with other boys. Brian Melchester, for instance, who had entered the house the same Half as Philip, wanted to 'mess' with him, but Philip settled to share his teas with Nat Levine who was an older brother of the small boy he and Brian had rescued at Tudor Court. The friendship of 'the short and the tall' was regarded as something of a joke by the boys in the house, but the housemaster was delighted that the diminutive Jew had found a champion – definitely a good mark for Mortimer-Wotton in old Ullage's retentive mind.

By the age of sixteen, Philip had ambled without any great concern through confirmation and school-certificate. He had shown himself somewhat dangerous at the Field Game, Eton's peculiar form of football, and erratically fast as a bowler. But he had become chiefly notable among his companions for the care he took over his clothes. He managed in the most natural way to be a little bit more fastidious about his appearance than his contemporaries – to wear his 'tails' with a difference. The foible even showed up when he was parading with the College O.T.C.

Indeed, Philip's interest in military affairs was another oddity that interested Charles Ullathorne. Though he didn't subscribe to that nonsense about 'Waterloo being won on the playing fields of Eton', he could see Philip as a soldier: and he carried the idea of an army career a stage further after one of Arthur Waddilove's periodic visits to preach in the College Chapel.

As usual with these visits, Arthur made his preaching engagement an excuse for staying the night with Charles Ullathorne.

"And how's Philip?" the conversation had its usual opening.

"Fine," said the housemaster, "no trouble with his work, everybody likes him, he's becoming a very valuable member of the house, but . . . "

The canon interrupted, "I know what you're going to say, Charles. The boy lacks ambition, eh?"

"Ye-es, that's about right. But I really mean he hasn't a clue as to what he wants to do with his life. And that's a great pity with a boy who, to my mind, has real gifts of leadership. I've seen it before in boys like Philip who have been born into titles and great estates. Call it 'lack of ambition' if you like. But it's more a sort of bewilderment, a state of mind. I hardly ever find it in the sons of the new rich who pour in on this place now – the latter generally know where they want to go – as often as not in the opposite direction to their successful parents. Sometimes I wish the landed gentry would take a lesson from the tycoons. Another glass of port?"

Arthur refilled his glass. "Bewilderment," he said, "that's a much better word – particularly in Philip's case where the family's no help. As you know, the boy likes his father well enough, but sees very little of him since he's so often away from Ockenham. And during Philip's school vacations the step-mother seems so dominant that he cannot contemplate life at home with anything but apprehension."

"Any trouble with the younger step-brother who's due to enter the house in a year's time?" asked the housemaster.

"Luckily, none at all. As far as I can see, the boy thinks the world of Philip. And provided he's not spoilt by Eleanor, Bobby's going to do very well for you at Eton. But of course, he's a different sort of problem. He won't inherit Ockenham unless Philip pulls out, as his uncle did. You remember, the artist and mountaineer? But I'd be surprised if Philip took after his Uncle Charles. For one thing he hasn't that sort of talent. For another – and much more important – I believe he's got a deep, deep love for his home."

"So you reckon he'll go back to his acres when the moment seems right – perhaps when he marries?" the housemaster suggested. "Well, in that case, why not ease him forward to a short-term commission in the Guards and hope he finds the right girl in the allotted time?"

The decanter was empty. There was no more to do except translate the plan into action – a task which Charles Ullathorne performed with the practised skill of a good schoolmaster fully accustomed to handling such matters in days when 'careers masters' didn't exist.

He broached the matter to Francis and Eleanor when they next visited the College. "Philip's beginning to think about the future," he said, "and I can't help wondering whether he shouldn't try for the army. He certainly looks the part, and for his sake I think we ought to give the thing a chance. Would you agree? Good, then I'll get him posted into the army class. It shouldn't be too testing for him and the Sandhurst exam is a useful target to aim at. After all, we can always scratch the fixture if you or he have other ideas later on."

Philip was delighted with the plan and really started working. In 1924, having to his surprise been elected a member of the Eton "Pop", that most coveted of honours, in his last year at School, he entered the Royal Military College – his eyes firmly fixed on a Guards commission.

From the very start of his training, he enjoyed the army life. Sandhurst – Salisbury Plain – Wellington Barracks – Philip's military progress was entirely unsensational to the extent that he got on well with his instructors, his fellow officers and, in due course, the men he found himself commanding. Especially the men and the N.C.O.s who, the adjutant noted, took a liking to this big newly gazetted subaltern who was prepared to work at his job and take his duties seriously.

What Philip could not stick was the endless social round. In company with his fellow subalterns, he was smothered with invitations galore from a new generation of Honourable Mottinghams, all hunting for escorts for their flat-chested protégées, all chirruping away with mindless references to 'Welly B' and 'have you met dear Noel'.

It was suffocating. Dinner jacket or tails, night after night. Dear Lady A. who knew a distant cousin in Sussex and was so anxious to introduce Philip to her Anne, such a sweet girl – or was it Amelia? He couldn't care less and he couldn't understand his fellow officers' enthusiasm – "free champers dear boy, wizard band, super food, get away from the mess bores."

"It's no bloody good," he told Brian Melchester. "I smoke too much, drink too much . . . and even pay too much. I'll find a woman my own way."

But occasionally he got caught in the network of invitations. Would he ever forget the night when Giles Arbuthnot, Guy Venables and Melchester – all from his year at Sandhurst – persuaded him to join a dinner party at the Coq d'Or before moving to somebody's dance in Knightsbridge? "All for free, Philip: Penny Bridlington's father's as rich as Croesus: and Penny promises there'll be no over-weight non-starters among the girls. It will be a great evening."

A great evening, in a sense, it was. The dinner was great – as a matter of fact, old Bridlington was damned interesting about his activities in the General Strike. The drink was great – champagne to start with, then a very decent burgundy, Hine V.S.O.P. with the coffee and on for more champagne in Knightsbridge where the numbers, the noise, the lot . . . great, great. The four girls – what energy, what capacity for enjoyment – kept with the four officers till one o'clock when Giles suggested a change of scene. "Café de Paris, come on, make your getaway all of you and I'll find the cab. Got some cash on you, Philip?" And away in a single taxi they went – four girls perched on the laps of four young men – and so, laughing and chattering, down the stairs off Coventry Street to Giles's favourite haunt.

"Table for eight . . . champagne? Certainly, Sir" – the party was well into the new day when Penny Bridlington drew Philip's attention to a middle-aged couple moving on to the floor in advance of the other dancers. "Gosh, that old boy's a beautiful dancer . . . good looking too for his age, must be fifty if he's a day . . . Look, Philip . . . Oh, I might have known . . . you're gawping at his woman, aren't you? Can't blame you, she's stunning and what a dress, absolutely divine . . . straight from Paris I'll bet."

Philip turned with a smile to the girl beside him, gave Melchester a warning kick, and said carefully, "'S a matter of fact, I know the old boy pretty well. When he and his floozy finish this caper, I'll go and find out where she got the dress – probably, on the cheap, in Shaftesbury Avenue. What?"

The band took a break, and Philip sauntered across the floor as casually as he could – his mind seething. What the hell was his father doing with this bird? And why, in God's name, should he choose this night of all nights to take her out to the Café de Paris? Francis suddenly recognised the tall young man approaching his table. "Philip, dear boy – what a turn-up for the book." Philip had never seen his father so animated. "Fancy finding you here. Let me introduce you to José." And turning to his partner he announced with mock solemnity *"Madame Josephine de la Vendée, j'ai l'honneur de vous présenter mon fils, Philippe."*

"*Enchantée, M'sieur, mais . . .*" and the lady continued, "your father ees veree pleased with 'is French but me – how you say? When in Rome I spik zee Eenglish, eh François?" and she gave Francis a dazzling smile, as he held her hand. Francis turned to his son.

"You understand, Philip? José's a war-time friend of my Salonika days, spending a few days in London. Hush-hush visit, very unexpected . . . you know the line?" His finger was on his lips.

"Of course, Father. Brian Melchester's the only chap in my lot who'll have a clue, so not to worry." He turned to José. "But tell me one thing, Madame. Where did you buy your dress? I've promised to find out."

"Oh Philippe. 'ow you are charming and . . . yes, bold like your father." Taking two visiting cards from her evening bag, she wrote on the back of one of them the name of her couturier in Paris. "*La voilà, mon ami. Deux cartes: L'une pour vous, l'autre pour la 'girl friend'. Moi, je suis d'une type généreuse. Au revoir, Philippe.*" And it sounded like a welcome to Paris rather than farewell.

Philip went back to his friends. "Penny's bang on target," he laughed. "French woman, French dress, French *chic*: body and all, straight from Paris."

A little later, the party broke up – separate taxis this time – and Philip took Penny back to Chelsea, the girl snuggling happily in the big man's arms, letting him feel her warm young body close against his. She kissed him a gay goodbye, broke away, fumbling in her little diamanté bag for a latch key. "See you again soon," she said, and her lips touched his cheek. "Thanks again, Philip, for a divine evening." And off she went without a backward glance, dancing still light-footed up the steps to the Bridlington front door.

Eventually the taxi homed on Birdcage Walk. A sweet girl, Philip said to himself. But no . . . nothing serious . . . too young for one thing, hardly more than a schoolgirl . . . won't wait anyway . . . a bit spoilt, I shouldn't wonder . . . ought to get a job. His thoughts meandered on. Everything seems divine this season bar the price of champagne at the Café de Paris . . . Still not a bad evening apart from running into Father. Wonder what the hell the old boy's up to . . . Must warn Brian to keep his trap shut . . . Wonder if I shall see

103

Penny again or that French bird Father's had in tow? Now stop thinking, you silly twit . . . Time to catch up on sleep . . . A great night, my foot!

The next morning Philip went down to Ockenham. His spirits rose as he broke clear of London. Home again, he stood at the window of the bedroom he now occupied at the south-west corner of the Great House. To his left he saw the Ockenham woods stretching along the high ridge of the hill – oak and beech and Kentish cob. They were, he used to think, at their most beautiful in the spring when bluebells and primroses grew in profusion at the foot of the trees: but now in summer they were still lovely to his sight, the leaves so fresh in contrast to the dusty fatigue of the trees bordering St. James's Park.

His eyes turned to absorb the old familiar features. In the foreground he looked down on the walled kitchen garden, carefully hoed: beans for the picking and cabbages; orderly rows of leeks and carrots and sprouts; clear space where the potatoes had been dug; and against the south wall the espalier peaches and the protective leaves of the old fig tree. Someone had been doing a dam' good job – even old Larkin would have to admit it, though he was invincibly obstinate as all good gardeners are.

Further to his right Philip could just see the reeds at the western edge of the lake from which the 'America' had once been launched on her maiden voyage: and beyond, the willows bordering the trout stream. From the lake's bank, his eyes traced the well-trodden footpath westwards past the beech clumps to the Dower House, glowing red and graceful in the sunshine, with the roofs of Little Ockenham showing up across the Chartham road. The picture, he knew, would always travel with him wherever the army sent him.

But wait a moment. Beyond the Dower House, though the contours of the fields were gently sloping as of old, hedges had changed their courses – disappeared by the look of it. The cluster of buildings at Dark's farm seemed to be in a new setting. And – right to the far horizon – Philip saw the gold of ripening wheat. So this was the 'distance farming' Eleanor had mentioned to him. As if to emphasise her responsibility for the change, Eleanor's Lancia came cruising along the Chartham road, turning off to cross the Dower House bridge, and so along the cart track to the out-buildings of the Home Farm.

Philip went down to meet her at the stables where she kept the car. Eleanor, too, seemed changed. There was a new animation, a sort of enthusiasm he'd never noticed during her dreary visits to Eton with his father and those rather ghastly holidays when father had been in the house. And, wonder of wonders, she was pleased to see him.

"Philip," she exclaimed as he opened the car door, "good to see you. I've been just longing for your arrival. Do you know something? I've fallen in love with this place. Yes, honestly. Can't think now why I ever wanted the lights of London when I first came from America. Of course, the change didn't happen all at once. There was a war and you and young Bobby in between. But gradually during these last few years it's hooked me – this parcel of land and the people who live on it. And I'll tell you something else, I'm a British citizen now. That visit last year to Cleveland settled it. What do you think of that?"

Philip was both surprised and delighted. That evening he and Eleanor dined together, almost like partners engaged in a new enterprise. Eleanor had, as he knew, travelled alone to America earlier in the year ostensibly to see her family, but actually to examine some of the new farm machinery being manufactured in her home town and Chicago and Detroit. Now it transpired that she'd found little point of contact with the Ohio Fletchers, been disgusted by her home town's ignorance of the European scene and lack of interest in anything outside its own boundaries. She described the citizens of Cleveland as "cocooned in their own affairs, just like they were when I said goodbye to them in 1912." Impulsive as always, she had literally transferred her loyalties to England – even to the extent of selling her American holdings, which she'd done while pre-slump prices were still riding high on Wall Street.

Now, with a couple of dry Martinis inside her and a shared bottle of claret, she was bursting with ideas. "It'll be a good wheat harvest, Philip: and the apples look like fetching very decent prices in the autumn. But we want to make plans for the next five years –

and it's more than a question of growing and selling the produce of Ockenham. That's something John Williams can organise perfectly well."

Philip was intrigued. "What are you getting at, Eleanor?" He'd always found it impossible to call her Mother.

"Well, my ideas come under two headings," she said, "only with Francis spending so much of his time in London and Paris, I really need your help."

So she knows about this French woman was Philip's first thought. But he replied easily enough. "Let's have a brandy to settle the meal – and then we'll get the future in focus."

Eleanor had clearly done a lot of thinking. "First," she said, "there's all this house property the family owns. None of you seem to be worried that the village houses haven't a bathroom between them and are only equipped with outside privies. But it won't do, you know. The younger people are going to want something better soon, whatever your grandmother's generation may think."

"And how do we set to work?"

"Perfectly simple. Start our own building firm. The basic requirement is three men – a carpenter, a brickie and a plumber. And I've got two of the three willing to give it a go. I reckon they can be occupied on this property for at least five years, working in each cottage as it becomes vacant. We'll see they have a share in the success of the business. And of course, I'll have to help them with the costing and accounts."

"So the Mortimer-Wottons set up in business?"

"That's right, Philip. Only I think it's two companies we're talking about, because I've already taken over that derelict forge at the Canterbury end of the village."

"Good heavens, what the devil for?"

"Well, I've figured it out like this. Horses on the farms are virtually a thing of the past. The new equipment and the tractors will need expert maintenance. And my new Ockenham Motor Engineers will give us just what we need – and fuel supply into the bargain. 'Q.E.D.' as that horrible Maths master of Bobby's used to say."

"So what's my role?" said Philip.

"Why, you're the boss, you silly man. It's going to be your show.

Indeed with your father up to his own devices it's really yours already. So I don't move far without your say-so. But, in addition, we've got to raise more cash to get things started. And I'm wondering whether you're good for a touch."

Philip burst out laughing – but not unkindly. "I wondered when you were coming to that, dear Eleanor. Better sleep on the ideas, I reckon, and count the cost in the morning, eh?"

And step-mother and step-son turned out the lights and went to their rooms.

As he meticulously put away his dinner-jacket (he really was becoming a creature of habit), two 'musts' kept recurring to Philip. He 'must' see his professional advisers and get their views on these heady proposals before he got swept away by his step-mother's enthusiasm. And he 'must' put his father in the picture however little he wanted to hear about Ockenham. But now, lights out. Eleanor, he had to admit, was quite a woman when she set her mind to something. Wasn't life odd? To think that on two successive evenings he should have met his father and step-mother, each in the most terrific form – on the one hand, the owner of the Great House with a French girl in a night club and, on the other hand, his American wife planning a one-woman agricultural revolution on the Ockenham estates. What had Arthur said to him? "Find out the reason for change and then you can adjust to it?" Something like that, but time to stop thinking. Leave the action to tomorrow. Philip slept well that night.

11

SIX WEEKS after his dinner with Eleanor, Philip was back at Ockenham, sitting in the rose garden in front of the house. He gazed across the lawn to the lake and the park. But his mind was analysing his recent activities and wondering how they fitted in with the harvest supper due to take place in the tithe barn in three hours' time.

He knew well enough the ritual attached to this annual event – it had happened at Ockenham every September of his twenty-two years of life, and for generations before he was born. At the end of the long day, the farm carts – they'd be tractors now – would return from the fields along the old cart track, carrying the men, women and children who'd been sweating it out through the weeks of harvest. John Williams would be driving the last tractor, a victorious general in a triumphal procession. He'd wave to Gran and her people as he passed the Dower House and give a second salute to those who lived in the Great House as he came within hail of the Home Farm. The journey completed, the farm hands would disperse to clean themselves up in time for the harvest supper, food for the most part from the Mortimer-Wotton kitchen and drinks by arrangement with Jack Kemsing of the Wotton Arms down in the village. Yes, he knew the routine by heart.

Philip's grandmother and the other members of his family, the vicar and any weekend guests would sit down to supper with the regulars and the irregulars who'd been helping in the fields. Then, after the meal, when the dancing gathered pace, Mrs. Mortimer-Wotton, followed by the rest of the top table, would make a discreet withdrawal. No doubt it would be just the same this year except that, following the death of Ben Wilson the postman in the previous winter, the excruciating noise of his fiddle was to be replaced by a hired trio from Canterbury. That, at least, was a tactical gain.

Why, then, was he so damned nervous? Somehow, it seemed to him, his old easy relationship with the farming people was changing. A process of change – he could see it now – starting from the day he'd moved from the village school to Furnival's. He was no longer one of them. Yet he was too closely involved, or was he too young, to play the squire's part. The feeling of unease had been growing since he'd worked with Eleanor on her new plans. He doubted whether he or his step-mother would fit the traditional picture much longer. It was all very well for Gran, or his father if it came to that. They had remained high above the dark circus, shining down on the performers below from an unchallenged eminence. There they were, high up, honoured by the locals – in Gran's case greatly loved – because they'd been honest in their dealings with them, generous with help, just and caring people.

But he, like Eleanor, was right in the middle of the ring. He went over in his mind the events of the past month. He'd seen old Justin Leadbitter as he told Eleanor he would. The old solicitor, his mind ranging back rather than forward, seemed chiefly concerned that Philip should discuss these new-fangled companies with his grandmother. So to the Dower House where to his surprise, the old lady showed herself entirely happy, particularly with the plans for renovating the village houses. "You and Eleanor are quite right," she said. "It's what your father ought to have done ten years ago. But there you are . . . he's got other interests. So you've got to take the decision now, Philip . . . only be careful not to go too fast or spend more than you can afford."

Next he visited his City stockbrokers who controlled the investments he'd inherited from his mother. Bill Govain – an Eton near-contemporary – was re-assuring. "I guess you're right, Philip, to get involved in these company formations though it's outside my field. And nothing wrong in the senior employees having an interest in the share-holding, so far as I can see, though I've never thought of you before as a leader of the social revolution. Just two points. If you go ahead with these subsidiary companies, get the Articles of Association buttoned up so that any of these guys who want to leave your employment gives up his shares for the benefit of his successor. And for goodness sake find yourself a decent accountant. From your story of what's been happening at Ockenham in the past I'd say nobody's ever troubled to add up anything. If you're going into business, do the thing properly."

The two of them lunched at Sweetings and within a few days sufficient stock had been sold to swell Philip's bank account by £10,000.

Finally, he managed to fix a date to meet his father at White's. To say that Francis was not interested in Eleanor's plans would be an understatement. It would be more truthful to say, in his grandmother's words, that "Francis had other interests." It was these interests that his father wanted to talk about. "Not José, dear boy, she's, as you might say, a divertissement – and a very jolly one, too. But she has other uses, you see. She makes it easy for me to meet some of the high-ups in the French army and at the Quai d'Orsay. Think of her, if you like, as part of my passport whenever I cross the Channel."

"The best-looking passport I've ever seen," said Philip. "But . . . but what's the idea?"

Francis looked round the club to see that no member was within earshot. He made that characteristic gesture of his – finger on lips. And his voice dropped. "Not a word to anybody, Philip – certainly not to Eleanor or my mother. For them, I'm an irresponsible fool, in the middle of a reprehensible love affair with a French woman of uncertain age. But the truth is – and it's right you should know it – I'm occupied up to my eyes and ears in more important business. Some of us are convinced that these damned politicians – don't bother to differentiate between the political parties – are pulling wool over the nation's eyes about the changing scene in Europe. Sooner or later, Parliament and the nation have to face facts. And it's facts I'm collecting. Believe me, my spare time is well and truly employed in Paris, Berlin, the Balkans and er . . . Chartwell. So I hope you'll give me the benefit of the doubt, old lad." Francis smiled and raised his voice. "About this plan of Eleanor's. I don't think we've ever really understood each other, so I wonder if my advice is much use to you."

"Can't you be a bit more explicit, Father?"

"Well, let me try. As I see it, Ellie's a clever woman who for some obscure reason is dominated by a succession of single-minded, over-mastering enthusiasms. Suddenly, she changes from interest A to interest B. Once, before the war, it was London and the arts – I reckon now I was only the means to an end. Then in the war came nursing and – don't let's put too fine a point on it – a succession of lovers. I've never confronted her with these things – but of course I know. My friends would tell me, if I didn't. That's all finished except that Bobby remains a link between us. Now she's gone farming mad and become more English than the English. All I'll say is this. Whatever you do, don't let her run away with all your money. And don't be too sure that her present enthusiasm will last for ever. She's a woman with a one-way mind. But she reserves to herself the right to change direction."

With that Philip had to be content. He'd returned to Justin Leadbitter, got him started on the company formations and, on the old solicitor's advice, met a City firm of medium size accountants who specialised in farming accounts. Eleanor said she was grateful for what he'd done. He'd kept his father and grandmother informed.

By way of double insurance, he'd put Arthur Waddilove in the picture. For old time's sake, they'd made a Wednesday excursion to Sandwich where Arthur – what a good athlete he must have been in his youth – continued to play off an eighteen handicap. Philip played off eight. But the old man, with the aid of eight strokes, beat Philip on the last green. No shop, while they were playing – that was canon law, as he liked to call it. But in the car – Philip's this time – they had talked about Ockenham non-stop.

As to the new developments, Arthur was re-assuring. "To get involved and bring the people in. That's the way it's going to be. And you're right to give a lead, Philip." But soon he moved on to other subjects in his casual sort of way, almost in the form of questions.

"Your grandmother, Philip – what a wonderful woman. She is now over seventy, you know. Do you think she's beginning to feel her years a bit? Seemed a bit tired last time I visited her: but she was very happy about you and Bobby, and genuinely pleased about Eleanor's interest in the estate." Then, a few miles later, "Have you heard that Edward Pendlebury's resigning the Living at Ockenham? Going to live in a cottage in New Romney, I gather. That means Francis will have to think about a successor. Let me know, if I can help, won't you? I might find an opportunity of talking with Francis in London." And then back to Philip. "Enjoying soldiering, Philip? When's the Battalion moving overseas? Egypt for Christmas, eh? You'll enjoy getting away. Only sorry it's not the North-West Frontier where I could give you one or two introductions which might not reach the Mess in the normal way. Still, another year, perhaps . . ." How Philip wished his old tutor was twenty years younger. As old as Gran, he could scarcely believe it.

But it was time to prepare for his harvest grind. Philip put out his cigarette and buried it carefully in one of the rosebeds – the fastidious tidiness of the Brigade of Guards came automatically to him. He changed into smartly cut fawn trousers (wouldn't be seen dead in those Oxford bags) and the new shirt he'd bought at Hodgkinson's in Jermyn Street earlier in the week. He topped himself out with an Eton Ramblers' silk square and joined Eleanor and the rest of the household as John Williams and his troops came up the track from the direction of the Dower House.

Two hours and two pink gins later, he walked across to the Dower House to join his grandmother in the black Rolls which Parkinson was to drive along the main road to the lodge gates at the end of the village and up the beech drive to the barn. Constance sounded pleased he had called for her. "It's good to have you with us this year: and nice for me to have an escort. Gives a bit of tone to the show." They were joined by Eleanor at the letter box outside the garden gate of the Great House and together they drove the last four hundred yards to the tithe barn. As Gran got out of the Rolls, she pressed Philip's hand and whispered, "You look fine. Now, for goodness sake, get some fun out of the evening. They're all your friends, you know."

As harvest suppers go, it went. The meal was served fast. The vicar hoped he'd see everybody at the harvest festival services next day. Barrels of Kentish brewed hops from Faversham were tapped by men with apparently unquenchable thirsts.

In due course old Mrs. Mortimer-Wotton rose to make her

departure while the going was good. Philip was leaving with the rest of the party when a commotion broke out at the far end of the room where a table of younger people had been making a fair amount of noise during supper. "High spirits, natural enough, nothing to worry about," was the verdict of those with long experience of this annual party. Or rather, that would have been their verdict up to the moment of the family's exodus: at which point somebody lurched noisily against a trestle and overturned a couple of beer mugs.

To those at the table it was the signal for an explosion which had been brewing in the village for weeks past. Eddy Kemsing, Jack Kemsing's eldest boy, leapt to his feet. "You silly little drunken twit," he shouted at Amos Williams. "If you can't hold your liquor at this time o' night, you ought to be in bed." His sister Margie had the air of an outraged Fury. Amos, red-faced and distinctly unsteady, was shouting at her brother.

Philip, looking over his shoulder, got the situation loud and clear, his mind flashing back to earlier arguments at Miss Millie's school. Trouble for sure. One could see it a mile off. Eddy Kemsing, tough and bad-tempered, a natural trouble-maker, spoiling for a fight. Amos Williams, strong and stocky, who could fight well enough when baited ... but in no state to slog it out tonight with anyone, least of all a bruiser like Eddy. Action – and quickly, before the fighting started. Philip, bigger than either of the combatants, quietly detached himself from the family and moved across to his boyhood friend. "Hey, Amos ... good to see you ... must have a talk ... long time since we met ..." With the practised grip of one who had, on other occasions, helped inebriated companions to their quarters, he steered the reluctant Amos firmly into the night.

They moved away from the barn towards the Williams house, leaving the noise and the dancing behind them. "Hope I haven't spoilt the party." Philip hung firmly to his man. "But I'd call it a day if I were you, Amos. How the hell did you get into this state?"

"'S that bastard Eddy, o' course. 'E must 'a been doctorin' my drink. 'E's got some pal over at the Fox an' 'Ounds on the Canterbury road oo's keen on Margie ... knows I've been goin' with 'er all summer ... tryin' to choke me orf ... but Margie won't let 'im boss

113

'er, you see." The words came out in a defiant rush.

"Eddy's a bloody man," Philip agreed judiciously. "Still, best to sort it out in the morning. Don't worry about Margie – I'll see her home. Now here's your backdoor. Sure you won't fall up the stairs and wake the baby? Wait half a tick, I'll loosen your tie and get your shoes off – much quieter that way."

Nobody saw Amos again that night.

Philip returned to the tithe barn, his silk square adjusted, immaculate, for all the world as if no 'incident' had taken place. He looked round for Margie. There she was, sitting with Dorothy Evans and a lad from Chartham. No sign of Eddy, thank God. Philip joined the party. "Shall we ... er ... dance?" he asked in a slightly hesitant voice, wondering how best to cool the situation. Margie looked up, nodded as if in gratitude and they moved away to the rhythm of the band from Canterbury.

After a time, she said, "Thank you for coming to the rescue." It was virtually the first time the two of them had been together since the early school days with Miss Millie. Later she said, "You've got mighty good-looking, do all the girls tell you that?"

And he replied, "Well, what about yourself? You'd make all the girls in London jealous as hell."

What more was there to say? Only, he thought to himself, that this girl really is beautiful and I mean every word I've said. They danced and he looked down on her short-cropped brown curls – normally unruly, so she must have been to the hairdresser specially for this evening. They danced and she looked up at the big man, her grey eyes inquiring, her lips – no make-up on them – half smiling. They sat and they danced again, their hands and their bodies suddenly electric to the touch, live wires in contact. For them, all at once, there were only two people in the world.

She said, questioning, "Time to get out of here?"

"Bed-time?" he replied, unwilling to say goodnight, his heart beating.

"That's right, my fine soldier, time for bed," and her eyes were shining as she led him out by the hand. Down the drive they went, making for the village. And then abruptly, without a word, she steered him to the left through an opening in the trees, emerging on the edge of the park.

Still no word between them – they just stood and looked at the full moon lighting up the Mortimer-Wotton lands. There was magic in the air. Then turning, they kissed each other, as if discovering a new world made only for themselves. She drew him down to the grass bank on the edge of the wood. There was a new urgency about her. "Make love to me, soldier man," she whispered. "No, don't tell me – girls always know – you've never done this before, I'll show you how . . ." She was sitting up wriggling out of her knickers, unbuttoning her dress, no bra, her full trim breasts white in the moonlight, inviting him. Who was he to protest? "Come, look at me soldier, let me feel you." She lay back and pulled him close to her, guiding him very gently. "Easy, my lover, easy . . ." They were together now, she the mistress, he the slave. The grey eyes, so close to his, closed . . . "Now, my fine man," she said, as their lips parted "now . . . now." And they shared in an ecstasy, as simple and natural as life itself.

For some little time which seemed as blissful as eternity they lay relaxed in each other's arms. Then Philip stirred and they came together again. It was new and different this time – the man masterful and demanding, the girl accepting . . . receiving him. Long, long after – for time had no meaning for them – they got up and dressed each other, laughing like children as Philip showed Margie how to fold and knot his silk square. All innocence was in their loving.

They moved softly down the drive. They stopped just short of the lodge gates and Margie looked up at Philip for the last time that night. She said very softly, "You've given me everything, Phil . . . I'll never forget. Thank you, thank you. And thank you for being so good to Amos. I'm glad you're fond of him. He's a lovely man, too: and I expect I shall marry him. You'll understand, won't you? But remember: you and I keep our own secret. This has been our night – yours and mine together."

They kissed again, holding each other close. So small she seemed to the big man, so vital, so different from the girls he'd met in London. He could not bear to part. At last Margie pushed him gently from her and moved away into the night, her quick footsteps echoing down the village street, her head held high. In her carriage there was a sort of pride.

Philip returned to the Great House, his mind in turmoil and yet exultantly happy. This night and this girl – her hair, her lips, her body, her invitation – to be wanted as she had wanted him, for himself alone – here was fulfilment. In him, too, there was a sort of pride.

12

NEXT DAY, Philip returned to London, fortified by Sunday breakfast on a scale that suggested the Victorians would hold sway for
ever at Ockenham – porridge, boiled eggs (brown of course), cold
ham (carved off the bone), coffee, cream, marmalade, honey – take
your choice – and stewed fruit to suit the season.

A quick farewell to Eleanor – and he was away, heading for
London via the cart-track and the Chartham Road. He stopped at
the Dower House to tell his grandmother not to expect him at the
harvest service as he had to get back to his duties in London: and
he had a quick word with Gwynedd and Mrs. Constant. But one
thing was certain. He wasn't going near the village until he'd
sorted out the euphoria of the night before.

Later, as his Riley, recently supplied by Ockenham Motors,
purred along the winding road to Maidstone and London, he kept
thinking about Margie. Yes, she could trust him to keep their
secret. He'd promised, hadn't he? Of course, of course ... no
question about it. Indeed, what could be more revolting than
talking about her to his fellow officers? Above the noise of his car
engine, he could already hear their cynical, disbelieving laughter.
Some ass would probably make a hideous joke about 'les droits de
Seigneur'. And his father? No, not on your life.

Philip's one-man argument continued all the way to Birdcage
Walk and on through the next two weeks. The memory of the girl
simply wouldn't leave him alone. The gentleness of her loving, the
touch of her hands and her whispered words insistently kept him
company. Question tumbled over question. He must see her
again, feel her close to him. No, he'd promised not to do so. On the
contrary, he must keep away from the village, leave her to make
the next move. Did Margie really mean she had made her choice?
What if she should be willing to marry Philip Mortimer-Wotton?

At the moment, he convinced himself, he loved her more than he would ever love any girl of his own class, whatever that might mean. To hell with the County and the innuendoes of Society mothers as they crossed off another 'good match'! Had not his family always preserved the freedom to ride rough-shod over convention when it suited them? And how would his colonel wear it? Did it mean chucking up his commission? In all probability Philip would be discreetly discarded as a rotten card in an otherwise good hand. Even if the old man backed him, there were those idiotic army regulations about officers not marrying before they were twenty-six – how would he get round that one? He wanted Margie now, today and tomorrow, not in five years' time. And the Battalion off to Egypt within four weeks? God almighty, where did he go from here?

He thought he'd see Margie again on his embarkation leave, that would be best. Come to some understanding, some decision before he left the country. But when, fourteen days later, he reached Ockenham for a last weekend, he remained as indecisive as Hamlet, his mind fuller than ever of 'ifs' and 'buts'.

He decided to clear his mind by taking a walk, as if delay could help! Deliberately, he headed away from the village past the Dower House and Dark's farm, along the field path towards Chartham, occasionally slashing with a stick at the long grass bordering the track. His course took him over the wheat stubble to the wooden bridge at the trout stream and across the Chartham–Ockenham road to the water meadows beside the Stour. He moved along the bank westwards, up-river to the boundary of the Mortimer-Wotton land and then back by the high fields the far side of the Ockenham woods. But his eyes saw little of the glowing early autumn colours or the beef herd of which John Williams was so rightly proud. He was so preoccupied that when he had a chance encounter with Guy Hogben, the most successful of the three remaining tenant farmers, who farmed three hundred acres south of Chartham and was one of the best sheep men in the County, he scarcely recognised him. He couldn't have told anybody what the man had said to him.

He was entirely alone with his thoughts except that, in his imagination, Margie Kemsing seemed to be walking beside him,

arguing with him, telling him his thoughts were a great foolish-
ness. "All this is Mortimer-Wotton land," he was telling her.
"Come and share it with me."

And she, the pub-keeper's daughter, was laughing at him, her
eyes sparkling. "You're making it up, Phil, just like you used to do
when you made ridiculous additions to Gwynedd Morgan's
stories. You know it's impossible. Don't be so daft. Tomorrow's
another day."

In his mind the argument continued, thrust and parry, half
serious, half an exercise in apologetics, until he emerged from the
woods above the Great House. There he stood transfixed, suddenly confronted with reality. To his right beyond the house, he
caught sight of Amos holding Margie's hand outside the Williams
home: and Margie looking into his eyes as if there was no one else
in the world.

Philip backed into the cover of the trees. Never had he felt
loneliness like this. He must talk with somebody, unburden himself . . . Right or wrong, he would break his word to Margie – the
little bitch. Striding down the hill, he went straight to the telephone in the library.

Arthur Waddilove was just back from matins in the Cathedral
when Philip's call came through. "Off tomorrow? And you'd like
to have a word with me before you move overseas? Why, I'd like
that too. Four-thirty this afternoon? Fine. Emily will be out, but
we'll rustle up something for tea. See you then."

It was just like old times, sitting in the canon's small room, the
familiar furniture unchanged and the picture of St. Francis above
the desk. There and then Philip stuttered through his story, until
Arthur stopped him. "That's enough," he said – and there was a
great sympathy in his voice. "You have done well to come, my son.
You won't have studied theology at Eton or Sandhurst. But I can
tell you, on the authority of the God we both serve, that a man
cannot enjoy the peace of forgiveness unless he does what you
have done. That's what Confession is all about. Because you have
had the guts to come here today, you will, I assure you, find peace.
As for breaking your word to Margie, you've also done right.
Principles, like laws, are not to be taken lightly but, as St. Paul
made clear, they are not the source of life. You'd be surprised how

many secrets are shared with parish priests. Your story stays here," and the older man put his thin hand on his heart.

"But there are three people in your story, you know. What about Margie Kemsing? Don't judge her harshly. From what you say, it sounds as if she has decided what she will do. I think she had decided before she met you at the harvest supper. If Margie marries Amos, you and she will keep your secret as lovers have done down the years. If she does not, she will certainly let you know, for this is the way of the world. There will in any case be sadness, and perhaps loneliness, for one of you. Few people have lived a full life without the hardship of sacrifice. It's something, my son, that God asks of most of us. Come now with me."

The soldier followed the priest across the Precincts and entered the Cathedral by the small north door, passing the Warrior's Chapel with the regimental colours of The Buffs bravely hanging above the sad memorials. The two men descended the steps to the Norman crypt, low-vaulted, mystical in the half-light. There they knelt in silence. Then the old man said very quietly, "O God, look down in mercy on us, thy servants . . . Grant us thy forgiveness and thy grace. And may thy peace and thy direction inspire all those wayfaring men who, like Philip, stand at a crossroads and seek thy guidance. O Lord, in thy mercy hear our prayer."

And in strange compulsive obedience Philip whispered the old time-worn response. "And may our cry come unto thee."

As he drove back to Ockenham, he made no effort to define or explain his actions. It was as if for once, he had made a journey into a land that was not his own. For the moment, at least, there was peace in his heart.

Ten days later he sailed for Egypt – but not before he had received a further letter from Arthur Waddilove. Outwardly, it was very matter-of-fact.

Dear Philip,

I've had a word with your father about a vicar to succeed old Edward Pendlebury who, as you know, has resigned from his Living at Ockenham. With the help of one or two friends in Canterbury, I hope we can find a worthy successor. But finding the right man takes time. Indeed it may be sensible for your family, in whose Gift the Living has always been vested, to pass over its ancient responsibility to the Archbishop. But such legal changes take even more time. So you may like to know that I have arranged to take all services at St. Dunstan's during the interregnum following Edward's departure. With the help of your grandmother and other good people in Ockenham, I'll do my best to fulfil those duties of comfort and counsel which daily reach a country parson. It will be a new experience for me and I look forward to it. Meanwhile, my best wishes go with you on your travels, and remember, your secret is always safe with me.

Yours, as always,
Arthur.

P.S. I have an idea that, in the next few years, Ockenham is going to see much more of your father. I believe *everybody* will be glad to have him back, however difficult it may be for him at first.

A.W.

In November, about the same time that Philip's Battalion was disembarking at Alexandria, Amos and Margie were married by Arthur Waddilove in Ockenham Church. A great village occasion it was – John Williams's eldest son getting fixed up with the Kemsing girl from the Wotton Arms. The celebrations continued long after Amos and Margie had clattered away by hired car to Canterbury, and thence by train to Deal for a long weekend. Indeed, the village gossips were still talking about their neighbours' indiscretions under the stimulus of Jack Kemsing's hospitality when the couple returned to their new home in one of the old cottages at Dark's.

Eleanor had happily agreed to John Williams's suggestion that his son and daughter-in-law should set up house at Dark's Place. She had already arranged for Ockenham builders to bring electricity and main water supply to the farm. Only the date of the wedding took Eleanor by surprise. But no matter. The work would be a doubly good investment if it ensured that Amos stayed on the farm. The young man seemed to possess many of his father's qualities – a hard worker, she reckoned, shrewd and reliable, and

121

with a good head for figures if Millicent Taylor was to be believed. And Margie would make him a good wife.

In Cairo, Philip was kept posted about these events by his grandmother. As to Margie and Amos – he'd come to accept the situation even before the wedding took place. But now, as he read about it in his grandmother's firm, no-nonsense handwriting, he was assailed by a new wave of depression. He suddenly found he could not stick the company and conversation of the officers in the Mess. He manufactured excuses to go off by himself – to fix up some golf at Gezira, to visit the amber sellers in the Bazaar, to walk in the gardens across from Shepherd's, or keep some imaginary appointment at the Turf Club where he could eat and drink by himself. Anything to be alone.

It wasn't long before his behaviour was noted by his company commander, who reported to the C.O. The latter had a word with his adjutant, Jack Biddulph, who quickly posted Philip from company duties to Battalion headquarters. The army is wise in such matters, especially when it has a good officer on its hands – and the adjutant was in no doubt about Mortimer-Wotton's quality.

"Time for a change of scene," Jack Biddulph told him. "Easy to go stale in this sort of posting."

During the next few months, Philip had little time to himself. Attending the C.O. on a visit to the navy at Alex. A long trip with Jack, west of the Delta and the desert road, helping to work out a succession of defence positions in the event of armoured attack from the west: and again, into the Canal Zone, to assess the possibilities of a sea-borne landing to immobilise Suez. Biddulph gave him little time for brooding about home. And he enjoyed working with the navy on the Suez trip: a bit casual, you might say, in their approach, but you could be certain that the sailors would get you there, whatever the odds. Occasionally, he'd get away to the races or have a round of golf. Once he spent a few days shooting duck and snipe at the Wadi Faiyum fifty miles south of Cairo.

Regularly every fortnight, he heard the latest Ockenham news from his grandmother – Bobby's success at cricket, Eleanor taking a motor mechanics course, Mrs. Constant's rheumatism, a hundred and one minutiae from the home scene, news flashes which added up to the conviction that life in an English village is rarely dull, and never without incident.

Constance's letters, always factual, were re-inforced by Arthur who was making regular weekend visits to the Dower House. Reading between the lines, Philip surmised that the old lady was not unhappy about the delay in appointing a new vicar.

The canon stayed Saturday and Sunday night at the Dower House. His weekly visits began with Saturday afternoon tea – silver teapot, Indian tea from Jackson's, scones or crumpets and a slice of Mrs. Constant's fruit cake: Arthur was always good on detail. Then, after two hours to himself with his sermons and service arrangements, he would sit down with Constance to a simple but beautifully served dinner. "Your grandmother," he wrote, "looks as splendid as ever in evening dress, though she doesn't expect me to wear my gladder rags. What style she has. She seems to enhance and bestow her special charm on the Georgian rooms and those remarkable pictures which she tells me your mother bought on her honeymoon in Paris. Sometimes there are one or two guests for dinner, your step-mother for instance or the doctor who is one of the church wardens. One way and another, I hear a lot about what's going on in Ockenham and Little Ockenham. I can tell you, fielding as substitute for Edward Pendlebury is no sinecure for an old man like me."

And that was something of an understatement. Following the Sunday morning services, Arthur had lunch at the Dower House, and after taking evensong returned to a light supper served by Gwynedd Morgan in the morning room. Finally he visited various parishioners through Monday, driving back to Canterbury in the late afternoon with a surprising amount of correspondence and notes in his suitcase.

Weddings, funerals, christenings, visits to the school, illnesses, village rows, meetings with Dr. Guthrie who had taken over Sam Gardiner's practice, and with the new district nurse who also had a strong interest in the Church – these commitments gave the old priest enormous pleasure.

People liked meeting him and weren't frightened of him. One day in late May he was button-holed by Gwynedd Morgan. Could she, being a strict Baptist, be god-mother to Margie Williams's baby? "It's due any time now, Sir: and Margie and Amos have specially asked me, remembering how I used to look after them in the old days. But I wouldn't like to do the wrong thing."

"Bless you, Gwynedd," Arthur replied. "I'm not a very orthodox theologian but I'm sure God and the baby will approve. As for me, I don't believe Amos and Margie could make a better choice."

And so in due course Gwynedd Morgan found herself nursing a strong little baby boy at the Norman font beside the west door of the old parish church; and Arthur Waddilove named the child Alexander John Williams in accordance with his parents' wishes.

13

APART from his regimental duties, these letters from home were for a time Philip's chief solace. But after a few months at Battalion headquarters, he began to receive various invitations to parties given by members of the British community in Cairo, and time off-duty passed more quickly. It was at one of these local parties that he first met Anne Sherwood.

The affair started casually enough at a villa in Heliopolis. Philip, taller than the other guests, caught sight of an outstandingly beautiful woman standing alone at the end of the veranda. She was gazing out into the dark of the night – thirty-five to forty years old perhaps, the light from the house outlining against the night sky her classic features and the fair hair swept back from her forehead. There was an air of sadness about her, a sort of cool, elegant isolation which in his present mood Philip found intriguing.

He turned to a friend for information. "Oh, that's Annie Sherwood," he was told. "The wife of a banking type, name of Harry Sherwood–d'you know him? No? Well, you haven't missed much. They say Anne has the hell of a time with him. Drink, chiefly: but there are other stories running around – and most of them unpleasant. Probably time he was posted somewhere a bit less exotic. Meanwhile, the lovely Annie is stuck out here, wondering what to do about her husband. She's quite a girl. Come over and meet her."

It was the first of many meetings. The attraction between the young subaltern and the older woman was immediate and mutual. Philip had eyes for nobody else that evening. Soon he was familiar with Annie's story – army family, her father killed on the Somme, her mother remarried in 1920. Annie, the only child of the first marriage, had escaped from Camberley immediately on leaving

125

school: and while working as a full-time secretary in the Bank of England, met and subsequently married Harry Sherwood. At that time he was a well-built athletic type with considerable ability and a driving ambition to get ahead. The marriage might have worked, she said, if Harry had not accepted this job in Cairo where he found himself moving into wealthy circles hitherto closed to him. The change of station went to his head – an unmitigated disaster. He was now impossible to live with – overbearing and neglectful in turn: and by the time Philip met his wife, gross in his habits and drinking like a fish. Annie said she would have left him years back, had she known where to go. As it was, she stayed around, befriended to some extent by other residents, but at heart desperately alone. It was no comfort to know she was not the first wife to discover in an overseas posting what a hopeless choice she'd made for a husband.

If Philip's sympathy meant something to her, she recognised in him a corresponding loneliness. "Tell me," she said, "tell me about yourself."

And here, on the outskirts of Cairo, Ockenham was re-created for her. The setting and the shape of the Great House. The people for whom the Mortimer-Wotton home was the fulcrum. Francis, Eleanor and Bobby, Gwynedd and Miss Millie, the people at the Home Farm, Arthur Waddilove and the grandmother who had been so concerned with his upbringing – Philip made them live. But . . . but there's something missing, Annie thought to herself. This picture, painted with such affection, is the story of a boy growing up. Never a word about a woman except the occasional reference to some débutante party. She sized him up again – easy of address, tall, good-looking, essentially masculine. Women of Anne Sherwood's experience aren't easily deceived. There's been a girl in his life, she concluded, as sure as there's a sun in heaven. And for some reason or other, she's let him down. But as she lay in bed that night, idle speculation turned to exciting resolve. This lad was vulnerable. Whatever might have happened with this other woman, Annie knew she passionately wanted Philip to be her lover.

One evening the two of them dined at Mena House. He's a good host, she noted, orders sensibly and always gets attention. They were taking coffee on the terrace. Philip had just received one of Gran's fortnightly letters – a lot of miscellaneous information in it. Bobby getting a place in the Eton side, a reminder about Gwynedd Morgan's birthday, Margie pregnant again . . .

"Margie?" Anne broke in. "Who's this Margie?"

Philip surprised her with his answer. "You know perfectly well, you witch. She's the girl you've been wondering about since we first met. So I'll put you wise. Present company excepted" – he smiled at his companion, "she's the loveliest girl I've ever seen. She was our local pub-keeper's daughter and I wanted to marry her."

"And she turned you down – didn't want to be the Lady of the Manor?" Annie was incredulous.

"That's right," said Philip. "You see, she was clever as well as pretty – generally top of the form at Miss Millie's. She knew it wouldn't work in the England we live in. So she married Amos Williams at the Home Farm – and a very good man he is."

"Poor Philip." Anne's sympathy was genuine. "It must have been shattering when you were ready to bust all the conventions to get her."

"Silly, wasn't it? Feeble, really? But Margie's always had a mind of her own – and it was her decision. So let's forget it, shall we?"

"Forget?" Her slim fingers rested lightly on his hands. "I suppose we both share this need to forget. Time to go, I think. But thank you for a lovely evening."

"Let's do some more forgetting sometime," Philip said as they rose. "I'm on duty for the rest of the week. But any evening free after that?"

Anne looked at her diary – Harry would be away in Alexandria all next week. "Today week, Tuesday? Lovely. Come to my house and I'll introduce you to our little French restaurant in Heliopolis."

She had chosen the Tuesday rendez-vous with care. French cuisine, but adapted to the Egyptian climate: a chilled, flowery Moselle: the service unobtrusive but attentive.

She took Philip back to her villa. Without haste they sipped their coffee and brandy outside on the veranda, prolonging their easy dinner-time conversation, laughing about people they knew,

127

capping each other's stories that had no point for anybody but themselves.

Suddenly, Anne pushed back the table. As they rose from the swinging hammock seat, the timbre of her voice changed. "Philip, darling," she whispered. "You know what I really want?"

"Yes, I think so," he replied and as he spoke she was in his arms, her eyes looking up in pleasure, her body pressed against his. "Yes, Annie, I think I do."

"Come then," she said and they moved from the veranda into the house. The bedroom seemed suffused with her personality, cool and elegant as he had first seen her, yet wholly feminine. He noted the slow grace of her movements as she slipped out of her dress and shook out her fair hair. She was very beautiful. She watched him undressing in the adjoining bathroom, her eyes alight, a little smile of invitation parting her lips. Then, as they lay together, she held him tight, her hands running over his strong athlete-fit body, his lips caressing her hair, her mouth, her breasts. Now, now he was hers: and she gave herself to him.

"Egypt is for lovers," she whispered. "This is how it has always been. To love is to forget everything but the present."

Two more nights they spent together, blissfully happy in their lovemaking, sensitive only to a physical need for each other. But on Friday Annie said in a strained brittle voice, "You must go away, Phil. Harry's phoned from Alex to say he'll be back tonight. He musn't find you here."

"Then you must come away too." Philip's voice was clipped and commanding. "I won't let you live in the same house with him. It's horrible. You hate him, despise him. I'll fix up something – a bolt-hole while you decide your next step. I'm going to take you away. Come on, my darling. Pack some clothes, don't write any note. Keep him guessing." His words, tumbling over each other, brooked no argument or hesitation.

Annie pulled herself together. She swept into a suitcase everything she could lay her hands on – jewellery, bits and pieces off her dressing table, a selection of dresses and nighties. The valise was already stowed in the back of Philip's car, when Harry Sherwood stormed into the house hours before he was expected.

He confronted Philip on the veranda. "So it's you, is it, you bloody young bastard?" he shouted. "The latest in my wife's collection of fancy men. That's it, isn't it?" Harry's face was flushed and his words slurred.

Philip stared at the older man. He was dangerously calm. "You seem to be having difficulty with your speech. But perhaps I misheard you."

"So you're insolent too, you blue blooded young lecher, are you? By God, your commanding officer's going to know about your behaviour. Didn't hear me first time, eh? Then I'll say it again. I don't like fancy men around here – least of all, the latest addition to Anne's over-sexed poodles."

A wiser man would have chosen his words more carefully – but Harry Sherwood was anything but sober. Philip's full-blooded pile driver to the man's stomach was aimed with a heavyweight boxer's precision and delivered with all the strength of a very angry young man. With an agonised grunt Harry slumped to the floor, out for the count.

Philip turned from the inert body on the veranda. He was calm as they come.

"Sorry, Annie, about the commotion," he said. "I get no pleasure from hitting a drunk like that, but somebody was bound to do it sooner or later – and by God, he deserved what he got. Don't worry about Harry. Leave him to the servants. They'll dust him down if he doesn't pull himself together. We'll put a few miles between us before the great awakening."

With that he steered a shaking terrified Annie down the veranda steps and eased her gently into the car. He drove away fast without a backward glance, following the road signs for Ismailia.

From time to time she looked at her lover, his eyes concentrating on the road illuminated by the car headlights, his strong face thoughtful. Occasionally, he would murmur, "Don't worry, Annie. Don't worry. Shut your eyes and try to sleep. You've done the right thing. It'll work out, you see."

Eventually, they reached Ismailia. He found a pleasant little French-run hotel in a tree-lined square not far from the French Club, booked her in, using her maiden name of Bennett, told her he'd be in touch and kissed her goodbye. God knows what happens to us next," she said, "but thank you for being such a very

129

sweet man." Abruptly she turned on her heel. She mustn't let Philip see her cry. It wasn't as if she was a child.

Philip reached Cairo in the early hours. He found himself echoing Annie's words, "God knows what happens next." He was very short on sleep. But drumming in the recesses of his mind was a phrase from the distant past – Eton, was it? Or Arthur Waddilove? He couldn't be sure – but it hammered away in his head. "Confession is good for the soul." Silly how words, long forgotten, come back to you when you're tired.

He spruced himself up and made an early appointment with the adjutant.

"Sorry to bother you," he blurted out, "but I'm in right trouble . . . knocked out that drunken banker, Harry Sherwood, last night and removed his wife to the safety of an hotel in Ismailia . . . thought I should let you know at once."

"You did what?" Jack Biddulph played for time while Philip repeated his story.

"That's exactly as it happened. Couldn't help myself. What do I do next?"

"Do?" the adjutant said. "What do you do? Good God, man, it's what I do that matters." He thought for a minute, tapping his pencil on the desk. Then he looked up at Philip. "You really are a bloody fool. I'd heard, some weeks ago, you were getting involved with Anne Sherwood – a beautiful woman, I grant you. But knocking out her husband . . . Dear God, preserve me from the stupidity of subalterns in a hot climate." Jack wiped his forehead with an immaculate handkerchief.

"Now listen hard. By way of a start you leave me to tell the colonel, see? Next, you get out of the Delta P.D.Q.: I reckon you're due for some fresh desert air – not a bint for miles. I'll have you posted to our company in Mersa Matruh. You replace Brian Melchester who's due for a spell here anyway. Give me Anne Sherwood's address – Anne Bennett, you say? And don't write or speak to her until I say the word. That's an order, understood? Now off you go, chop chop."

"Er . . . thanks very much," Philip started. "But what about . . .?"

The adjutant looked straight at him, but perhaps an onlooker would have seen a hint of humour in his eyes. "There are no 'ifs' and 'buts'," he said. "Just accept the fact that you've made a fool of yourself and leave me to sort out the pieces."

Philip's subsequent dressing down by the C.O. was most deflating – he hadn't felt so small or silly since he left school. But Jack Biddulph must have been a good diplomat. A few days later, Philip decoded a signal from Battalion headquarters. "Personal from Biddulph to Mortimer-Wotton stop expect letter from A.B. stop take no action till letter received stop not to worry."

Shortly after, Anne's letter arrived by army post office.

My darling Philip,

I'm still at the little hotel in Ismailia where you left me – living a quiet life and often thinking of you. But you must be wondering how my little drama is unfolding, so I'll bring you up to date.

First there was a surprise visit from your Captain Biddulph. He told me where you were and suggested no letters either way till he gave me the go-ahead. Hence my silence till today.

What a nice man he is. He thinks a lot of you: so do I (but that's by the way). So far as I was concerned, he couldn't have been more helpful. He was sure I would want to sort out my life with Harry in my own way. If I decided on some sort of separation, fine and dandy; and he recommended the name of an English lawyer in Alex. But if I could keep your name out of the proceedings, so much the better. Of course, I will: though I don't know what Harry's going to do.

A friend tells me he is O.K. Since seeing Captain Biddulph, I've been to Alex and shall only correspond with Harry through the lawyers. They know that I won't go back to Harry *ever*. If he demands grounds for divorce, I'll do what's required. But that's all for the future – these legal proceedings take a long time and have to be finalised, I believe, in England.

From what I know of Harry, I don't think he'll be taking you to Court. Whatever the legal grounds, he wouldn't emerge with much credit and his 'ego' has taken a big enough knock already. Me, I hope he'll leave Egypt and start again. It will be the best solution for him as well as me. Poor old Harry, he wasn't always like this.

Meanwhile, this letter brings my fondest love. I'm sorry to have caused your exile – it sounds like a replay of the sort of thing that was always happening in Imperial Rome! But I'm so grateful for the love you brought me and so glad you bullied me into choosing freedom.

No more for the moment. It will be many months before I shall be able to see clearly into the future. But our days and nights together remain for me a living joy. If they helped to free you also from the past, then they were doubly well spent.

As always,

Your loving,

Annie.

P.S. Sorry if I seemed a bit feeble that night. I've never seen anyone knocked out cold before – and all for my sake. Bracing but unnerving at the same time!

Later, many months later, after the Battalion had returned to England, Philip learnt that Annie had decided to stay on in Ismailia, having picked up an English teaching job in one of the French schools there – "much more interesting," she wrote, "than the sort of secretarial job for which I'm properly qualified." And her hunch was right about Harry who had accepted a posting to Singapore. For some years she and Philip continued to correspond, she telling him of her new friends and assignments in Ismailia and he keeping her up to date with events at Ockenham and in the regiment. They were, after all, his first loves as Annie Sherwood shrewdly understood.

More immediately, Jack Biddulph managed to have a word with Philip in Mersa Matruh when he accompanied the colonel to watch some desert exercises. "Don't worry about the Old Man," he said. "He never lets the sun go down on his wrath. As far as he's concerned the Sherwood affair is over – finished, dead. Actually, he's very bucked with the way these exercises are going. And back in Cairo he speaks of every officer in his team with the fervour of an Arsenal supporter. Believe it or not, that includes you."

Biddulph laughed. "But for heaven's sake don't get involved again. With a bit of luck, Anne will fight clear of horrible Harry: and find her future out here. But you keep off the grass, my boy, until you get home in two months time. This sort of thing has a bad effect on my digestion."

Philip's face was as eloquent of gratitude as his silence. Thank God for men like Jack Biddulph.

14

RETURNING to England, Philip spent the first part of his leave at the Great House. It was reassuring to see the place again and tramp the familiar fields. Although Bobby was up at Oxford, Gran was delighted to see him. Arthur Waddilove was often at the Dower House with news of Canterbury and the village: and Eleanor was anxious to bring him up to date with the farm problems and developments at Ockenham Motors. There was a great welcome, too, from the old servants who had originally followed his grandmother to the Dower House. Yes, it was good to be home again.

It was in Mrs. Constant's kitchen that he first met Margie's little boy. "Two years old, would you believe it?" said Gwynedd, who appeared to be taking charge of Alex while Margie was awaiting the birth of her second child. "A sturdy little chap, too: knows how to wheedle goodies out of Mrs. Constant, don't you Alex? Just like Amos and you, Mr. Philip, in the old days at the Great House." She turned briskly to her charge. "Now come along, young man. Time to take you home to Mother." Philip watched his old nurse struggling to get Alex into his coat for the return journey to Dark's Place.

"That boy's too strong for you already, Gorgon," he laughed, and lifting the child high in the air, dumped him with a flourish in the push-chair. Just what any man might have done for any little boy, you might suppose. But in the child's delight, Philip found himself face to face with the bright, friendly, daring eyes of Alex's mother. It was very disconcerting.

His leave ended, and he returned to the Battalion – the same round of duties, the same old timetables, with occasional courses and field exercises to break the monotony. Yet he was strangely reluctant to escape to Ockenham from the claustrophobic atmosphere of Wellington Barracks and the London scene. Somehow, he felt unsettled and ill at ease.

Now, Egypt. It had been different in Egypt. There at least a man could enjoy some variety. He surprised himself by developing in retrospect a genuine taste for the place – the colour of the Cairo street scene, the noise of the crowd and the clatter of the over- loaded trams, the sails at sunset on the Nile, the haunting minor key melodies intoned from the housetops. The nostalgia of hind- sight, no doubt. But he recalled with pleasure his journeys around the Delta – past the patient cattle and the toiling Fellaheen by the Sweetwater canal, out to the ancient monuments of the Pharoahs with their eternal reminders of an Old Testament world, even the endless distances of the desert . . .

Inevitably, his mind went back to Annie. She'd understood him – yes, that was it – as no other woman had ever done: a lovely companion until that ghastly scene with Harry. "The latest of her over-sexed poodles" – he could still feel the anger in him. Oh, it's all over now. Forget it, you fool. That's what you were ordered to do, wasn't it? Subalterns of twenty-five are not for marrying – see army regulations on officers' marriage allowances. Anyway, she's too old for you. Stop looking over your shoulder and decide what you want to do next.

One thing Philip knew. Whatever might be said of Ockenham, London in the Thirties was not his scene. Even his closest friends were getting on his nerves. Why the hell had Brian Melchester needled him in the Mess last night: "Still pining for the lovely Annie, Phil?" And why, in God's name, had he rounded on Brian and told him to mind his own bloody business, as if Annie still mattered? Surely by now he should know how to keep a poker face. Oh well, he'd put it right with Brian next time they met over a drink. A good chap, Brian: too old a friend to take offence . . . Still, you've got to watch it.

Unhappily, Philip soon had to face trouble more serious than boredom or Annie Sherwood. Bill Govain put it to him, over lunch at the Great Eastern Hotel. "Afraid there's bad news for you, Philip." His stockbroker spoke like a consultant bringing his patient news of a fatal diagnosis. "I've just heard that the former Hollingbourne companies will be passing their dividends again.

My scouts tell me they're in right trouble like most of heavy industry."

Philip tried to reassure him. "No need to kick yourself. You told me to get rid of my mother's shares years ago, remember? It was I who told you to hang on – sentiment, I suppose. But where do I go from here?"

Bill Govain considered. "Well ... there's no point in selling now. The bottom's dropped out of the market. Better wait and hope for recovery, I'd say. Any chance of getting back some of the £10,000 you let your step-mother have before you left for Egypt? We might put that to work."

"Bill, don't make me laugh. That went down the Ockenham drain long ago."

"So you have to make out on a subaltern's pay and allowances? What about the old man?"

"Not a hope," said Philip. "Cash reserves are not father's strongest suit as you and your firm should darn well know after dealing with him for thirty years."

"Perhaps your step-mother ... or a sale of land ... or something ..." Bill's voice trailed away. "Anyway think around it and give me a ring if you've any good ideas."

Think around it? How silly can you get? thought Philip as he hailed a passing taxi. Think around it? There's only one thing to do – make a clean break and get a posting away from London.

Next day he managed to have a word with Jack Biddulph who very decently promised to sniff round for some service attachment where the outgoings might be less onerous. Then he made a date with his father.

Francis was genuinely concerned. "Very sorry to hear of your problem, old lad. Only wish I could bail you out. But alas, life in London costs a packet, and at the moment I can't give up my present activities. Still, no reason why we shouldn't take a modest lunch. Come on." And Francis shared a half-bottle of Bollinger with his son before moving into the Club dining room.

Afterwards, on the spur of the moment, they drove down to Ockenham in Philip's Riley. As they descended Wrotham hill with the panorama of the Kentish Weald stretching out before them,

Francis was positively expansive and Philip became increasingly aware of the change in his father. No signs any more of the listless depression of malaria. The man beside him was full of a new vitality that showed in his physical response as well as his speech. "Tell me more about your job," Philip said. "The new life with Winston seems to suit you. Any room for me in the wings?"

Francis thought for a moment. "Well," he replied carefully, "I wouldn't like to make any promises. The trouble is we're a strictly civilian outfit, mostly unpaid amateurs. And, honestly, I don't like the idea of your leaving the Guards. They like you there, you know, even though they don't say much. Still, trust me to keep an eye open."

They were driving through the woods above Charing when Francis returned to the subject. "Look, Philip," he said, "I think I ought to tell you the real reason why Ockenham's likely to see more of me in the immediate future. The fact is I'm keeping a boat at Ramsgate, strictly concerned with *l'entente cordiale* – big enough, y'know, to make the Brittany crossing." He put his index finger to his lips. "That means squaring Ellie – no, don't worry old lad. She knows all about José ... But outside the home circle we've got to work up a bit of a cover plan. You know the sort of thing ... 'Odd feller, Mortimer-Wotton' (Francis was a good mimic), 'gone crackers on sailing, taken up with some naval type, what?' 'Something to do with that French bit, I shouldn't wonder.' 'Could be, could be.' Or for the County, 'Good to see old Francis back at Ockenham. Reconciliation with that American wife, do you think? Quite like old times.' We want to keep 'em guessing, Philip, if you see what I mean." Francis was thinking aloud. "Ockenham's nicely placed for future operations. And I've got a hunch that Ellie will enjoy the mystery game."

But when they reached the Great House they found that Eleanor had more immediate concerns on her mind. Old Mrs. Mortimer-Wotton had suffered a stroke that very morning. "Paralysed down one side," Eleanor reported. "No warning of trouble. Gwynedd found the old dear helpless and called me over. Dr. Guthrie came very quickly and says it might be worse. Her mind's clear and speaking's reasonably distinct, but she's over eighty, you know. I'm just back from the Dower House. The old lady seems comfort-

137

able – just irritated she has to alter her routine and cancel her engagements. We've got a night-nurse coming in, but the important thing, doctor says, is to keep her from worrying. She doesn't know you or Philip are here, Francis – so I wouldn't visit her till the morning."

The three of them talked far into the night, partly about the family but chiefly about farm losses and the difficulty of maintaining the house and estate. Next day, Francis and Philip both saw Constance, but there was nothing they could do. Eleanor had taken every sensible step and both men returned to London before nightfall.

As for Gran, she clung to life through the summer with characteristic tenacity. She saw many of her old friends and, with Millicent Taylor's help, sorted out her affairs, paying the tradesmen with unaccustomed speed. Arthur Waddilove was a frequent visitor and she took great pleasure in listening to Philip's account of his day-to-day activities and to small talk from Bobby now at the end of his first year at Oxford. But in the autumn, following some circulatory problem, she suffered a second stroke. Francis was out of the country – no address given. But in answer to Eleanor's call, Philip hurried down from London.

He reached the Dower House just as Arthur was leaving. "Oh Philip, thank God you've come." The old priest's face showed his relief. "Gwynedd is with your grandmother, but she's been calling for you all the morning. It's like an answer to prayer. Don't disturb her peace, my son. Just stay beside her as if she was a sleeping child. She'll know you're there. Peace be with you both. I don't think she'll ask for me again. But if she does you will find me at the Great House with Eleanor."

Philip entered the old lady's room. Gwynedd looked up at him from the window seat where she was sitting with her Bible and her sewing beside her. He bent down to kiss the old nurse, then moved quietly across the bedroom to the chair beside his grandmother's bed. "What style she has." He found himself repeating Arthur's words. "There is dignity even in her dying."

Gran's eyes fluttered open. They moved slowly from one of Charles's Alpine paintings on the far wall to the silver framed photograph of her husband standing on her bedside table. Then they focussed on the grandson to whom she had for so many years been a mother. Philip's big clumsy hands instinctively smoothed her forehead and her lips moved. He could just hear her last hesitant whisper, "Goodbye for the present, dear boy . . . Henry says . . . form and breeding count . . . can't all win the race . . . if only . . . if only Bertha . . . had lived."

That was all. A sudden contraction of the frail hand resting on his, one last convulsive indrawn gasp: and Gwynedd was leading him gently from the bedside. It was the first time he'd ever seen anyone die.

At Ockenham the death of Constance Mortimer-Wotton marked the end of an era. It was as if a queen had died and her court circle could not adjust itself to a new ruler. The Dower House servants went about their duties, all purpose lost. Mrs. Constant missed her routine of daily consultation. There were no words of encouragement or thanks to Ted Larkin hesitating to cut a cauliflower. Parkinson polished the black Rolls with grim determination wondering who would give him orders now. And Gwynedd? No clothes to lay out, no tea to prepare. "She was so good to us all, Mr. Philip. A very wonderful woman . . . we shan't see the likes of her again." The Welsh woman's dark unfathomable eyes filled with tears as she spoke. It was a time for mourning.

Millicent Taylor, less emotional, found temporary relief in answering the letters which continued to reach the Dower House from all over the world, bringing news of the unfortunate girls and troublesome lads whom old Mrs. Mortimer-Wotton had helped to find new hope and new life. But to the family one unsentimental fact stood out crystal clear. Gran's death did nothing to ease their financial problems. When her will was proved, they had good cause to remember those words of Francis long ago, "My mother is a natural spender."

Early in 1935, Francis, Eleanor, Philip and Bobby held a conference at the Great House. All sorts of minor economies were suggested – Bobby to come down from Oxford, Philip to resign his commission, Eleanor to cancel some orders for new farm equipment, Francis to give up the lease on his Ryder Street flat. Suddenly, Francis took control.

"Time to cut the cackle," he said. "Philip and I will do our own thing in our own time, but Bobby dam' well completes his last year at Magdalen and Ellie presses on with her farm mechanisation. Meanwhile, we have to raise more capital to run Ockenham, right? More cash. So this is what we do. Flog the land on the Canterbury side of the village and leave the buyers to develop it for housing the Canterbury over-spill. That leaves us in possession of over 2000 acres of good farming land, while the new residents will bring a bit of new life to the place as well as new customers for Ellie's garage. How's that for a plan?"

Francis's enthusiasm was catching. "I'll tell you something else," he said. "As tenancies in the village lapse, we'll sell the freeholds and pick up some extra boodle that way. Don't know what my old mother would have said. But something on these lines ought to take us over till we see which way the cat jumps."

"What exactly do you mean," Bobby interrupted him, "about the cat jumping?"

Francis's commanding mood changed to that of confidential conspirator. He winked at Bobby and with that familiar gesture of his put his index finger to his lips. "Bit of a gambler's throw," he laughed. "You never can say for sure. But I'm prepared to bet all Lombard Street to a China Orange that within the next few years farming will be booming and the steel industry in Sheffield going at full blast."

Francis wasn't to be drawn further. But within weeks lawyers and estate agents and civic authorities were pressing forward with his plans. Not quickly enough to stop him surrendering the lease of his flat off Piccadilly. Not quickly enough to change Philip's decision to leave the army in favour of more lucrative employment. Time would be needed for the gambler to win his bet.

Philip, however, enjoyed one last soldiering assignment. Returning to Birdcage Walk, he was greeted by Jack Biddulph. "Got something good for you at last, Philip – right up your street. It seems our lords and masters are taking a new interest in Italy. Anyway, they've decided to send four officers, *'en civile'* you understand, to take a look at the place. They've already collected a Gunner, a Sapper and a chap from the Tanks: and I've put up your name as the fourth member of the party. Interested?"

"Sounds terrific." Philip was really excited. "Thank you very much. Tell me more. When do we start? Is there a plan?"

"You'll get the details from the War Office," the adjutant replied. "As far as the Brigade of Guards is concerned, you are granted extended leave of absence. Call it a nice Italian holiday, if you like. Fast train to Milan, then bus and bicycle across the North Italian plain as far as Venice. Just to indulge a natural interest in military history, you'll take a routine look at the '14–'18 battle zone – the Trentino above Lake Garda, the Isonzo river and the Piave line: they're all easily reached from Venice. Then, off you go south to Florence, Rome and Naples, south until you can't go further without swimming. I expect you'll be given a few extra chores by the bloke in the War Office: but I'll leave the briefing to him. Oh, by the way, you're likely to be the youngest in the party. Good luck and keep out of trouble."

So, in due course, Philip and his three more senior team-mates presented to the War Office a report on the problems of landing an army corps in Italy and advancing into Germany through the Northern passes. A damned depressing report it was. Little chance of using armour except in the Po valley: rivers flowing in the wrong direction, narrow coastal plains, dominated by gun emplacements on the Apennine foothills. Any advance from the South would require mountain troops, probably Indian Divisions: and need support from sea-landings up the Peninsula. The four co-signatories, enjoying a farewell dinner at The Senior, drank with cynical humour to the report's perdition in the certainty that it would end up in the dusty pigeon holes reserved for such documents at the War Office.

It was not until 1937, after Philip had resigned his commission and was working on the personnel side of a light engineering firm in Ashford that he heard more about the Italian report.

The occasion was the wedding of his brother, Bobby, to Penny Bridlington, the girl Philip had known in her débutante days. It was the strangest coincidence. On leaving Oxford, Bobby had charmed his way into a job with old Bridlington's printing company in Rochester, met the boss's daughter and heigh ho, the wedding bells of Chelsea Old Church were ringing for them. "Just like a fairy story," Gwynedd and Mrs. Constant agreed. "Bobby has all the luck," said his Oxford friends at a time when graduates were swelling the unemployment figures. But all were glad for Bobby and Penny – they were so clearly happy.

It was at dinner after the wedding that Francis took his elder son aside. "A word in your ear, old lad," he said. "That was a damned good report of yours on Italy. As you know I'm in pretty close touch with Mr. Churchill these days. And the old man, by methods best known to himself, winkled it out of the War Office and got very interested. He growled a bit about the defeatist mentality of all regular soldiers – that's Winston all over. But he took it all in, I can tell you: and asked me to give you his congratulations."

Not for the first time Philip gained the impression that his father had more strings in his hands than he cared to mention, even to the extent of influencing his selection for the Italian mission.

What was now beyond doubt was the fulfilment of his father's prophecy to the family conference at Ockenham. A stream of armaments orders was beginning to flow to Sheffield and the great industrial cities of the country, and farmers were receiving financial encouragement to double and redouble home food production. By 1938 war was a near certainty. Early in 1939, Philip was recalled to the army like other members of the Army Reserve of Officers. The coming years were going to require every trained soldier as well as every ton of steel and every acre of corn.

15

By some quirk of chance, Philip was posted back to Cairo within a few months of the outbreak of war.

Eight years had passed since his first tour of duty in Egypt, but the place still retained for him its nostalgic, unchanging familiarity. Unchanging, that is, except for the absence of Annie Sherwood. As he knew from a letter received before the war, she was now married to a Frenchman in Ismailia – an ex-regular officer working for the Canal Administration. Her husband, Pierre Leduc, was older than Annie, but remarkably young for his sixty odd years: and Annie had apparently found in him the qualities of charm and personal consideration that Harry Sherwood so conspicuously lacked.

An invitation to her home gave Philip a surprising piece of information about his father. It was while Anne was busy getting some drinks that Pierre exclaimed, *"Mon Dieu*, but you remind me of your father."

"My father?" Philip was taken by surprise.

"But yes," Pierre replied. "Didn't you know? He and I met long ago in Salonika on the staff of General Sarrail. In fact, we made a little journey together to Bucharest, *une excursion très amusante*: and then of course we share the memory of the lovely Madame Joséphine, the only attraction in that very dull headquarters. But perhaps the lady would hardly find a place in your father's *mémoires* – the English are very discreet, *n'est-ce-pas?*"

"On the contrary," Philip laughed. "Father's not a lover of France for nothing. He has introduced me to the lady and . . ." Philip abruptly checked himself – there were so many doubtful allies in Cairo. "But that was many years ago." Pierre did not appear to notice his hesitation.

"C'est incroyable. So you will know how your father was

banished because he taught too well the English?" Pierre's humorous eyes lit up at the recollection. "And Annie says – *voyez*, we have no secrets – she says you in your turn were banished from Cairo? There is a similarity, *plus ça change, hein*? But I tell you this, *mon ami*. François would have applauded the blow you struck for Annie. And me? How otherwise should I have met this abandoned English lady in Ismailia? *D'accord, chérie*?"

Pierre turned to Annie and raised his glass. "We drink to our friendship with you and your father."

It was a gay evening and nobody was embarrassed by the past. But Philip returned to Cairo with the bitter-sweet certainty that Annie's future lay in Ismailia with this inquisitive Frenchman.

Her absence from Cairo provided at least one reason why he was now sitting by himself on the terrace of the Gezira Club, idly contemplating an empty glass on the table before him.

Rousing himself to action, he snapped his fingers. A young Sudanese, brown of face and smooth of skin, approached silently, removed the glass and returned a moment later with further replenishment.

"Whisky – moya, Sah," the boy said softly and inscribed a fourth mark on the table mat before returning to his position against the wall of the Club-house, whence he contemplated this solitary Englishman sipping his solitary drink. He saw before him a tall aloof man of splendid physique: with a carefully trimmed Guards moustache which gave a military look to a typically English face, wide-set eyes, auburn hair, straight nose, skin tanned by the Egyptian sun: a man he'd often served after swimming or a round of golf. He, Abdul Hassan, prided himself on his ability to distinguish a British regular officer from the rest of mankind. He could recognise authority in the wearing and cut of khaki drill shorts and shirt, in the style of footwear. This one was 'big shot' for sure, deep in thought about his own country. Otherwise he would not command a fourth whisky and he wouldn't be drinking alone. Was not he, Abdul Hassan from Khartoum, also an exile? He understood these things: and with time on his hands, he fell to imagining the country, the women, the children, the castle of which this fine milord would be dreaming.

In point of fact, Hassan's imagination was very close to the truth.

Philip was feeling thoroughly frustrated. The chips weren't falling right for him. And in a state of introspective depression, he was reviewing his present plight.

Here he was, in the midsummer of 1940, looking over his shoulder and moaning to himself about the England to which he had returned in 1932 – an England where soldiers were underpaid, business friends went bankrupt and farming was a short cut to poverty. He reviewed those years of appeasement in which England had gone soft while this damned house painter, Adolf Hitler, had strutted the stage: years in which a British Foreign Secretary made a secret deal with that little crook, Laval, to allow Mussolini to invade Abyssinia: years in which England was more upset by the marriage of Edward VIII to an American divorcée than by the bombing of Guernica. The all-time low had been reached when a British Prime Minister returned from Munich crying, "peace in our time," after being bullied into permitting the Germans to dismember Czecho-Slovakia. God, it made him boil even to think of this government of fifth rate men. And look where it had got them all.

Philip regarded his diminishing drink without enthusiasm, and turned his thought to the domestic scene for which he and his family held a more personal responsibility. Looking back, the fact that stood out a mile was the vitality of the father he had once found so hard to understand. It was a point re-emphasised in the past week by Annie's French husband. The slightly feckless, indeterminate father Philip remembered from his Eton days looked very different now. Not one of your soft Joes, lulled into silly security by these appeasement politicians, but one of the few men to see the future and do something about it. And, by all that's wonderful, he'd found his métier in these cloak-and-dagger adventures of his. Strange how it needed the threat of war to bring his father to life. But that seemed to be the size of it. Perhaps it was the quality of the gambler in Francis – the gambler who enjoys playing for high stakes and, like every successful gambler, sees further than the rest.

Or was everybody's life a question of luck – gambler's luck?

What price Eleanor, for instance? First cutting herself off from Francis, even accepting the place of José in his life. Then, almost by

145

way of compensation, taking a passionate interest in the farming and in the build-up of Ockenham Motors. And now, after all these years, regaining status as Francis's confidante in these clandestine adventures... Here was something more than a live-and-let-live rapprochement. Was it also to be ascribed to the chance of war? God, it's a funny old world. He needed Arthur Waddilove to sort it out.

Philip's thoughts moved in logical progression to consider the case of his brother. Now that boy really *was* born lucky. Not just on the cricket field – an Oxford 'blue' and a trial for the County were fair enough, considering his father's prowess at the game. But what about the other things? Sailing straight into a job with old Bridlington, marrying his daughter, starting a family – one daughter already and another baby expected: and now commissioned and on active service with The Buffs ... while he, Philip, a trained regular officer, was kicking his heels in a minor staff job at Grey Pillars.

Philip pulled himself together with a visible jerk. Go easy, Philip. Cool down. For God's sake, keep jealousy out of it. Bobby's had the lucky break. That's all there is to it.

"Ismah," he called. The Sudanese boy arrived with another whisky and Philip returned to his own predicament. Here he was, a dedicated soldier missing out on the best jobs and losing seniority because a shortage of cash had caused him to resign his commission at precisely the wrong moment. Here he was, stationed at H.Q. British Troops in Egypt thanks to some scruffy clerk in Whitehall. Hanging around in the hope of a staff course at Haifa: for all the world like one of those old lags at the Depot sipping whisky and waiting for something to turn up. Philosophers the fools called themselves. Was it his fate to be one of them – a 'born loser' as the golfers say? No, he was damned if he'd accept that.

Yet something surely was conspiring against him. He could forget Margie who'd chosen Amos Williams: and Annie who'd married Pierre Leduc ... after all, they had made the running, so why should he feel hurt? Philip dismissed them from his mind. But back came those last words of Gran, "if only Bertha had lived." How decisive his mother's death had proved: decisive for so many

people beside himself – for his father, for Ockenham . . . no
Eleanor, no Bobby . . .

He began to repeat a jingle he'd read in a life of Lord Fisher,
picked up casually in the Mess –

"Time and the Ocean – and some guiding Star
In high Cabal – have made us what we are."

So that's what Admiral Jackie Fisher thought directed his
actions. Stars, eh? Certainly, they shone clearly in the night sky
over Cairo. A more ancient text tumbled out of the past. "The stars
in their courses fought against Sisera." As a boy, he'd always felt
sorry for the poor sod, quite apart from his nasty death. Just one of
that long line of generals who'd never been given a fair chance.
Nowadays they were two-a-penny in Cairo: perhaps they too
were blaming the stars in their courses.

Heavens, he was getting maudlin . . . must be the whisky. He
shook himself back to reality, paid his bill, summoned his staff car
and returned to Abbassia across the Nile bridge and through the
teeming streets of Cairo. Soldiers all over the place: spies, too, he
wouldn't wonder. But war for him seemed a long way off – as far
away as the Gezira Sporting Club was from the Great House at
Ockenham . . .

There was a chill in the evening air as Philip's car turned past the
guardroom into the barracks at Abbassia. He changed before crossing to the Mess where Guy Venables, now a G.S.O.2 at Grey
Pillars, looked up from a long letter just received from his latest
girl.

"Hullo, Phil," he said. "Looks as if you've got the posting you
wanted: and there's a heap of mail from England."

Sure enough, there was an official confirmation of a place on the
Haifa staff course waiting for him and, in addition, three letters
from home.

The first, from Eleanor, was full of local and family news – two
landgirls at the Great House, the new Allis Chalmers combine-
harvester assembled and ready to go into action, Bobby on embar-
cation leave, a second daughter for Penny, mother and children

147

evacuated to the Great House, and a cryptic sentence about Father making a good recovery. The letter was dated 15th June 1940.

Another, bearing the same date, came from Arthur Waddilove, the old priest's writing as firm as ever. His chief concern was with the civil defence of Canterbury and the protection of the Cathedral. But he added two items about Francis. "Your father," he wrote, "is recovering marvellously well from his Dunkirk ordeal. Three times over there at the age of sixty, bringing back far more men than you would have thought his boat could possibly carry – not to mention a few dogs who are still roving the Dover streets: and by some extraordinary stroke of luck, no enemy damage to the boat. The experience certainly took its toll and your father's only just beginning to sleep soundly again. But his vitality is truly amazing. And Eleanor has nursed him with great understanding. While the boat is being fitted with a new engine, he has indulged his fancy – believe it or not – by buying an old fire-engine for the defence of Ockenham. Apparently the staff at Ockenham Motors is putting the engine into good shape, Eleanor and the landgirls will be painting it red in their spare time (if they have any) and Gwynedd Morgan – here surely is the stroke of a master – has been ordered to polish the brass bell until she can see her face in it! Your father certainly adds colour to our somewhat sombre scene. And behind the façade, Philip, there's a very warm place in his heart for you. Keep in touch if you possibly can."

Finally there was a rambling undated letter from Margie. "Thought you might like to take a look at Ockenham as seen from Dark's Place. Amos is very busy, having been given overall charge of the farm machinery by his father who, I'm glad to report, keeps in good health. Everybody on the farm is working too hard though the landgirls are a great help. Sometimes Amos gets annoyed he's not in uniform with the rest of the boys. But I tell him we're all part of this war and a farmer's skills mustn't be wasted.

Of course, the colonel's fire-engine is the talk of the village. Young Alex tells me that when it's ready to take to the road, the children at the school are to be given a free ride round the district – great excitement. Alex will soon be moving to a senior school. He's very good fun, big for his age: and teacher says he's got the brains to go places. But it's early days. Now he's ten, he helps me a lot with Mary (7), Alice (5), Paul (3) and even with the new baby. We've decided to call him Arthur, after Canon Waddilove who still manages to see us quite often. We are so very fond of him.

Gwynedd seems much happier now she's settled into the little cottage next to us. She really loves the children. It's like turning back the clock, seeing her first with our lot, then with Bobby's little girls, and a moment later finding both families on her hands. Our three-year-old Paul had an argument with one of your little nieces the other day and Alex overheard the Gorgon saying it was a case of 'the pot calling the kettle black.' Can you remember her using the same words to us? Actually, she finds a lot of time for Alex – she takes her godmother's duties very seriously! And she often brings him books from your library at the Great House. So you see we are very grateful to the Colonel and Mrs. M-W for letting us live at Dark's. Meanwhile everyone waits for news from you. If you can find time to write to the Gorgon, you can be sure we shall *all* know what you're up to – and you can be sure of a reply, too! P.S. Alex is very excited about you beating the Italians at Sidi Barani and says will you please get him a Desert Rat badge." A smile spread slowly over Philip's face. A staff course for him: and Ockenham unscathed and working up to the annual climax of harvest. Margie, Amos and Penny: Alex and all the other children endowing the place with new life: Gwynedd Morgan fussing over the new generation like an old hen with new-hatched chicks. This surely was reality. This was what life was really about. The stars were shining. "Yes, thank you," he assured Guy Venables as they sat down to eat. "Good news from home, all good news."

It was only after reporting to Haifa for his staff course that Philip heard of a German bomber which, in a cloud-dodging daylight raid, had dropped a string of bombs on some cottages at Chilham and unloaded the last of them on the Great House at Ockenham.

16

THE unimportant incident of a small H.E. bomb shattering the north-west façade of Ockenham Manor holds no place in the war annals of the County of Kent. By the grace of God and the strength of the building there was no loss of life, though the kitchen staff was badly shaken by the blast and one side of the house was a complete 'write-off'.

As to the rest of the household, Francis and Eleanor were away from the Great House on their respective businesses. So were the two landgirls, while Bobby's small daughters were over at the Dower House with their mother. Taken by and large, the affair was dismissed as a lucky escape, and soon ceased to be a talking point at the Wotton Arms where the bomb-incident-bore was already recognised as a man to be avoided.

After a quick inspection of the house, Ockenham Builders reported that, by blocking off the north wing, the south side of the Great House which comprised the oldest part of the structure could be made habitable on the ground floor and that the cellars could be used safely. Full restoration would be out of the question while the war continued.

Francis, returning from Ramsgate where he'd been inspecting his boat's newly-fitted engine, viewed the remains of his ancestral home with aristocratic detachment and almost cynical good humour.

"Never liked that eighteenth-century front," he confided to his friends, "altogether too pretentious, too ornate – and pretty poor material at that. Typical of that Italian fellow, Palladio, who charmed my forebears into these expensive follies. Anyway, there's no time for tears. What annoys me is that the Ockenham Fire Service wasn't ready for rescue operations. It would have provided a good opening match for the boys."

With that, Francis arranged for the Great House to become the Command Post of the newly-formed Home Guard detachment, the running of which he delegated to Guy Hogben. For all practical purposes, the Home Guard and the fire fighters of Ockenham were identical and interchangeable.

Philip reacted to news of the Ockenham bomb with the same air of detachment that his father had displayed. "Knocked off the front of the house," he told his Haifa friends. "The Luftwaffe must have been in a panic. A lot of rubble but no lives lost." He seemed to have dismissed the matter from his mind.

His thoughts, however, became more positive during a forty-eight hour leave in Jerusalem when, following guidebook directions, he walked out to the Mount of Olives. He found a seat in the shade of the trees and looked across the valley to the walls of the Old City, its roofline dominated by the Dome of the Rock.

An old monk, seeing him with a sketch book, thought he must be making his own drawing of the immemorial scene, as tourists have done down the years. But peeping over the big man's shoulder, he noticed that the sketch depicted a two storey house in an English park setting. The old man paused. Then he said in excellent English, "It is right, my son, that in time of war the peace of this garden should make you think of your home. May God be with you and those you love." And smiling he continued his perambulation.

In due course, three missives reached Ockenham from the Middle East: one for Colonel and Mrs. Mortimer-Wotton containing a sketch entitled "Ockenham Manor Mark III": one for Master Alexander Williams containing a Desert Rat badge, kindly supplied by an officer of the Seventh Armoured Division: and finally a picture postcard for Miss Gwynedd Morgan on the back of which Philip informed his Bible-reading old nurse that the supply of milk and honey in Palestine was nothing like as satisfactory as in Joshua's time. Gwynedd proudly showed her postcard to everyone she met, from the Baptists at Chartham to the Dower House staff. And the people of Ockenham concluded that their Mister Philip was in good heart.

All the family and staff were now living at the Dower House, except for Francis who fixed up a bedroom for himself in the cellars of the Great House, and established his office in the undamaged sitting room and library where his mother had once spent so much of her days. Life quickly settled into its new grooves, and the fire-engine, resplendent in red paint and complete with pumping equipment and turn-table ladder, completed its maiden journey from Ockenham to Chartham and back, the schoolchildren alarming the cattle by ringing Gwynedd Morgan's shining brass bell every inch of the way. "This village of Ockenham," they proclaimed to the countryside and the beasts of the field, "is ready for anything."

The same confidence was reflected by their parents and the casual drinkers at The Wotton Arms. The colonel's fire-engine was the symbol of Ockenham's confidence. Whatever the shortcomings of the fire-engine and its operators, none of its drivers – not even Joe Fagg who worked at the garage but came from the other side of the County – would lose his way in the maze of Kentish lanes from which all signposts had just been removed. This was their corner of England and they would guard it. God help any German who asked the way in the neighbourhood of Ockenham.

Old John Williams was the only man living on the Mortimer-Wotton land who was not caught up in the general enthusiasm. He spoke to Eleanor, and for good measure, repeated his warning to Guy Hogben. "Now look 'ere, Mr. 'Ogben, ah don't want too many o' them practices an' military exercises an' gallivantin' at night. Ah've gotta get 'arvest 'ome yer know, an' me an' the girls canna do it by ourselves. First things first, ah say, an the reapin' comes first round 'ere."

The arrival of Philip's letters from the Middle East also coincided with the start of the Battle of Britain. Above the fields of Kent, the fighter pilots from Biggin Hill and beyond engaged the enemy in furious daily combat. Houses were destroyed at Thanington on the road to Canterbury. In the centre of the city the Deanery and some shops in Burgate were damaged. The men of Kent were once again called to be the vanguard of liberty.

Only once did Ockenham enjoy its little moment of fame when a Dornier 17, smoke pouring from its port engine, banked into the wind and crash-landed up on Hogben's farm. The duty man at the Great House sounded the alarm. It was repeated at the Wotton

Arms and the village post office. The Ockenham fire-engine, skeleton manned, careered up the Chartham road to find the crashed plane and cordon it off until the experts could inspect it. The other enrolled members of the Home Guard joined in a search for two crew members who had been seen to bale out just after steadying the doomed plane on its final course. One was found up by Ockenham woods, helpless with a broken leg, and was brought on a stretcher to the Great House. His comrade landed cushy and for five hours escaped discovery. But as the sun went out of the sky his courage ebbed away. At nightfall Amos and Margie Williams opened their front door to admit a very exhausted young German pilot and accept his surrender. Alex rushed off to tell the Home Guard – thus duty was done. Yet at Dark's Place there was pity rather than anger. Margie sat the young German down to high tea with the family. Amos watched him with a wary curiosity. There was no attempt at conversation. Suddenly, his hunger satisfied, the airman looked at the open fire and the children playing, and burst into tears. He was very tired and a long way from his parents in Hanover.

By the end of October, the Luftwaffe's losses enforced a change in enemy tactics: and London and the great cities of the Midlands and North became the chief objectives for the German bombers. The scare of invasion receded, and at Ockenham John Williams and his small staff directed the ploughing and the sowing as weather and the seasons appointed. In Canterbury there were public concerts in the Dane John Gardens.

It was about this time that Francis Mortimer-Wotton made the first of his disappearances. He told Eleanor not to expect him around for a spell. She understood that he and his friends in the Special Operations Executive known as S.O.E. – standing for Stately 'Omes of England, Francis told her – were planning a few surprises. On several occasions thereafter his little ship left Ramsgate at night with no lights showing and returned some forty-eight hours later with her crew slightly depleted. There were other missions when exchanges of goods and men took place secretly in out-of-the-way Breton harbours. In January '42, an onion-seller with a soiled beret on his head and a Gauloise drooping from his lips might have been seen riding an ancient bicycle in Calvados.

His tour included visits to Bayeux, Caen and Granville before he headed south-west and dismounted beside a small château between Rennes and St. Malo.

There, in the high vaulted eighteenth-century entrance hall, José identified Francis. She laughed and cried and laughed again as she embraced her evil-smelling lover. It was a most joyous re-union. Nobody would have thought from their behaviour that Francis and José were engaged in the world's most dangerous game.

"Tonight," they agreed, "we relax. Tomorrow we occupy ourselves with business." They bathed and dressed as if preparing for dinner at the Ritz – José splendid in an evening dress from Paris, Francis looking most distinguished in a suit belonging to the late Count from whom José had inherited the house. They opened a bottle of Margaux '27 to grace a most carefully chosen meal and their conversation sparkled over the ridiculous adventures that war imposed upon them.

"You, *mon cher*, head of the great house of Wotton, dressed up as an onion-seller. *C'est épouvantable.*"

"And you, my dear Contesse, directing a smugglers' ring from this fine mansion. It's most undignified."

"*Au contraire,*" she laughed. "It's a way of life in Brittany, as is well-known to certain boat-owners across the Channel."

They capped each other's stories about the *drôleries* of war and ranged over the shared memories of their first meetings in Salonika. Francis said, "That reminds me. Had a letter from my elder son some time ago. Remember Pierre Leduc? Philip ran into him in Egypt – apparently, he's an official of the Canal Company."

"Ugh, I don't trust that one, François. You tell Philippe to take guard. We came to call him Pierre Look-both-ways – I give you English translation – shifty-eyes you might say. He was no credit to the army of France. We exterminate him as a fly on the wall and remember only each other."

Thus they returned to the present. Late that night they went to bed and made love as they had so often done before. They slept peacefully in each other's arms as if war did not exist.

Next morning they dallied over breakfast in José's bedroom beside the big window overlooking the fields of Brittany – coffee in the French style and newly baked 'croissants'. "The French are invincible in peace and war," said Francis.

"And the English," said José, "are also invincible – but especially so when they dare to invade the homes of occupied France as lovers in disguise. But enough of your compliments." José kissed him on his forehead. "Now we make business – and where can we be safer than here in my own bedroom?"

She walked across to a tall chest of drawers, rummaged among her underwear and returned triumphant with a large scale map. "Now look, François. Here is where I stay with my cousins in April." Francis noted the exact map reference. "A dull countryside compared with Brittany – but is there any place in Northern France that is not blighted by these pigs of the occupation? At least, I can relax after dark with my little radio receiver. And I think of you, do I not, by tuning in to the French service of your B.B.C."

The conspirators completed their plans. José would listen in every evening from the first of April – "we call it April Fool's day," said Francis. Should she hear, after the news, a loving message addressed to José from her François, she would immediately communicate with a certain Raoul in Bruneval. *"Assez simple,"* they agreed. It would be left to Raoul to create *'un petit divertissement musical'*. It could be a noisy diversion that the excellent Raoul would arrange.

Well satisfied with his visit, the onion-seller made an inconspicuous departure, pedalling north-west towards Roscoff. At midnight he boarded a Breton fishing smack. Or so it would have appeared to a casual observer. But once clear of the harbour, the little ship detached itself from the rest of the fishing fleet and moved at unusual speed to Falmouth where the onion-seller changed into country tweeds more fitting to his station. Later that day Francis Mortimer-Wotton reported 'Mission accomplished' to Col. Buckmaster at Special Operations Executive in Baker Street.

When he returned to Ockenham, Eleanor asked no questions. Other people had no questions to ask – hadn't the colonel always been a law to himself, a bit of a mystery man? He was one of them; and yet apart from them, so to say. But towards the end of March the more observant Home Guard members at the Great House Command Post noted that the colonel was retiring very early to his

bedroom in the cellar. "'As a bit of a laugh with us each evenin',"
one of the duty men said to Guy Hogben, "bu' twoudna' surprise
me if Colonel weren't cookin' up somat in cellar. Seems a bit
excited like if yer get ma meanin'."

Down in the basement, Francis switched on the B.B.C. French
service. The familiar voice of the French announcer came on the air
loud and clear – "*Ici Londres, ici Londres.*" There followed some
guarded but depressing news of Rommel advancing in Libya, the
German successes in Russia, the Japanese swarming over South-
East Asia. Then a pause. "*Et voici un message personnel.*" The air was
electric ... Francis's hands were shaking with excitement. "*Voici
un message personnel. François embrasse sa femme, Joséphine.*"

Across the Channel near Bruneval José heard the same loving
message. Twenty-four hours later a fabulous explosion in
Northern France diverted members of the German occupation
forces from their normal duties. Simultaneously a gigantic storage
barn caught fire and engaged the full attention of the *Sapeurs
pompiers* of the locality. The same night a naval task force under the
command of Commander Rodney Slessor R.N.V.R. destroyed the
major Radio-location installation at Bruneval and returned to
England with a load of secret equipment which in that desperate
spring was of more value than much fine gold.

Two days later – it seemed eternity to Francis – the B.B.C.
announced the navy's success.

"We've done it, Ellie," Francis shouted, hurrying across to the
Dower House. "Heard the news? We've smashed the Hun's detec-
tion equipment at Bruneval. Champagne for dinner – time for a
break in training. What a day!"

His enthusiasm and excitement reached the Wotton Arms. That
evening the Home Guard detachment in Ockenham was in no
condition to fulfil its duties. They toasted the Colonel till there
were no bottles at their disposal. And Eleanor sharing Francis's
happiness seemed to recognise again the man she had met in
Cleveland long ago.

17

IT was about this time that Francis, casually passing the time of day with Gwynedd Morgan, learnt that Arthur Waddilove who had continued to visit his friends at Ockenham after the arrival of the new incumbent, had been talking with the headmaster of the village school about Alex Williams.

"Alex is my god-son, you see Sir," the nurse explained to Francis, "so I've a special interest in him. Well, last week Canon Waddilove took Alex into Canterbury for an interview with the headmaster of the King's School. He's another canon – Shirley or some such name – so I suppose he would know Mr. Waddilove. Anyway, it seems he'd already seen a report on Alex's school work. And the long and short of it is that in the autumn, when Alex is eleven and a half, he'll be off as a boarder to King's Junior School. It's been moved to a place near St. Austell – that's in Cornwall, sir – so it will be a long way for Alex to go for his schooling. But Mr. Waddilove has persuaded Margie and Amos that it's a great chance for the boy. So of course we're all very excited. He'll have to learn Latin and French, they say, but the headmaster has told Alex not to worry. All we have to do is to get him fitted out with the right clothes."

"And what of the lad, Gwynedd?" asked Francis. "Is he as excited as you are?"

"Ah now, I don't rightly know about that," she replied. He's a deep one, is Alex – one of those boys like Mr. Philip used to be, sir, who takes life in his stride. He's not given to showing his feelings. Very different, I must say, from his brothers and sisters. When I asked if he was pleased about his new school, all he'd say was that he'd always wanted to travel on a big express train: and though I might not know it – as if I wouldn't, really these modern children, if you please – the Great Western is the finest railway in the world. Just the sort of answer I might have got from Master Philip at his age – the young monkey. Ah well, I suppose boys are all much the same really" . . . and the old lady moved briskly away towards her cottage.

Francis marvelled at Gwynedd's constancy to his family which managed to embrace every man, woman and child dependent on it. Here she was, sane and balanced, concerning herself with the future of young Alex Williams. For her, though she often spoke of the might-have-beens of earlier years, the present was all-absorbing, all-sufficient.

Come to think of it, it was much the same with the others who lived in this lovely corner of Kent. London might be in ruins and military disaster be staring at England from the four corners of the earth. But those who dwelt in the farms and cottages and depended for their livelihood on the Mortimer-Wotton fortunes, still continued in their chosen ways, airing their daily fears and hopes – the shortage of sugar and oranges, the birth of a baby, the death of an old man, a boy's education. Didn't somebody write – perhaps it was in the Bible – about "The day of small things?" Would he have been happier if he'd had more to do with the small things? Or would he? Surely he would have been bored stiff.

Yes, you had to face it, there was a great gap between the village and the world of political and military decisions in which he and his friends were involved. It was a gap between town and village, a gap between the boss and the people he employed, a gap between the Great House and the ploughman's cottage – a gap so personal that he hardly liked to enter the Wotton Arms for fear of embarrassing the locals. Yet no armies could move without these good people, no nation fed, no parliament elected. What a rum world it was. Did it really require a state of war to bring them all together? That, after all, was what had occurred over the Dunkirk rescue, and the Home Guard and the fire-engine: and, most recently, in the spontaneous celebration of the navy's success in Northern France. These splendid people knew – and were proud – that the family up at the house was playing a major part in the action.

Francis's joy at the success of the Bruneval raid was short-lived.

One morning in May a despatch rider from Baker Street delivered two personal letters to the Great House.

The first, very splendid in its official envelope, informed Lt.-Col. Francis Mortimer-Wotton D.S.O. that he was to be recommended for the award of the *Croix de Guerre avec Palmes*, "for outstanding courage in the service of France."

The second, contained in an outer and inner O.H.M.S. envelope, was over-stamped 'Top Secret'. Francis tore it open, already forewarned that it was on its way. "From Raoul," the decoded S.O.E. message ran, "José arrested by S.S. in Brittany and moved to Fresnes woman's gaol for interrogation stop rumour not yet confirmed traces S.S. information to middle east axis intelligence stop check most urgently and warn Wotton. Message ends."

Francis acknowledged receipt and sent the Don R. on his way. Hours later Eleanor discovered him sitting motionless on his bed, his face haggard, his eyes unseeing. He hadn't even destroyed Raoul's message. She fetched him a double whisky. "Better read it yourself, Ellie." he said. "Fresnes . . . you know what it means for José . . . torture, disfigurement . . . torture beyond endurance." His voice broke with an emotion he could not control. Suddenly, he added, "That little bastard, Mr. Looking-both-ways. My God, is it possible? No, no, I can't believe it." He swallowed the whisky neat. And Eleanor urged him to get some sleep.

Yes, she'd be back again – just off for a late shift at Ockenham Motors – but she'd be back later with some food. "Yes, Francis, I'll be back. And tomorrow you can make further inquiries at S.O.E." She looked at his desk calendar. Tomorrow would be the first of June, 1942.

Then she left him, alone in his makeshift bedroom.

That same evening Amos Williams was on a routine Home Guard patrol which included a visit to the Wotton Arms. As he came out of the pub he saw flares in the sky over Canterbury. He returned to the bar and put a call through to the Command Post at the Great House only to learn they knew nothing. Jack Kemsing tried to phone a fellow publican in Canterbury and couldn't raise him. Amos moved at speed up the Beech Drive. The colonel was awake, took one look at the sky and ordered the alarm to be sounded in the village and Little Ockenham.

"I want the fire-engine manned in five minutes," he told Amos in a hard-as-steel voice which Amos hardly recognised, "fully kitted up with every fire-fighting appliance we've got. Those are marker flares for bombers, for sure. The bastards are going for Canterbury." And then to Guy Hogben, "You stay here Guy, with a skeleton Home Guard detachment. I'll go with the fire-fighters. If you can get a call to Canterbury tell 'em the fire-fighters of Ockenham are on their way."

The telephonist was still trying to make contact with the Dane John Control room when the fire-engine reached the Great House. Eleanor was at the wheel. She was just leaving Ockenham Motors when the call came, "I know this engine better than most," she said firmly. "Joe Fagg has the night off and is probably as tight as a tick, anyhow. And you're not going without me tonight, Francis, so where do we go from here?"

She would brook no argument. Francis didn't attempt it – he knew the look on her face of old. "O.K. Ellie m' dear. Let's make it a double act. Canterbury it is. We'll stop at Kemsing's to pick up the rest of the troops and then you point the old girl's nose to Canterbury." He jumped up beside her, gave a defiant tug on the bell-rope and the fire engine lurched off bravely into the night.

By the time they left the Wotton Arms the fire-fighters of Ockenham were at full strength. As they crossed the Stour bridge short of Thanington, bombs were falling on the city. The drone of German bombers was everywhere – background music to the devilish percussion which the citizens of London knew so well.

"Down Windcheap," shouted the colonel to Eleanor, "straight on into Castle Street, if possible, and head straight for the Cathedral." The fire-engine came to a halt in St. George's Place just as a bomb struck the eighteenth-century Corn Exchange right in front of them.

"This is where we stop and fight," said the colonel. "connect the hydrants, get the supports out and the turn-table ladder into operation. By God, we're going to need it."

Another bomb fell and fire enveloped the fine old Georgian building. Before anyone could restrain him, Francis Mortimer-

Wotton was on the ladder. Water pressure still coming on? O.K. Up, up, up, up. Now he could be seen balancing high above the building, a jet of water directed on the upper storey while men below were fighting the ground floor flames. Another bomb fell and the great red fire-engine gave a fearful lurch. For a moment more the figure of Francis Mortimer-Wotton could be seen silhouetted by the light of the flames against the night sky. Then he pitched into the holocaust below.

His charred body was recovered next day as the citizens of Canterbury set about restoring life to the City after the so-called Baedeker raid. All men must die, and Francis Mortimer-Wotton was only one of the fifty odd people killed by the Germans that night. Another casualty was Arthur Waddilove. The old priest, as his custom was whenever there was a bomb alert, was visiting a shelter near the Cathedral. He was talking to a mother and her small family when the bombing started. The family had come to know the old man well during constant visits to the shelter. He had a way of taking their minds off their own fears by telling them of the courage and good humour of other poor people in lands he had visited overseas. They began to comprehend they were just a tiny part of the vast family of suffering humanity. When the bomb fell, Arthur Waddilove was comforting the baby while the mother calmed the other children. He was killed instantly. By some miracle the baby was found alive, half enveloped in the long black cloak which the old priest always wore on his night patrols.

Later that month, the men and women of Ockenham were represented among the two thousand people who assembled in the cathedral to pray, with Archbishop William Temple,

> "for our fellow citizens in the Services that in
> wayfaring and in danger they may have success"
> and "for all our friends from whom we are now separated
> that God may keep them in the peace which comes
> from trusting in Him."

There were few in that vast congregation who did not believe that the Cathedral had been spared by a miracle: and few who did not feel, as their eyes travelled up the vaulting of the Nave towards the High Altar, that the preservation of the mighty building was the symbol of their own survival.

Only Eleanor knew of the Top Secret message handed to Francis prior to the raid on Canterbury. Brought back to Ockenham with the utterly weary crew of the wrecked fire-engine, she had gone straight to her husband's cellar to destroy any evidence of his secret missions. This, she felt, was what he would have wished.

It was then that she saw the citation from Free French Headquarters – "For outstanding courage in the service of France." And now Francis was dead, sacrificially dead, accepting death – and Eleanor's mind took to extravagant fancy – like a member of the *ancien régime* on his way to execution. No, that was too ridiculous. Who was she to speculate on the conflicting thoughts in her husband's mind? Since 1914 she'd hardly known him until the patched-up alliance of the last two years. She could only guess what this French woman meant to him. She clutched the citation, proud at least that she had fought beside Francis in his last battle. With a sad little shake of the head, a mixture of grief and resignation, she returned to the Dower House to look after her son's children and resume her work.

Only after the liberation of Paris was it confirmed that José had died in Fresnes prison, poisoned by her own hand rather than disclose, under torture, the names of her comrades in the Resistance.

18

PHILIP received the news from Canterbury in the desert, at the headquarters of an Armoured Brigade to which he had been posted after his Haifa course. By that time, Rommel's Afrika Corps had been halted by Montgomery's Eighth Army at the Alam Halfa ridge: and with Sherman Tanks pouring in from America and the desert air force establishing air supremacy, even the Desert Rats, 'browned off' with the successive advances and retreats of their apparently mindless commanders, were prepared to give their new commander a swing. Philip himself was delighted at being promoted brigade major. Life in the desert was looking up.

And now ... his father killed, Arthur killed ... Canterbury destroyed. He could scarcely comprehend the blow that had struck him. The brigade commander said, "You must go back, Philip. God knows we shall miss you here, but they'll need you still more at home. I'll arrange compassionate leave just as soon as I can." The brigadier's sympathy was of the heart. But even as he used the word 'compassionate', he looked up at his tall thirty-five-year-old brigade major to see a man he'd never met before, a soldier transformed into something hard and pitiless as an avenging Fury. His words of sympathy died in his mouth.

Philip mumbled his thanks, and asked in a toneless voice for twenty-four hours to think things out. Sitting on his camp bed, he fought to recover a sense of proportion. From his hole in the sand his mind was transported to his small village near Canterbury. How, he asked himself, could his anger be appeased by quitting the battle? He thought of the father he'd come to admire. Wasn't such a man, whose qualities flourished in war and languished in peace, bound to take one risk too many? Did not death always come to such men unexpectedly in unlikely places – a sort of accident, you might say?

And what of Arthur? God knows he'd never sought long life, nor the fame and fortune that were his for the asking – never sought anything except to lend his strength to the poor in spirit. What a travesty that this man of peace should die by enemy action! And yet, was not this the death that Arthur would have sought, fulfilling one final task in the course of his calling? Philip recalled the happiness of shared days: the Poor Priests Hospital, Eton, the Sandwich road, the little room in the Precincts where St. Francis seemed enshrined, the ancient Cathedral crypt. Memory stirred as he thought of his friend. How he would love to have seen the old priest once more, if only to thank him for his goodness. But that must surely have waited until peace was won.

Until peace was won . . . Philip's features hardened. He ceased to measure the inevitable rebirth of spring against the loss of his father and his friend. He no longer attempted to weigh the permanence of the land against the brevity of human life and see in the contrast a sort of balancing equation.

Sitting in this miserable hole in the desert, something antique and elemental seemed to fuel his anger as his mind moved to the destruction of Canterbury's ancient buildings and to the rubble strewn by barbarians over its little lanes and pleasant places. In a state of cold calculating fury he felt himself in the presence of murder most foul, the murder of all he held most dear. The time for argument was past. That same evening he asked for a posting to a motorised Battalion of the 60th. He had an overwhelming compulsion to meet the murderers face to face.

His motorised Battalion of the Rifle Brigade suffered comparatively few casualties as it moved with the Armour to Tripoli and then to Tunis. But the old regular elements blew their top when they heard they were booked for the invasion of Italy. It was too much for men at the end of a long haul, some of whom hadn't seen their homes since their peacetime posting to Egypt in 1937. Philip and his fellow officers found themselves in charge of some bloody-minded and utterly intractable mutineers. If they were not removed they would infect every incoming draft required to bring the Battalion up to full war establishment after its desert losses. The company commanders, under Philip's lead, persuaded the

C.O. to report the crisis to the Divisional commander. It was a wise move. Before the situation got out of hand, the trouble-makers were removed and the Battalion put into reserve in Tripoli where a vigorous retraining programme was undertaken.

It was a job Philip understood and enjoyed. It gave him time to learn more about the junior officers and N.C.O.s – and he liked what he saw. His previous training with the Guards helped him to gain the confidence of the new riflemen joining the Battalion. "A good bloke, the major," they agreed, "knows 'is stuff and don't throw 'is weight about." Meanwhile, among the officers, his pre-war journey in Italy gave him an unexpected authority which other desert warriors, for all their self-confidence, signally lacked.

This was particularly true of Douglas Haxton, the young and newly-appointed C.O., who had already collected a M.C. and bar in the desert fighting.

The colonel was a problem. Even before the Battalion landed in Italy and moved up the Adriatic coast to join the main body of the Eighth Army, Haxton was needling Philip. The antipathy was as inevitable as it was mutual.

The relationship between the two men eased as the Battalion began to gain confidence in a series of small skirmishes north of Foggia. Both the colonel and his company commmander could at least share a pride in their achievement. But that was before the Sangro débâcle.

There, in the most appalling conditions of rain and mud, the Battalion was among the first infantry units to cross the river and dig in on flat ground short of a line of hills strongly held by the enemy. The cover was limited. The hope was that the Eighth Army gunners, still on the south side of the river, would keep the Germans quiet until the armour could cross the river and cover the infantry's further advance. The orders were clear cut. Dig in and try to keep the cold out.

Philip was proud of 'A' company's performance. Officers and N.C.O.s had been remarkably calm and the riflemen in their first big test had responded admirably. No panic at the river, lucky in the crossing, only three men wounded in No. 3 platoon – one of those bloody schu-mines. But otherwise lucky, damned lucky.

And the boys were showing just the spirit which was so sadly missing in Tunis at the end of the desert run.

Suddenly, Philip and the other company commanders received orders to report to the C.O. They found Douglas Haxton fairly purring over the Battalion's achievement. But after giving them a tot of whisky, he came to the point.

"Take a look at the hill over there," he said, pointing to some high ground standing out a little from the surrounding line of hills. "It's Hill 601 on the map, see? It's a bit higher than the hills to the right and left of it and it's slap in front of us. I reckon the *Tedeschi* have had one hell of a bashing over the last twenty-four hours and it's ours for the taking."

"Fair enough," said one of the company commanders, "but what exactly are you proposing, Sir?"

"Why, attack tonight in Battalion strength. It's money for jam."

"But the men need a rest. They've had one hell of a day and must have a chance to sort themselves out."

"Rest?" said the colonel. "They won't sleep out there, you know. Too damned exposed. They'll do much better when they've moved the Teds off that hill. So that's what we'll do – get moving, say at one a.m. and rustle the Germans while they're out to the world. We'll be holding the hill well before first light. O.K.?"

Philip was so angry he could hardly control his voice. Then he said firmly, "I'm sorry but I don't like it. It's not a case of whether we can get on to the hill but whether we can hold it when morning comes and we are exposed to every bit of shit they can unload on us. I reckon the casualties will be far too great to justify the risk. And where does this fit in with Brigade and Divisional plans? I thought they'd told us to stay put."

"Come off it, Philip," said Haxton. "I've never been in a battle where tactical decisions in the field could be taken at Division or even Brigade level. It's a matter of taking your chances when they present themselves. The boys at Division are going to be very pleased with us when they hear we hold a strong point from which we can command the adjoining hills. I will of course ensure good communications with them and see that the gunners are ready to deal with tomorrow when it comes."

Haxton waved away all further argument. He was not going to

166

take 'No' for an answer. The inevitable casualties did not seem to worry him. These young men – the majority new to battle – might have been pawns on a chessboard for all he cared. Despite Philip's protests Haxton's plan to attack Hill 601 was laid on.

'A' company would lead on the left, 'B' company on the right – the rest in reserve, with the Battalion's anti-tank guns ready to move into position on the hill the moment the enemy was dislodged.

At 00.30 hours, 'A' company crossed the start line, 3 platoon leading and Philip up front with Sgt. Baker, a runner and a signalman.

They moved quietly enough in open order, their faces blackened, armed to the teeth. Such noise as they made was deadened by the wind and the rain. Philip prayed to God there were none of the wooden schu-mines on the first approaches. If the Germans had relied on anti-tank Teller mines which were unlikely to be set off by infantry the company would at least be off to a good start.

The ground was rising now. At two a.m., Sgt. Baker spotted the outlines of a Spandau position which had been pin-pointed the previous day. Philip stopped the leading rifleman and went forward on his stomach with the sergeant. Still no noise – and then an unmistakable snore. One of the enemy was asleep. Two bayonets were unsheathed. Two Germans died without a sound. First objective achieved. Philip had murdered a sleeping man in cold blood. Baker had dealt with the other poor devil and seen the fear in his eyes.

The climb continued around the shoulder of the hill. They'll soon tumble to it, thought Philip, when they buzz the Spandau post and get no answer. But we ought to be able to close on them from the flank if our luck holds. The important thing was to get there. The leading platoon worked its way round an old farm shelter. If there were any Germans there, they could fix them from above. Meanwhile, move upward, keep contact. Baker had No. 3 platoon under superb control.

It was then that all hell broke loose on the right. 'B' company had bumped the enemy with a vengeance – run into a patrol or set off a mine – who could say? A Very Light shot into the sky on the other side of Hill 601. Whistles were blowing as the enemy roused themselves. A spandau was loosing off to the right. 'B' company was in trouble – poor sods.

There was only one course for Philip – make use of the disturbance on the right, get the rest of the distance and flush the enemy defenders while their fire power was concentrated on 'B' company.

His orders rapped out. One platoon under Mr. Vintner to clean up the farm building – the rest to get up to Sgt. Baker's leading platoon and have a go. Shoot to kill. No mucking about with prisoners. Get there and make every possible use of the enemy's dug-in defences. Battalion H.Q. informed by field telephone – "'A' company attacking summit in full strength. Wotton requires immediately anti-tank guns, medical officer, hot tea in that order. Reserve company to prepare to follow guns up 'A' company's marked route."

Speed, discipline and darkness did the trick. The riflemen achieved complete surprise. They were all over the German company positions. The killing was horrible. There was all the difference between this sort of thing and taking pot shots at enemy patrols. One of the boys was sick, others were crying, somehow they stuck it knowing that the enemy would get them unless they struck and fired first. And anyway, they'd got to take the pressure off 'B' company.

Every rifleman was aware of the presence of Philip and his signaller and diminutive runner, as the major saw his platoon into defensive positions and checked the Brens' field of fire. A runner from Mr. Vintner's platoon reported that the farm buildings had been cleaned up – one German killed, four wounded, no casualties among the riflemen. He was told to stay put, but act as guide to the reinforcements now on their way. By dawn, 'A' company held Hill 601 and all anti-tank guns were dug in.

The casualties in 'B' company had been heavy. They'd withdrawn as best they could and the Teds who had gone after them seemed to be moving towards their comrades on the high ground to the East.

So what? Brew up, get down some food if you can stomach it and look out for trouble at first light. Sure enough it came. Mortars endlessly, a fair stonk from 88 millimetres, and then the first counter-attack. The riflemen with ground advantage and prepared positions beat back both the first and two subsequent attacks, but the casualties were mounting. 'A' company must be relieved within twenty-four hours. The situation was untenable unless a Divisional attack could be mounted to relieve the pressure and silence the enemy gunners.

In fact, Philip's company held out for forty-eight hours, aided by 'C' company which came up after dark on the first day. And then the full Divisional attack was launched. Under a fantastic barrage, the sappers got tank-bridging equipment across the river and the riflemen cheered as the armour fanned out. The battle of the River Sangro was joined in earnest. But there were 300 casualties in Colonel Haxton's Battalion of whom sixty were dead. Among them the M.O., 'B' company's commander and six other officers.

Philip, with shrapnel in his leg, refused to leave his command post until a relief Battalion took over. Then he returned with the remnant of 'A' and 'C' companies down the way they had come, across the level ground and over the river into reserve. Sgt. Baker, miraculously unharmed, came down with him and saw the stretcher bearers get him into an ambulance.

The remaining riflemen of 'A' company moved back in three tonners to a big house twenty miles behind the front line. Food, sleep, a new clothes issue and a grim sense of humour helped to restore them to sanity. But few of them could forget the two days and nights spent on Hill 601. The memory kept recurring in their conversation.

"I saw the major gettin' that multiple mortar goin'. 'E knew all about them German weapons." "Sure 'e did," said another. "'Anded me a spandau; 'e was calm as the boatin' lake at 'ome, yer know. Said to me, 'It's all yours, Johnny – works like this, lots of ammo, let 'er go an' use the tracer. It may persuade their O.P.s that their own men are still on this bleeding 'ill.' 'E found time to thank the cooks, too. Gawd, I 'ope we get 'im back soon."

The runner, a boy of eighteen, had his own story which he put in a letter home. "I was close to the major right through the battle," he wrote. "Told me to stick close to him and I'd be O.K. I fell over once and he pulled me up. Then a few minutes later, he handed me back that little book I was given in England – it was *A Shropshire Lad*, Mum, remember? – and he says he thinks it must have fallen out of my pocket. Afterwards, during a lull, he talks to me about Housman. I thought he might have thought me a bit of a cissy with my poetry – but not a bit of it. He says most soldiers, even Sgt. Baker, carry something like that in their battledress pocket and, sure enough, he pulls out of his pocket a picture of his home in Kent. 'That's my Housman,' he says. 'I reckon we both know what we're fighting for.' And then a bit of shrapnel rips into his leg and he has to get the wound dressed. But he won't leave us. He stays with us until a relief Battalion takes over. The other lads say – and so does Sgt. Baker – they've never had an officer like the major. As he went down the hill, they gave him a cheer such as I've never heard before. It was sort of spontaneous, Sgt. Baker said, which means that no one quite knows who started it but everybody felt they had to join in.''

Philip dimly remembered the lad waving to him but that was about all, for he couldn't hear a thing. Then somebody gave him a jab which knocked him out until he reached a Field Hospital where the shrapnel was removed from his leg and the wound properly dressed.

A nursing sister was watching him when he came round. Some days later she said: "You were fairly shouting the odds, major, under that Nitrous Oxide anaesthetic. They call it 'laughing gas' but you certainly weren't laughing. Told the world to watch out for somebody called Haxton and avoid him like the plague . . . seemed to be the biggest villain you'd ever met. Or maybe the second biggest, because you told me confidentially he was as nasty a piece of work as Furnival, or that's what it sounded like. And your language, major! It really was in a class of its own.''

The girl laughed and turned away from the bed. She didn't add that while the big man was still half-conscious, he had also broken out into a sort of sobbing and, again and again, a gabble of words – "You poor little German bastard . . . not your fault . . . not your war . . . not ours." Such memories were best forgotten if forgetting were possible.

Eventually, just after Christmas, Philip returned to Base Depot to learn that Haxton's Battalion had been merged and Haxton relieved of his command. But that was no longer his business. His deafness and leg debarred him from further front line service. But he was damned if he'd accept a home posting. Somehow, he'd keep in touch with Baker and his splendid riflemen. For the moment, he'd pick up some stooge job in the Naples area. With the aid of friends at Alexander's 15th Army Group Headquarters in Caserta he fixed himself a job in charge of a leave area near Salerno.

19

A SOLDIER on active service is always fascinated with the part chance plays in his survival. A senior officer is killed by a stray bullet and a man gains unexpected promotion. A last-minute order leads to some other fellow taking the seat on a plane that crashes on take-off. The front line fighting man miraculously survives while a camp commandant – safest job in the world, dear boy – is blown to bits on an undetected Teller-mine. Every fighting man is secretly aware that luck is his constant companion and becomes inbued with a fatalism as pervasive as that of the Arab.

So it was with Martin Harrison, once of Beckenham Grammar School, with a First in Law at Oxford, admitted Solicitor 1938, and five years later cross-posted from a T.A. Gunner regiment to a staff job at Eighth Army H.Q. His trained and orderly mind fully accepted that the logic of life ceased on the day his regiment became part of the desert war. For him it was just another piece of luck that in April 1944, some twenty miles south of Naples, he had his first meeting with Philip Mortimer-Wotton.

Actually, the two men met beside a culvert on a sun-kissed lane winding its serpentine way through the lemon groves behind Ravello. As the road followed the contours of the hill-side, Martin found himself gazing down to the blue of the Mediterranean and its white border of waves breaking against the rocks a thousand feet below. Another turn in the road and he had a bird's-eye view of the busy peaceful outskirts of Amalfi lining the route to the town centre and the port. Another change of direction and with his back to the coast, he was staring up, up, up into the hills of the Sorrento peninsula. Every slope was dotted with the homesteads of Italian small-holders, each of them apparently endowed with the same possessions – poultry, a cow, fruit trees and children innumerable.

No scene could have been more cut off from the bloated bodies and the wrecked tanks, the stench and the noise of the Italian battlefields which for the last six months had been the background of Martin's life. Here, at long last, was another world, and enchantment was in it. His thoughts began to circle round the endless questions that plague men who are weary of war. What were these battles really about – Tobruk, Alamein, the Mareth Line? Could a desert really be worth so much destruction? And what of Sicily and the costly airdrop short of Catania – he was one of those who had survived that near-miss at the Primasole bridge. And now, even with the Italians out of the war, the mud and the impossible rain of the Sangro crossing ... Where, for heaven's sake, did it end? And where did it all fit into the world beyond the bailiwick of the Eighth Army . . . at home in England . . . in France . . . in Germany? Speculation formulated useless questions and cried in vain for answers.

Suddenly reality returned in the shape of another soldier on the same road. The contrast between the two was indeed striking. The younger man walking up the hill was still light of step, of medium height but strongly built – a man who on a Saturday afternoon in England might have been a scrum-half or a wicket-keeper according to the time of year. His appearance gave no hint of his tired thinking. The other stood every inch of six foot three, full of authority but ponderous of movement. Despite his uniform, correct in every war-time detail required of an officer of field rank in the Brigade of Guards, he hardly seemed part of Martin's war. Probably it was the uniform that did it, for Martin was accustomed to the desert boots, the sheepskin coats and the grey New Zealand pullovers still affected by the best-dressed Desert Rats. But whatever his uniform, this bulky Guardee looked, in some odd way, old beyond his years.

As Martin drew level with him, Philip Mortimer-Wotton was standing beside the stonework of the bridge seeking, rather hopelessly and with temper rising, to find some point of understanding with a middle-aged Italian farmer. Both turned in relief to the new-comer.

"*Il Comandante*," pleaded the Italian relapsing desperately into his own language, "*Vuol portare via mia moglie! Spogliarmi della*

173

frutta, della verdura anche del vino – va bene! Ma rapire la moglie! Mai, mai, mai!!"

"Hell, I don't want your oranges." The major's voice was rising too. "Can't you understand, man? All I need is a woman to help out at the Villa della Robbia."

He turned in exasperation to Martin. "Look, I'm getting nowhere with this feller whose wife, I'm told, is the best cook in the district. Can you get it into his peasant mind that I'm in charge here as Town Major – the name's Mortimer-Wotton if he wants to know. I've taken possession of a house – the Villa della Robbia they call it – just off the main square. And I need a civilian cook to look after things at my headquarters. Tell him he can come along too if he wants to guard his wife from worse than death. For all I care, he can have a cut at the rations and the garden produce. For heaven's sake, get it into his head that it's a good offer of employment I'm making, not a lecherous proposal. I gather he once worked in London at the Savoy or somewhere . . . says he knows an English gentleman when he sees one. Well, who in heaven's name does he think I am? These Italian chaps are all the same," concluded the major. "Sing, think, talk women and expect the poor creatures to do all the work. I can't make 'em out."

Martin, wondering whether the major was at a loss with women or Italians or both, had a go with his *Teach Yourself Italian* which he'd been working on since the Sicily landings in the August of the previous year. Surprisingly – or could it be that the major was a bit hard of hearing – the matter was soon settled. La Maria would report *Domani pronto alle due dalla Casa del Comandante.* He, Giovanni Battista, would personally accompany her to the side entrance to the villa and ask for Sgt. Morgan – a card with capital letters EVAN MORGAN was thrust into his hand by the major. Maria's cooking skill would be put immediately to the test, as would Giovanni's gardening knowledge. If – but only if – Sgt. Morgan was satisfied with the results, Maria and Giovanni might reasonably expect happy employment, freedom from want and better take-home pay than any other married couple in Ravello.

At once, Giovanni was all Italian smiles. "O.K., O.K., *Signor Comandante. Tutto ben capito. A domani alle due,"* and moving away

174

with the slow, steady gait of a hill farmer, he set off up the track to tell his wife of her new assignment.

Philip Mortimer-Wotton took a seat on the bridge parapet, mopped his brow and inspected Martin Harrison from head to toe as an adjutant might inspect a newly commissioned officer reporting to the Depot. This appraisal, conducted with surprisingly kindly eyes, appeared to satisfy the major.

Suddenly, he broke out into a succession of staccato sentences: "Haven't seen you before, have I? Which mob d'you come from? Officers' leave camp, I suppose? Anybody with you? Which pub have you been allotted? Sorry if I seemed a bit short with that Italian feller. Fact is I've gone deaf. Devilish worrying, especially when the locals don't know any English. Or if they do, they speak it with a cockney accent learnt in the Spitalfields market which just isn't my wave length. Anyway, thanks for your help."

Martin did his best to answer this rat-a-tat of questions. Having been speculating on what he would do with six days of solitary leave, he was only too happy to find a listening companion.

The major was given to understand that Captain Harrison R.A. had arrived in Ravello that morning, complete with a jeep and his batman-driver, Fusilier Banks of the Royal Northumberland Fusiliers. The last thing Martin reckoned he wanted was leave, but he'd had the clearest orders from his G.S.O.1 to take a break. "No 'ifs' and 'buts' Martin," Col. Venables had said. "You're too damned conscientious. You've been flogging yourself silly since the Sicily landings. If you don't want to kick the gong around Bari or Naples, go find yourself a quiet spot in the Sorrento peninsula. I don't want to see you for seven days. By then, we shall need you in top condition. Off you go, quickly, while the going's good."

The Padre had recommended Ravello and fixed a room for him at the Grand Hotel Palladio which proved to be neither grand nor Palladian in conception. And so, here he was walking the Italian countryside, with an Italian 'Teach Yourself' book in his pocket and the three World Classics pocket volumes of *War and Peace* for company. As for Fusilier Banks, he'd report for duty every morning. If Martin had no use for jeep or driver, Banks would disappear to some local farm where, although he was speechless in Italian and monosyllabic in English, an Italian farmer's wife would always feed him and wash and mend his clothes and Martin's, as required. Martin had come to understand that the 50th Division in general and the Geordies in particular had no equals when it came to making the best of the war. It had been the same ever since Syracuse. The Italians understood the massive silences of Tees and Tyne. And Banks who had once been a miner outside Gateshead, knew the technique by instinct. He just appeared at an Italian farm looking extremely helpless, clinked a tin or two and was immediately accepted as one of the family.

Philip Mortimer-Wotton broke in. "Under Guy Venables, eh? He's an old buddy of mine. But the Palladio's the wrong *albergo* for you. Nothing against it really except that it's haunted by the Contessa. She's an old American bag who lost her heart and most of her money to some degenerate aristo twenty years ago. I'm told he died unlamented just before the war. And the Contessa, poor old thing, feels she's really helping the allies by sharing a bed with all and sundry. It can be a bit embarrassing if you're fussy. She's a bit long in the tooth for that sort of life though some think differently. Anyway, come back to the villa for a drink and I will give you the low-down on Ravello."

The two men walked down the hill together. From time to time, the major acknowledged greetings from the locals, all of whom seemed to have accepted him in a remarkably short time as the boss-man of the town. Martin began to get the impression that his companion was touring an estate he'd owned for centuries. Indeed, this feeling was intensified when he stopped in the main square of Ravello to buy three postcards and an assortment of sweets from a small shop which had once prospered on the tourists from Amalfi and Naples. "Pictures for the family," he explained, "and sweets for the local children who behave themselves and show us proper respect."

Next, he met an Italian priest at the foot of the Cathedral steps. The priest had a considerable smattering of English and while he conversed with the major, Martin had all the time in the world to look around. He noted that the shops in the piazza were uniformly pathetic except for the *café ristorante* at the corner where the towns-folk were discussing their world with much vivacity. He could discern no worried faces or suspicious looks. Ravello, it seemed, had escaped the ravages of war. Only the young men were missing. Taken by and large, not a bad place for a holiday.

As a linguist, the major was scarcely better equipped than the Victorian travellers who conducted their shopping sprees on the strength of two words, *'Quanto'* and *'Troppo'*. But concluding his conversation with a resounding, *"A rivederci,"* and the smartest of salutes to the priest, he led Martin up a small side street, doled out a few sweets to a bunch of delighted children who said, "Thank you, Sir" in the most charming manner, and continued his way to the fine wrought-iron gates of the Villa della Robbia.

"Sergeant Morgan," he shouted into the hall, "I think we've hired a cook and a gardener but I'm completely exhausted. Can you produce 'the usual' on the patio in five minutes time? And how's the shower working?"

Back from the cool recesses of the house came the Welsh accents of Evan Morgan. "It's all go, Sir. N.A.A.F.I.'s delivered the goods. And, surprise surprise, your friends at Fortnum and Mason have caught up with you. Oh, and I've fixed the shower provided you treat it with a bit of care."

"Excellent," said the major. "We'll look at the state of the game as soon as I've changed. Meanwhile, I have a guest with me. Fix him up, will you?" And with that, Philip Mortimer-Wotton mounted the splendid staircase as if he'd owned the villa all his life, leaving Martin Harrison in the entrance hall.

There were no carpets on the floor, but a chandelier of Venetian glass suggested that somebody of wealth and taste had once lived here, as did a delicate little virgin in blue terracotta set above the door on the right of the hall. Martin was just going to explore further when Sgt. Morgan appeared.

One could see at a glance that the sergeant was a professional soldier. Shorter than the average guardsman and certainly older than the major – forty at least, Martin reckoned – his bearing gave the impression of efficiency combined with fitness and physical strength. Greeting Martin with an unmistakable Welsh accent, he came straight to the point. "The 'usual', Sir, as the major refers to his whisky, is not really in good supply if measured by his daily consumption. But beer is plentiful and at this time of the evening the local 'vino' can be strongly recommended."

"I'm always happy to take the local recommendation," said Martin, and moved with Sgt. Morgan through a finely proportioned room towards glass doors opening on to a veranda and a garden suffering from wartime neglect.

"Sorry about the weeds," Evan Morgan was apologetic, "but the major and I've only been 'ere for a week or so, and I reckon the plumbing came first. But give us a few days and you'll see a difference. By September we'll be staging a garden party for the locals, you'll see. The major rather fancies it 'ere. In a funny sort of way, it's like 'ome to 'im. Anyhow, if you go to the end of the garden, Sir, you'll understand what I mean. This place 'as considerable possibilities."

Sgt. Morgan disappeared through another door which led off the veranda to the kitchen. Presently he returned to spread a newly-laundered table-cloth over a round iron table on the patio. "The major likes things clean," he explained. "Which reminds me that 'e takes much longer than five minutes in the shower – so you've got all the time in the world, Sir, if you want to 'ave a look at our view."

Martin strolled up the weedy path towards a sundial and the Belvedere beyond it. Here, in years past, some occupant of the Villa della Robbia had laid out a terrace and surrounded it with classical statuary. Overgrown though it was, the stonework seemed exactly right in its setting. As Martin reached it, he was confronted by a fabulous view. Below him, green wooded slopes fell away steeply to the blue of the Mediterranean. To his right, hidden from view, lay Amalfi. To his left, he could see afar off the Gulf of Salerno. In the foreground were the olive trees and the lemons and oranges for which the district was famous. On a slope of land lit up by the evening sun women were tending the vines against the day of the grape harvest some four months away. Martin was not surprised that the major fancied the place.

He returned to find Philip Mortimer-Wotton seated at the table on the veranda. He had changed into fawn coloured trousers with a knife-edge crease, a freshly laundered cream shirt, the open neck covered by an Old Etonian silk square. On the table was a carafe of red wine and beside it, a hip flask with a scale of measurement showing through a slit in its leather covering. With infinite care, the major measured a quarter into a tumbler – and filled it with water. Then he turned to Martin.

It was the start of a long friendship.

20

BEFORE Philip was halfway through his whisky ration on that first evening. Martin had accepted a suggestion that he should spend his seven days' leave at the Villa della Robbia. By nightfall he was installed in the best guest room of the Villa, with Fusilier Banks in a bedroom at the back of the house, and the jeep lined up in the garage with the major's staff car and 15 cwt. truck. By the following morning the major was, to use his own phrase, "getting things organised." In other words, the additional strength provided by the presence of Captain Harrison and his batman was to be used, "to make the place fit to live in."

The garden was to be tackled immediately. "All those weeds spoil the view from our patio. How are we off for garden tools, Sgt. Morgan?"

"All fixed, Sir. But what's going to be planted?"

"I leave it to you, sergeant. Ask that Italian Johnny who is coming round with his wife this afternoon. And Martin?"

"Yes, Sir,"

"If you want some exercise, you're welcome to help Morgan and your tough fusilier with the hedging and ditching. But with your Italian, I reckon your top priority is to get the place properly furnished. I bet the owner's stuff is stored in the neighbourhood. Anyway, be a good chap and have a go, will you? You know the sort of thing we need. Some rugs for the ground floor rooms. A dining table, some decent cutlery, a few easy chairs, a desk, beds of course . . . clean linen, pictures, perhaps. Get the idea? Right. Then I'll be off to fix things up with the Banco di Napoli where the army has organised our cash supplies. And may Maria fulfil all our hopes when I return for dinner this evening. *A rivederci*."

"Well, did you ever meet such a man?" asked Sgt. Morgan, as

180

the major, having expended his one Italian phrase, steered his car gingerly towards the main square of Ravello, miraculously avoiding the children who appeared from nowhere to salute him and wave him on his way.

"But does he really mean what he says?" asked Martin of the sergeant. "And if so, who pays for the furniture and the rugs?"

"Oh, you don't have to bother about that, sir. The major always does the paying. 'E's that sort of man. And believe you me, 'e really means what 'e says. 'Sgt. Morgan,' 'e said to me the day we got posted 'ere, 'we could be 'ere a long time, so we'll turn the villa into a place fit for gentlemen to live in. And we'll spruce up the town into the bargain.' That's what 'e says to me and now we're going to do it. You see."

Martin wandered into the garden. Banks was already at work, stripped to the waist, digging with the purposeful routine of a man trained in Warbank Colliery.

"Happy?" asked Martin. Banks paused for a moment, leant on the shaft of his long Italian spade and made a surprisingly long speech. "Ah'm used ter diggin' an' ah like gardens better than coal. Tell sarge 'e can leave this bit to me. Right warm day, though, could be thirsty work." Then Banks returned to his digging.

Martin came across Sgt. Morgan in the kitchen fixing a padlock on the store cupboard, while two Italian women were methodically cleaning the house. He told Morgan he was off on his shopping spree and could be expected back for lunch. "God knows where I start," he said.

"Oh yes, God does," replied Evan Morgan. "I'll bet 'e'd start with the old priest. Same as the minister back in the village above Merthyr. The major says the priest's the one what knows everything round 'ere. Try your luck with 'im, Sir. That's what God would do." And the Welshman returned to his self-imposed task of securing the safety of the rations.

Sure enough, Martin found the priest to whom he'd been introduced the previous day, on the steps of the cathedral. Having learnt of the major's wishes, he assured Martin that all would be forthcoming – if possible within the next few days. He and Martin took coffee together outside the café on the corner of the piazza. And the priest explained in halting English.

"You understand, *Capitano*, my people love your people. Before the war many of the *contadini* – how you say orange growers – had friends in London. They still pray for the safety of their relatives in Covent Garden and Spitalfields – may God bless them all. And then there was great English milord who used to live here long ago. I expect your *Comandante* knows him well. He also is highborn old family, *non è vero*? My people understand such distinctions. They like the older order of things. They don't like being told by government how to grade their oranges. They know good from bad."

Martin listened entranced. This surely was how it had seemed as he and the major crossed the square the previous evening. Here, in this little hill town, the major was in his element. As Martin took leave of the old priest he was determined to find out more about his new high-born friend.

Sergeant Morgan proved most revealing and, like all his compatriots, he told a good story. It seemed he'd first met the major in Abbassia barracks where Evan Morgan had graduated, in the course of years, to the position of chief clerk. There was not a thing he didn't know about form-filling which was not the major's strongest subject. But in addition he had impressed the major by his tidiness – a subject on which the major was very strong indeed. "Can't stick office wallahs," he said, "who spend their lives battling against a constantly rising tide of paper. Plain inefficient. Not my style at all. You're different, sergeant. Where do you come from? Family back home? How long have you been in Cairo?"

Sgt. Morgan had evidently received the same sort of rapid fire questions that Martin had experienced on the hill road behind Ravello. "And 'ere we come to the great coincidence," continued the sergeant with gusto. "I tell the major I got the missus shipped back 'ome with the three kids just before the declaration of war. Then I adds that Deal's not a bad place to live except the locals can't understand why a Welshman should prefer the Welsh Guards to their bloomin' Royal Marines – they being the pride of Deal, you know Sir, and much the smartest chaps to be seen in those parts. At which point 'e stops me dead in my tracks by asking if I'd ever lived at Prospect Villas. Which was strange because my father and mother lived right there. And so did I until I enlisted, not fancying coal mining which was my old man's job – and my elder brother's too.

'Sounds to me,' says the major, 'as if you're part of the same family as an old friend of mine called Gwynedd Morgan.'

"And do you know, Sir," concluded Evan Morgan, "this Gwynedd was my eldest sister, left 'ome when I was a baby, to work with the major's family on the far side of Canterbury. Still working for them too – part of the 'ousehold, I'd say. The major thinks the world of 'er. And so, 'ere I am. When the cards turn up like that, any soldier knows 'e's on a winner. Me and the major kept in touch, seemed sort of natural. At last I get clear of Cairo and then 'e smokes me out in Caserta and hey presto, I'm posted 'ere to look after his office and staff. Play your luck, Sir. That's the way it goes in the army."

Luck, coincidence? Maybe, thought Martin, but the major was no fool. In Sgt. Morgan he'd picked a sure winner, a fact quickly emphasised when the Battistas arrived at the villa at two p.m. Martin was fascinated by the speed with which the sergeant got his message across to the natives. *"Mangiare alle otto, understood? Il Comandante . . . buon appetito a fame, right?"*

"Si, si, ben capito," chorused Giovanni and Maria: and it was understood that some Neopolitan dish, parmigiana di Melenzani, would commend itself to a hungry man returning from Naples. From that moment, Maria took charge of the kitchen and Giovanni went up the garden to make his number with Fusilier Banks. Sgt. Morgan had a good look round the establishment, cleared up his office and arranged for tea to be served to all.

The major returned about six o'clock in a state of great excitement. When he had signed for the 'impress' account at the head office of the Banco di Napoli, an interpreter sitting with the Pay people had scrutinised his name very carefully, left the room and returned a moment later with a senior Italian official of the bank.

"You are by chance of the Mortimer-Wotton family of Ockenham Manor near Canterbury, England, Sir?" the man had asked Philip. "Then you are related to the artist, Charles Mortimer-Wotton who banked with us many years ago?"

"Why, yes," replied Philip, "he was my uncle, but he died long ago in a climbing accident."

"Ah, that was very sad – he was great artist," said the banker. "Alas, I did not know him, though I have acquired two of his Calabria paintings. But he left certain instructions with the bank which were to be carried out in 1950 or thirty years after his death whichever should be earlier. Thus, in 1942, the matter was duly brought to my attention and now, in 1944, the matter is still fresh in my mind. Naturally, we saw no way of communicating with his family in England until peace should be established. But now? Perhaps we could talk together when your army business is completed."

Half an hour later, Philip was in possession of a sealed envelope addressed to "my brother, Francis Mortimer-Wotton or his successors" of Ockenham near Canterbury, England, together with the knowledge that a sum of over £50,000 had accumulated on deposit at the bank for which disposal instructions were now requested.

Philip thanked the manager for his courtesy, told him he would consult his family about the money and left the bank after signing a receipt for the sealed envelope.

He stopped at the Excelsior on the Via Partenope, ordered a dish of Capri crayfish and a bottle of Soave Secco, and with great deliberation opened the envelope. In it he found two documents. The first was a will, formally typed in English, witnessed and registered by a Neopolitan *avvocato*, and dated 1910. It said quite simply that, "having given my house on Capri and such of my paintings as it contains to Giles Gaveston and having met in full my obligations to him I hereby bequeath all my remaining property in Italy and unsold paintings in England and Italy of which I stand possessed at the time of my death to my brother, Francis Mortimer-Wotton of Ockenham Manor in the county of Kent or, in the event of the prior demise of Francis Mortimer-Wotton, to my nephew and god-son, Philip Mortimer-Wotton of the same address." It was the last will and testament of Charles Mortimer-Wotton.

The second document was written in Uncle Charles's own hand. The artist's hand-writing, beautifully controlled in its calligraphy, showed that it had been most carefully compiled and fair-copied by the author. It was also dated 1910 and headed *Apologia pro vita mia*. Philip read on.

From the day I met our family solicitor, Justin Leadbitter, in the lounge of the Danieli Palace in Venice in July 1908, I have felt the need to explain why I decided to leave England and surrender to my brother the right to inherit our family house and estate at Ockenham.

I do not know what Justin said on his return to England. When we met in Venice, he was so devious in his approach that I did not attempt to explain that I was in love with beauty – and not simply in love with Giles Gaveston. Giles had always fascinated me not just because of his charm and marvellous companionship, but because he was, so to speak, the key that opened for me the whole world of painting and music which we discovered together in Italy. Justin, no doubt, labelled me a homosexual – a dirty word in his splendidly respectable vocabulary, though it could have been applied to many of the greatest names in history from Alcibiades onwards: and even to some of those who have inherited the great houses of England. In any case he would have been in no doubt about my wish to remain unmarried and to ensure, so far as I could, that my god-son Philip should eventually inherit Ockenham Manor and its land.

But in the following two years the need to express my whole 'raison d'être' became compulsive for three separate reasons. First, there was my final break with Giles in Capri. He used to say that he had been fascinated by me physically ever since our Eton days though he never mentioned it there. But as my painting developed, his obsessive desire to be always with me became irritating and oppressive. There was a series of silly, spiteful rows. He became jealous and resentful of my concern for my painting. Then I discovered that when I went on my painting tours through Campania and Calabria, the house I had bought on Capri was used by Giles for depravities which were utterly repugnant to me – as they would have been to him in the earlier days of our friendship. Something devilish had come to him in the south – something, perhaps, from Calabria itself with its pagan age-old customs. I gave him my house and returned to Venice. I have never seen nor heard from him again.

Secondly, there was my passion for climbing which I tried to explain to Mother when I visited Ockenham at the time of Bertha's death. I think she partly understood, for it was my Swiss landscapes that she wanted to retain. But she may not have realised the risks a mountaineer is bound to take every time he plans a new ascent never before attempted. Calculated risks, not silly risks. But the overriding desire is always there – to achieve something where others have failed; to seek and find the unknown. If one day I should not return from the high places of the world, I would like posterity to know what urged me on and what happiness and fulfilment I found there.

But there is a third reason for this 'apologia' – and the one which has caused me to leave orders for this document to remain unopened and unread until after Mother's death. I am a convinced pacifist, as are my two friends, Kurt Ulrich and Gianni Donati. We have come separately to the conclusion that all war is futile as well as wicked – in my case, as a result of reading Norman Angel's book *The Great Illusion*. The three of us – a German, an Italian and an Englishman – are horribly aware of the European jealousies which are beginning to fan the flames of war. We have sworn that together we will fight this most evil thing and we will never fight against each other.

But I am aware that, unlike Kurt and Gianni, I am breaking with a family tradition which is commemorated in many corners of the world – a tradition which Mother holds very dear because it embraces the father that neither I nor Francis can really remember. Much can be forgiven, but not the crime of refusing to fight for one's country. In the world in which I have been brought up, to be a pacifist is the ultimate disloyalty.

My actions since leaving England will be variously construed. As I write these words, I know I am labelled as an outcast from society and a quitter from the responsibilities I inherited – Justin Leadbitter, in his kindly roundabout way, made this very clear. And if war should break out in Europe – which God forbid – I shall be called a coward for refusing to fight.

But I am what I am. I like to think that the future will be kinder in its judgment than the present. If long life is granted to me, I may even be understood in my own lifetime. And then I shall destroy this document. But the mountaineer's life is always at risk. If death overtakes me, this 'apologia' may help my family to know the motives that possessed me. As to the greater world, I only ask to be judged by the paintings that bear my signature. They will be more lasting than this document. Yet every one of them is in some sense inspired by the vision of beauty which I have discovered in the course of my journey away from responsibility. They will, I pray, prove my justification. For them I make no apology.

Philip read his uncle's words three times. Then he drove slowly away from Naples, south along the coast road. On his left he passed the sinister layer of lava, spewed out by the recent Vesuvius eruption. On his right he looked across the bay to Capri and the Sorrento peninsula. All the time his mind was seeking to fit Charles Mortimer-Wotton into this landscape of extraordinary contrasts. On the one hand Vesuvius which could destroy impartially the ancient civilisation of Pompeii and, with even less justification, today's small-holdings of these humble Italian peasant farmers. On the other hand, the island out to sea and the Sorrento peninsula, apparently so peaceful in the afternoon sunshine, oblivious to the war that had passed them by. This had once been Uncle Charles's scene. It was out of this land that his inspiration had come. Now, thirty years after his death, did his motivation matter to anybody? Was it not better that his pictures should speak for him?

He must consult somebody about the envelope in his pocket. What would his father do? Or Arthur Waddilove? Neither could help him now. Then he thought of Martin Harrison. Why not? A solicitor; and a lot of common sense. He liked the lad. Yes, that was the answer. Philip put his foot on the accelerator and took the hill road to Ravello.

That evening at the villa, after a splendid dinner from Maria (sign her on, Sgt. Morgan, sign her on), he told Martin of the document which had been handed to him by the bank official at Naples.

"Now you understand, young Martin, I'm consulting you as a solicitor, not as a gunner. You have to treat this document as confidential to you and me. Take it to bed and let me know tomorrow morning what you advise your client to do about it. I think you'll agree that it's not easy for me to make a decision by myself. I need outside reinforcement. Yet there's nobody in my family whom I can consult. Do we post it to England to moulder in the Mortimer-Wotton archives or in a solicitor's strong box? Or what?"

Next morning, Martin came up with his answer. "As your newly-appointed legal adviser," he said, "I would suggest you are the only person who has any right to read this document. There are, you tell me, no other members of the family who knew your Uncle Charles or remember him. Those that remain – your brother and step-mother for instance – are therefore part of the greater world to which he refers in his apologia. In my opinion, they should come to know Charles Mortimer-Wotton by the pictures that bear his signature."

"And the document, Martin?"

"Banks and Giovanni have started a first class bonfire. I hate to destroy such remarkable hand-writing, but I would advise cremation."

They went together to the end of the garden and Philip fed the pages, one by one, to the flames. The wind was blowing the smoke out over the Mediterranean in the direction of Capri.

"And the money, Martin? Any views on that?"

"That's not so simple. There could be difficulties – even exchange difficulties – about moving it to London. And I doubt whether the lira will hold its value after the war. In such circumstances, a quick investment in property could be a possible answer."

"You mean ... you mean?" Philip looked at his new legal adviser and suddenly burst out laughing. "So you advise a little property speculation do you, young Martin? In Ravello, perhaps? A little place like the Villa della Robbia, eh? Maria and Giovanni as housekeepers? A swimming bath, do you think over there? And one or two of Uncle Charles's paintings to give a bit of tone to the place?" Philip Mortimer-Wotton laughed as he had not laughed for years. It was useless for Martin to protest that this wasn't what he meant.

"It's a great idea," Philip continued, sweeping away all objections. "I'll start to fix it this very day. And if you ever find yourself a wife, young Martin, you can bring her here for your honeymoon."

21

PHILIP was as good as his word. Forty-eight hours later, he and Martin enjoyed a gargantuan lunch at the Excelsior with the bank director and his friend, *il Dottore Tibelli*, who proved to be the senior partner in the legal firm which had witnessed Uncle Charles's will.

The Italian advisers were charming and amenable. *Si, si* they would set the wheels in motion at once. They had already ascertained that the family which owned the villa could no longer afford its upkeep. The matter would be arranged and the house purchased with the funds in the Banco di Napoli, as soon as Philip's legal title was established. The major's wishes, suitably re-inforced by the Excelsior's wine and cuisine, would receive the highest priority.

Martin, slightly intoxicated, stepped into the blinding sunlight of the Via Partenope, vainly trying to adjust his mind to the transaction in which he had been a fascinated non-playing partner.

How simple, how ordinary an affair it seemed to Philip Mortimer-Wotton! Anything odd about an English country gentleman of ancient lineage wishing to own an Italian villa? Or gratifying his wish as if money and the vagaries of war had no significance? But no, it wasn't the major's decision that took Martin's breath away so much as the manner of its execution. The ease and assurance of it – the head waiter leading Philip to the best table in the dining room, the *camerieri* dancing attendance, the chef making a brief appearance to accept the thanks of the English milord: an Italian banker and a lawyer accepting Philip's instructions as if issued by royalty. It was positively eighteenth century in style, fantastic, crazy, out of this world – or at least out of Martin's world centred on London's south-eastern suburbs. They'd never believe it at home.

Here he was, in the middle of a ruddy great war, hurrying along a Naples street beside this larger-than-life character, as if the two of them were returning from a successful business lunch in peace-time London.

His companion was in high good humour. "That's the way to fix these Italian Johnnies," he said with satisfaction. "Nothing like a good lunch to get people off the mark. Very decent types, actually. And efficient, eh? Seem to know all the landowners round the district. Struck me they might be doing a bit of land-grabbing on their own account. I shouldn't wonder if, one of these days, our licentious soldiery don't return to enjoy the Italian sunshine in better conditions. And then our new friends will be in the money. What was it Noël Coward wrote about mad dogs and Englishmen sitting out in the midday sun? But don't worry, young Martin. You think I'm crackers, eh? Well, let me tell you that my family were in love with Italy long before the days of Uncle Charles. So why should I be different?"

And, as the two of them drove back via Sorrento and Amalfi, Philip threw out odd items of information about the English in Italy – not just about his own ancestors, but about Byron and Shelley, Dickens and Florence Nightingale's father, Milton picking up the idea for *Paradise Lost* in Calabria, Shakespeare getting most of his plots from the city states of the North ... "My view is," he con-cluded, "the Italians have got what the English lack and vice versa. We are – what's the word – 'complementary'. It's utterly ridiculous to be fighting each other. Mussolini's the biggest villain unhung – yes, much worse than Hitler who was at least reflecting the bloody-minded ambitions of a majority of his own nation. What do you say?"

But Martin was peacefully sleeping, replete with the finest meal he'd every enjoyed.

They returned to a scene of great activity at the Villa della Robbia. Sgt. Morgan was directing Italians with rugs, Italians with furniture, Italians with chandeliers. His orders were being inter-preted by Giovanni with much noise and gesticulation and children were chattering everywhere.

"It's Bedlam," Evan Morgan confided to Martin, "but your clothes are laid out on your bed – or so Banks tells me. And there's enough 'ot water for two, according to the *idraulico* 'oo's been workin' up there all day. That's what they call plumbers round 'ere, Sir. And now I'm closing down the show for the night. The old priest'll be presentin' 'isself to the major in the morning."

For Martin the next few days passed like a dream. Afterwards, he remembered a day trip to the ancient Greek colony of Paestum, south of Salerno, where Banks grudgingly conceded that the pillars of the temple of Neptune might be bigger than anything to be seen in Newcastle. And a visit to Pompeii where a salacious little pimp spent too long expatiating on the sexual deviations of the inhabitants and led to one of the fusilier's classic statements. "Reckon earthquake served 'em raht. Must 'ave been a lot o' dirty boogers livin' 'ere in them ol' days."

But most of all, Martin remembered Philip. There was the charming little dinner he gave to the old priest, Don Pietro whose gastronomic tastes were clearly well understood by Maria. There was the courtesy with which he treated the local people, especially Maria and Giovanni: and the respect (it was almost devotion) that he inspired in them. There was the authority and understanding with which he worked with Evan Morgan. Above all, there were the evenings spent out on the patio or up on the Belvedere looking out to sea. It was then that Philip, having completed his office work and his daily rounds of the leave areas, revealed something of his own life to the fascinated Martin.

Partly he spoke of the Great House and the Mortimer-Wotton land and the chain of events which now made him the indisputable owner of the family inheritance. It was as if he felt a need to explain himself to some chap who'd never shared the same background. Martin sensed the love Philip felt for his home, but also a sort of foreboding (or was it doubt?) about his ability to meet the responsibilities it entailed. "You see, young Martin," he said one evening as he savoured his final whisky at the table on the patio, "it's all going to be different when this war's over. Here, with these local chaps, I know what I'm doing. These Italians accept me as the Highlanders accept their Laird – they're still feudal. But serving up front with those cockney riflemen, I've had my eyes opened to what's going on in the rest of England. Now don't misunderstand me. Those lads in the Rifle Brigade would never question my authority in the field. I'm a professional soldier, trained for the job. I'm a safer bet than some of the others. But back home? What right have I got, they'll be asking, to all this land acquired so long ago – back in the early Middle Ages, I suppose, when men were building the great cathedrals? Isn't it too big a thing for one man or one family to hold? Should I not share it with those who work it? The post-war world of Ockenham won't be the world of old John Williams or Miss Millie or Evan Morgan's sister who knew my grandmother and helped me grow up. That's one reason why I've asked Evan Morgan whether he and his family might like to move to Ockenham when the Germans pack it in and he's demobbed. He's a first-class chap. And I reckon I'll need to be surrounded by people whose hearts are in the right place."

Philip never spoke of his own battle experiences though he laughed about pre-war incidents with the Guards in London and Cairo as if he wanted Martin to understand the kind of world he'd lived in, before and after leaving Eton. But on his last night at the villa, Martin caught a glimpse of the high-ranking soldier that Philip might so easily have become if the luck had gone his way. Philip was in an expansive mood.

"You've got to face it" he said, "our only purpose in Italy is to draw as many German divisions as possible away from Western Europe and France and Russia. The Eighth army's no longer in the centre of the stage. Our star performer has gone – and you'll find he will take some leading members of the cast with him. I wish to God he was still here. For all his silly little conceits (that damned beret and his Australian hat) Monty's a professional, trained in a tough soldier's world of mountains and mud where there's no sand to get between the toes. Too many of the desert commanders play at war as if it were a game of chess. Monty's different. He knows the grim reality. That's why he's always avoided battle until he was sure of an advantage in armour and air support and fire power. He never forgets the casualty list when he's fixing his objectives. Take these latest affairs. If Monty had ordered the landings at Anzio, he'd have gone straight for the Alban Hills with every stitch of armour at his command. The landing had no other purpose than to cut the road to Rome and trap the German armies in the south. And if he hadn't got the strength to do it, he'd have cancelled the exercise – and damn the politicians. It's the same with Cassino. We've staged three costly and useless battles. Remember, I've been over this gound before. Even the Indians and the New Zealanders – and there are no greater fighting men in the world – had no hope of making it in winter, with the Rapido and Garigliano running high and the Appenines forming a natural defensive position." He paused for a moment. "But don't worry, young Martin. The fine weather's on its way now. I know the new army commander – used to meet him before the war. He's a good man and I think you'll soon be chalking up another Eighth Army victory. So here's to our next meeting – in Rome."

The following morning Martin and Banks left the villa to re-join army headquarters, following its move from the Adriatic coast to a point north of Naples. Apart from their memories of Ravello, they took with them a letter for delivery to Major R. Mortimer-Wotton M.C. 5 Bn. Royal East Kent Regt. (The Buffs). "That's the brother I was talking about the other day," Philip told Martin as he sealed the envelope. "Married just before the war, two little girls to show for it and a super cricketer into the bargain. Ought to play for the County when the war's over. Quite a lad. You should find the Battalion with 78 Division. Nothing important in the letter. Just to tell him my leg's doing well and I'm buying a house here. Haven't mentioned my hearing. He's probably got enough on his hands without having my worries too."

Then Philip paused, looked up from his desk at Martin, and said, "You won't have much time for peace-time plans when you're fighting a battle. But it helps, sometimes, to think about the future . . . if you ever consider life as a country solicitor I might be able to help. Anyway, Martin" – and there was a quizzical look in the grey eyes – "thanks for your company and a lot of good advice."

Banks was driving, speechless as always, his silence only punctuated by an occasional grunt at a hairpin bend or a fearsome oath if an Italian chicken or cow disputed his passage. Martin liked it that way: it gave him time to think. As the jeep threaded its way through Naples and out on to Highway Six, Martin was temporarily back in England. A solicitor out of London, a family firm in Canterbury perhaps? That, surely, was what the big man was hinting. Judged by his performance in organising the purchase of the Villa della Robbia, he had a way of getting people to do what he wanted. No, Martin corrected himself. It's not just what he wants. It's what I want. And at the moment I can't think of any man I'd rather serve than Philip Mortimer-Wotton. He smiled to himself. It was rather reassuring to think that, if they survived the battle, he and Philip and Evan Morgan might all meet again.

22

MARTIN HARRISON reported to Col. Venables at Main Army head-quarters. "Met a friend of yours, Sir, name of Mortimer-Wotton, running the leave area."

"Oh my God. Poor old Philip. In a stooge job down there? He really has the most appalling luck. Did he tell you about the Sangro affair?"

"Not a word, except that he got a nasty bit of shrapnel in the leg. He's rather deaf, too."

"That's Philip all over. I met him first at Sandhurst, and then in the Guards. We all thought he'd end up with a Divisional command, at least. But just before the war, he ran out of cash and resigned his commission – he's a real compulsive spender, you know. Still, he comes back; and, after a bit of a wait, gets appointed brigade major with an armoured Brigade in 10 Corps. Super job, just what he wanted. Everything seems set fair and back on course, when he insists on returning to regimental soldiering. Just don't know what came over him. But once he makes up his mind, wild horses can't stop him."

"Yes, I know that," Martin laughed. "I've seen him in the process of buying an Italian villa for himself."

"Come off it, Martin. Buying a house? You're joking. Where's the cash come from?"

"No, it's a fact, Sir. Fell on a Mortimer-Wotton nest egg in Naples. Told me his family has a link or two with Italy, dating back to Elizabethan times – Sir Henry Wotton started it, I think. Anyway, he took a fancy to this house in Ravello, so he bought it – just like that."

"Good God, what a man. Must have made up his mind his war's over. I suppose it is, after that Sangro business."

"What happened?"

196

"Nobody's really put the story together beyond the certainty that Philip's C.O. made a dam' silly decision, got his Battalion massacred and lost his job. But a chap in the 60th has told me since that Philip's company put up a miraculous performance – just what I'd expect. They're sore as Hell Philip didn't pick up a gong. But I bet you'll never hear Philip talk about that. No V.C.s for failures, you know. Only the survivors could tell you what Philip did up on that hill – and there aren't many of them to tell the tale. Just his luck."

"Anyway, glad you've brought me up to date with Philip. Win or lose, you won't meet a better soldier anywhere. Let's hope he gets some fun out of his new house."

Venables turned to the map behind his desk and gave Martin a brisk run-down on the position of the Eighth Army Divisions preparing to move up towards the Garigliano river. "If the plan works this time, there won't be any property speculation round here for a few months," he said.

The final battle for Cassino began on the moonlight night of 11th May 1944 when Alexander's Army Group launched a simultaneous attack across the Garigliano river. It was the biggest 'set piece' of the war in Italy, with the American Fifth Army in the coastal sector and Juin's Free French Corps and its fearsome African *Goumiers* in the centre, directed towards the high ground between Highways Six and Seven. To their right were the Eighth Army formations – Canadian, Indian and British Divisions directed on the town of Cassino and Highway Six, with the Polish Corps in the hill sector above the monastery. Opposite the Allies stood Kesselring's Germans, with orders to defend to the death the hitherto impregnable Gustav Line. His Mountain Corps held the hill sector which included the town and monastery of Cassino. His Panzers and Panzer Grenadiers were deployed in the Liri valley to the south-west. There was not an Italian to be seen.

On 15th and 16th May, the 78th 'Battle-axe' Division crossed the Garigliano in support of the two forward Divisions of the British XIII Corps. Somewhere in that brilliantly executed manoeuvre was the 5th Battalion, the Buffs. Somewhere in the thick of the battle was Bobby Mortimer-Wotton. And somehow, in the carnage and destruction, his luck held as it had done since he'd landed in North Africa twelve months earlier. On 18th May he witnessed that final act of chivalry when the three British corporals, each decorated with the military medal, crossed Highway Six to greet the heroic Poles as they descended Monastery Hill, two miles west of Cassino town. Above the ruins of the monastery he saw the Polish flag raised by a squadron of the 12th Podolski Lancers and flying triumphant – or was it in homage to the Polish dead? Bobby was still young enough, romantic enough to savour the excitement of victory.

That same day he turned off Highway Six to reconnoitre a decent lager for the night. An undetected mine exploded under his jeep. He and his nineteen-year-old companion were killed instantly. They were surely too young to die.

Bad news travels fast in the army. The report of his brother's death filtered through to Philip well before the end of May while the Allies were still fighting to link up with the Anzio divisions for the final advance on Rome. The news only served to confirm the nagging anxiety in Philip's mind.

Weeks before the battle he'd been assailed by this premonition of tragedy. Hadn't he spoken about Bobby to Martin Harrison? Yes – and many times to Evan Morgan, too? Could his letter, he wondered, have reached Bobby before he died? Now he felt unbearably lonely. Slowly he walked down the narrow street from the villa and crossed the piazza, unconscious of the children and the little groups observing him. His dragging feet climbed the steps to the west door of the little town's cathedral. Somewhere in the cool dimly-lighted interior, he stumbled to a chair. Did someone join him there, a tall thin man he'd known long ago in Ockenham . . . in Canterbury? He couldn't be sure – it was so dark in the place. Nor did he ever know how long he was there. But he heard other voices – Eleanor, Penny, two little girls, Gwynedd – startlingly clear. He was not alone any more. Somewhere a bell chimed.

From a corner near the west door, old Don Pietro saw the big Englishman straighten himself, walk across to an offertory box, stuff some notes in it and leave the cathedral. He watched him stride across the piazza towards the villa, a new resolution in his step. The old priest returned to his cathedral and knelt unseen before a crucified Christ in one of the side chapels. "Blessed are they that mourn," he whispered, "for they shall be comforted."

Returning to the villa, Philip poured a whisky for Evan Morgan and himself. He was in command once more. "This is the moment, Evan, when our ways part," he said. "At first light tomorrow I leave for army headquarters where I know my brother's death will be confirmed. I shall arrange for compassionate leave and hop a lift to England with the R.A.F. Before I go, I'll return here to pack: and then I'll need you to drive me to the airport. But – here's the point – I've no intention of changing my mind about this house. I shall see Tibelli when I pass through Naples. I shall arrange to keep in touch with him and I shall see Captain Harrison at Army H.Q. and tell him the form. Meanwhile, you can help by putting Don Pietro in the picture; and also Giovanni and Maria. You're a persuasive old Welshman, and I'm relying on you to persuade the Battistas to continue as housekeepers after the leave areas move forwards to Rome, Get the idea?"

A week later Philip took leave of Evan Morgan at the airport. He'd been taught all his life to distrust emotion but the final day at Ravello was altogether too exhausting. There were the kindly platitudes of dear old Don Pietro. There were the tears of Maria and the black tie of Giovanni. There was the pathetic little bunch of flowers on his desk presented *a nostro Comandante* by the children down the street. And now here was Morgan finding it hard to keep his voice steady.

At long, long, last, he was airborne – over the sea to Algiers, Oran, Casablanca. On again, he supposed, to somewhere in England. He was too tired to care. At Casablanca he was transferred into a big U.S.A.F. transport plane, flying out of Africa towards the setting sun. Intermittently he slept. Once he woke in a fury uttering a string of obscenities that startled his companions. Then he slept again. In his half-conscious state, he dreamt of Martin and Evan Morgan, of Sgt. Baker and the Shropshire lad, of Don Pietro and the Battistas, of Dr. Tibelli, of an Italian villa, of lemon trees and vineyards in the sunshine . . .

He woke with a start as an American shook him gently. "This is where we say goodbye Major – somewhere in Cornwall, I guess. Here's your seat belt. Gee, I'd say you gotta lot of sleep to catch up with. Never seen anyone sleep so sound when Hank's been at the controls. He really is a God-darn awful pilot." But Hank, whatever the strictures of his crew, made a perfect dawn landing on an R.A.F. landing strip near Truro. And two hours later, Philip Mortimer-Wotton was train-bound for London. His war was over.

Book Three

A Gentleman at Home

This man is freed from servile hands,
Of hope to rise, or fear to fall:
Lord of himself, though not of lands,
And having nothing, yet hath all.

SIR HENRY WOTTON (1568–1639)

23

ELEANOR received the phone call from some unidentifiable R.A.F. station. All very matter-of-fact and impersonal. "Major Mortimer-Wotton will be travelling on the Truro-Paddington morning train. He expects to reach Ashford, Kent, between four and six p.m. and hopes you can arrange for a car to meet him."

Yes, yes, of course she'd meet Philip. She longed to meet him. Get out the M.G. and give it a run. He'd have so much to tell her. News from Italy, news of what happened to Bobby . . . She must know, though she couldn't bear to think of it . . . And, let me see, he'd want first hand news from her of England, of Kent, of Ockenham, of the people here and of his father's death . . . of the state of the farming . . . of the lawyers' dilemma over Francis's estate duties. Eleanor's mind began to complicate the simple fact of Philip's return until it became one more problem in her increasingly confused life. She went over to the whisky decanter, poured herself a generous measure, drank it neat, felt better and called for her daughter-in-law. It was not yet ten o'clock in the morning.

"Penny darling," she said. "An R.A.F. type has just phoned to say that Philip's arriving at Ashford this evening. I'm not quite sure whether I feel up to meeting him. The car hasn't been out for weeks and what with one thing and another, I wonder if you can possibly manage . . ." She lit another of her endless succession of cigarettes.

Penny broke in – she was getting used to what she and the staff called 'possibly manage' requests from her mother-in-law.

"Why, of course, Mother, one of us will get over to meet Philip. Don't you bother yourself. He'll be desperately tired, I should imagine; but I'll see that we have a meal and a bed ready for him. He'll probably want to sleep round the clock. My goodness, it'll be nice to have him back." And Penny, trim and efficient, hurried away to tell the staff, wondering to herself whether Philip had any suspicion that his step-mother had become an obsessional drinker even before Bobby's death. Already the woman positively stank of whisky.

The first person Penny encountered was Margie Williams who'd brought her younger children from Dark's Place to the Dower House where they, together with Penny's two small daughters, attended Miss Millie's little school for the 'three to sevens'. This – the most remarkable of Ockenham's war time institutions – took place in the rooms over the Dower House stables where a marvellously rejuvenated Millicent Taylor kept an assortment of small children happily occupied from ten to three o'clock each weekday while their mothers went about their wartime business. She kept the children up to seven years old, if necessary, at which point they moved on to the village school. She also arranged for the youngest to sleep at midday (duly tucked up by Gwynedd Morgan). At one o'clock the whole pack of some twenty children enjoyed a meal supplied by the Dower House kitchen. All were agreed that Miss Millie was a genius. To those in touch with the play groups of a later generation, the premises might have appeared sub-standard and the Mortimer-Wotton contribution of staff and premises positively feudal. But the village schoolmaster was on record as saying that no child ever came to him from Millicent Taylor who couldn't read nor any who couldn't blow their noses and do up their shoe laces, and you cannot say fairer than that.

Margie greeted Penny's surprise news with unfeigned delight. "But I'll be over in Ashford anyway – with Amos. It's market day: and I'm due to meet Alex who's coming back today for the summer holidays. So the old Standard can do the fetching and carrying – you can save your petrol. You say Phil's on a train from Truro? Why, that's probably the one that stops to pick up the King's boys at St. Austell. What's the betting that Phil and Alex are on the same train? Anyway, you can spare yourself this journey, Mrs. Robert. Amos and I will wait at Ashford until we have both our heroes in the back of the car. It's going to be quite a day and no mistake."

Gwynedd was equally excited. "Yes indeed, Madam," she'd be happy to make up a bed for Mr. Philip and have it properly aired, just like the old days when he returned from school – no trouble at all. Then she paused, looked at Bobby's young widow and added very softly, "It won't be easy for you, dear, when your heart is so sad. I know, I know, I really do. It was the same for me a long time ago; but there, I've found much joy in my life since then. May God help you too – and your lovely little girls."

Gwynedd bustled off about her business and Penny cried for Bobby as she waited for Philip's return.

Philip and Alex met at Paddington. The boy, approaching the barrier, heard the big Guards officer in front of him ask about a taxi for Charing Cross and suddenly realised that the officer could only be Philip Mortimer-Wotton. "Excuse me, Sir, but you'll be hard put to it to find a taxi these days. The best way to reach Charing Cross is underground by tube to Trafalgar Square. Actually I think we've met before, haven't we? I'm Alex Williams, back from school for the summer holidays."

Philip looked closely at the schoolboy beside him. Fifteen years old or thereabouts, a big fourteen perhaps: lightish hair, a bit gangling, growing out of his trousers; but fine features too, and the grey eyes he'd recognise anywhere.

"Alex," he laughed, "What a moment! And we've been in the same train from Cornwall without knowing it? Well, at least we can travel the last leg of the journey together, and you can bring me up to date with life in England. How's your mother? She's about the best correspondent I've had these last four years. My goodness, you've grown a bit since we last met." And the two helped each other with the baggage, down the stairs to the tube, up again at Trafalgar Square, across the Strand to Charing Cross and into the Ashford train. It was the first time Alex had ever travelled first class.

Margie was at the station to meet them. Philip saw her first: her trousers and light blue shirt showing off her still youthful figure, her skin clear, her eyes sparkling, her smile of greeting taking in the man and the boy in one combined welcome. "So you two met O.K.," she said. "I told Mrs. Robert I knew you would." And she led them to the Standard. "Amos is staying on at market," she explained, "and returning with the three tonner. So we ought to be able to get all this clobber into the car. Hop in the front, Major: Alex can ride in the back seat with the luggage."

205

The three of them chattered all the way to Ockenham. Of Philip's journey home, of Alex's exams, of Gwynedd dashing about the Dower House with hotwater bottles, of Miss Millie's school over the old stables, of Margie's parents at the Wotton Arms and John Williams and his wife at the Home Farm – and the strain of war.

"And Eleanor and Penny, how are they taking it?" prompted Philip. Margie's words became more guarded. She hesitated. "Er ... it's been terrible for them ... terrible, the news about Bobby. Of course, it's very recent really ... Only two months ago. Penny has been wonderfully brave. And the two little girls, Susan and Kate, are really too young to understand. Only five and three – you see. For them life goes on as usual – and that helps their mother, I think. But Mrs. Francis ... first your father, then Bobby – you'll find her greatly changed I'm afraid, Phil, sort of withdrawn and depressed. Maybe you'll be able to help ... Everybody in the village and on the farms is so sad for her and feels for her, but somehow none of us, except old Fagg at the garage, can make contact with her. And the fact is that Amos and I have never trusted Joe Fagg."

Margie concentrated on her driving, wondering if she'd said too much. She and Alex dropped Philip and his luggage at the Dower House, before driving on to Dark's Place.

So Philip was home at last, a change, a kiss for Gwynedd, a chat with the people in the kitchen, a light supper with Eleanor and Penny, and so to the joy of freshly aired pyjamas and a warm bed, though not before he knew exactly what Margie meant about his step-mother. Poor Eleanor, he thought, as he fell asleep. I'll have to find out more in the morning.

The months that followed weighed heavily on Philip. The army had no use for him. Nor was he needed at Ockenham where the harvest took its orderly course under the general direction of Guy Hogben and John and Amos Williams. He occupied his time – there was so much spare time – in following the Allied advance in Europe. With a professional soldier's appreciation, he marked on his maps the breakout from Caen, the relief of Paris, the flushing out of the V bomb launching sites in Belgium and Northern France, the opening up of Antwerp, the setback at Arnhem, the Rhine crossing ... and, finally, the German collapse. Every time he tried

206

to get back to an army job, there came some irritating reminder that the nerve deafness that had been with him since the crossing of the Sangro was the hidden enemy he had to fight.

It was hard to insulate himself from the war he understood. But gradually he forced himself to concentrate on the problems of peace.

The most pressing of these was his father's will: and one of Philip's first calls in Canterbury was to the family solicitors. By some miracle, the eighteenth-century offices of Dawson and Leadbitter in Castle Street had escaped serious damage in the Baedeker raid of 1942. Outwardly, the old firm's premises looked much the same as they had done for the past fifty years. But old Justin Leadbitter had died during the war. He had no sons to follow him and the other partners knew little about the Mortimer-Wotton estates. Nor, indeed, did Justin's chief clerk, the ageing Mr. Septimus Tomkins, in the sense that Francis Mortimer-Wotton had failed to keep in touch with the firm during the years following his mother's death – and more especially during his cloak-and-dagger activities of the early war years. It now appeared that, even after the land sales in the Thirties, Francis had managed to accumulate considerable personal debts as well as mortgaging the Estate. These complications had only come to light after his death, when the problems of death duties had to be tackled.

Tomkins was very apologetic to Philip and also very tactful about Eleanor. "You see, Sir, the colonel fixed things up with the bank without telling Mr. Justin: and Mrs. Mortimer-Wotton didn't seem able to help us. Of course, we've been very short of staff these last few years, especially after Mr. Justin's death. But it looks to us as if you won't be worried by death duties so much as by the colonel's creditors."

With that opening Philip found it fairly simple to suggest to the senior partner, a member of the Dawson family, that a young qualified solicitor might usefully be introduced into the firm with a view to eventual partnership.

When the call came, Martin Harrison was waiting. For him it was a dream come true. The seven days at the Villa della Robbia had remained an unforgettable memory of his war service. By comparison, the fact that he'd risen to the rank of lieutenant colonel at 15 Army Group, with an O.B.E. to show for his services, didn't mean a thing. From the day he waved goodbye to Philip at Ravello, he never doubted that his destiny lay within the orbit of the Mortimer-Wotton world. And in the succeeding two years his youthful eyes magnified Philip into a man of heroic proportions who measured up to the Greek ideal. Here, in Martin's eyes, was a man endowed with natural authority, against whom the gods of Olympus had unleashed their wrath but had not prevailed. Surely this proud and generous soldier deserved the loyalty he unconsciously evoked.

After a series of meetings in Canterbury and London, Martin joined Dawson and Leadbitter, and Philip was cock-a-hoop at the success of his plans. But depression set in as he wondered what on earth he ought to do about Eleanor. Could she snap out of this drinking? Or was it a case for the doctors? He and Penny managed to get some control over the home liquor supplies, but they were both aware that Eleanor was getting gin and whisky under the counter. They traced the source quickly enough to Joe Fagg down in the village at Ockenham Motors. He might be a good mechanic, but he'd been messing about in the black market and nobody in the village wanted anything to do with him. Joe Fagg must be eased into another job – the sooner, the better.

Philip remembered his offer to Evan Morgan – just the sort of man to tell Mr. Fagg where he got off. Encouraged by a long talk with Gwynedd about her brother, he visited Evan Morgan's wife in Deal. Subsequently, he drove her and the four children over to see Gwynedd and in the course of the journey discovered Sgt. Morgan had already alerted his wife to the possibility of a move to Ockenham. In that quarter at least, the wind was set fair. And arrangements were made for Evan Morgan and his family to move to Ockenham.

On most days he was in contact with Penny. She was effectively running the Dower House and seemed very relieved to be able to share her problems with him. They were, after all, old friends. Had they not both known and loved Bobby? And now they shared responsibility for Eleanor.

Philip delighted Penny with the story of his villa in Ravello. "I was mad, Penny, utterly mad," he told her. "But it's when you're in that sort of mood that all the exciting things in life seem to happen. You must come and stay there – Susan and Kate too. They'll love the oranges and the bathing and the sunshine and Maria Battista will make you free of all house-keeping worries."

He rambled on, telling her of Evan Morgan and Martin Harrison. "You've heard all about Evan from Gwynedd, I expect. Anyway, I've found a vacant house for him in the village and he and his family will move in just as soon as he's demobbed. Evan Morgan's got just what we're going to need – toughness and efficiency as well as loyalty. We'll set him to reorganise the building and engineering operations that Eleanor set up before the war. And the first thing he'll do is to get Joseph Fagg out of this village. Don't ask me how; but I bet Mr. Fagg will ask to be clear of Ockenham within three months of Evan's arrival.

Still, Martin Harrison – this lad who's joining Dawson and Leadbitter – is the real hero of the villa," he continued. "Clever chap, scholarship type, comes from Beckenham, qualified solicitor, keen on games. Literally gave me the idea for buying the house after I talked with him about Uncle Charles." And Philip told Penny of the fortune accumulated in the Banco di Napoli. "By the grace of God, Martin Harrison was on seven days leave when this banker fellow sprang the news on me: and now this same lad is sorting out father's will in Castle Street. Amazing isn't it? I hope you'll like him, Penny. I've got a feeling that young Martin's going to be very useful to us."

Penny interrupted him. "Makes good sense to me, Philip. You'll need a bit of extra support round here. Perhaps, with these two in residence, you'll be able to get away more easily. One day I want you to show me the villa ... take me to the place where Bobby died."

Philip nodded. "But of course I will."

"Dear Philip, you're very kind. It will be a sad journey – a once-for-all journey, I expect. But I must do it. After that, I can try to look forward again."

Penny hesitated for a moment. Then looking down at the pattern on the morning room carpet, she spoke as if putting into words her own most private thinking. "You know, I don't think I can go on living at Ockenham now Bobby is dead. Everything . . . everybody . . . yes, even you . . . remind me of him. No, it's not the problem of living with Eleanor – I'll visit her as often as I can. And the children will want to come down to stay with you and keep up with the friends they've made here. But somehow I've got to separate myself from the past . . . I can't explain it very well. But to me Bobby is here – not in Italy. I sense his presence in every corner of the house and every patch of green in the park. I'm sure it will be best for me and Kate and Susan to get away. You understand, don't you?"

Her eyes looked up at him. How pretty she still was, but how different from the eighteen-year-old he'd once known. Sort of responsible . . . mature . . . tragic: he searched for a word, wondering what changes she saw in him.

In due course they made their pilgrimage to the British cemetery outside Cassino town – a garden beautifully tended by an old Italian peasant, row upon row of headstones identical as soldiers on parade, distinguished only by name and regimental badge. Bobby lay there among his Kentish companions – Major Robert Mortimer-Wotton M.C., the Royal East Kent Regiment. Was he really no different from the rest?

Penny and Philip stood sad and silent before the headstone. After a time their eyes turned to the tall cross at the far end of the cemetery and thence to the monastery of St. Benedict standing sentinel on the hill above the town. A swarm of Italians was busy up there, reconstructing the great building as it had been before its destruction by the Allies.

The builders' activities brought Penny out of her rêverie. "There's too much sadness down here in the plain," she said with a sigh. "Those Italians are right. Let's get back to England and do our own rebuilding."

Philip understood. They never continued the journey to Naples and Ravello. A few months later, Penny and her two little girls left the Dower House and returned to her old family home.

Penny's departure left Philip with the grim and lonely prospect of coping with Eleanor. He was acutely conscious of the way Bobby's young family had eased the process of his return –

especially the two little girls with their constant presence and clamorous requests. Like all children, Susan and Kate were far less concerned and far more patient with his deafness than people of his own age who expected him to be as he had always been. Perhaps he could persuade the girls to stay with him at the Great House from time to time. But not Penny. For her, Philip knew, there could be no substitute for Bobby in the house and fields which had once echoed his laughter. Penny must travel a new road.

Indeed, that is precisely what happened. Within two years of the Cassino journey Penny remarried. A quiet wedding in London it was, to a wing commander she'd met during the war. "Nice type," Philip reported to Eleanor who couldn't 'quite manage' to get to the wedding. "Right age. Clearly in love with Penny. Gets on well with Susan and Kate."

His objective report to his step-mother held no rancour or regret. But the feeling of isolation, intensified by his deafness, began to oppress him. It was in this mood that he decided to go forward with his half-baked but constantly recurring plan for sharing part of his inheritance with those who worked the Mortimer-Wotton land.

24

As a first step Philip decided to try out his ideas on Amos and Margie. He came to this sudden decision when approaching Dark's Place on one of his afternoon walks.

The little group of buildings, set in the very centre of the Mortimer-Wotton land, looked beautiful in the sunshine. His spirits rose at the sound of the children playing in the yard. As he passed Gwynedd's cottage, the children ran out to welcome him. The elder girl – that must be Mary, he thought – dashed into the house to alert her parents. Alice and Paul danced round him, while the little three-year-old boy stumped across the yard and a moment later was riding in triumph on Philip's shoulders.

Margie came to the door. She took the little boy from Philip, handed him back to Mary and chased the lot out of the house. Then she called to Amos. "The major's here. There's beer and glasses in the kitchen. Bring them in, love, will you?"

The three of them sat down together and suddenly burst into laughter. It was really very funny. In that split second 'the major' disappeared. And Margie, Amos and Philip were back to the days when they had sat side by side in Miss Millie's village school. Now over a glass of beer in the sitting room at Dark's Place, they rediscovered their childhood friendship.

Margie talked of the children. "All present and correct, Sir," she said in a mock parade ground voice. "Except for Alex who has cycled to Canterbury to meet a school friend."

Amos talked of the farm. "Glad you're pleased with what we've achieved, Philip. Things we'd never have done if there hadn't been a war. Government subsidies, Lease-Lend, replacing the earlier machines with Case tractors and balers and the Allis Chalmers Combine Harvester. You name it. Guy Hogben and I reckon to run the whole show with fourteen people, one of whom is a landgirl who wants to stay on. Mind you, we have to rope in the village for help in the high seasons. But it's staggering what the new machines and government help have done. I only wish the book-work didn't take up so much of my time. I understand it well enough, but it's just not my line, is it Margie? Trouble is, there's nobody to take it on."

"Maybe that's an area where a deaf man can help." Philip checked himself: the bitterness was involuntary. Then he said – "That's a pretty sick joke, but I'm sure I can do something about the form-filling. Meanwhile, I've an idea to put to you. If I turned the farming into a company, would you like a share in the investment? Haven't worked out the details yet, but a company means shareholders and I'd like Amos to hold some shares and be managing director. What do you say, Amos? And if you'd be happy to work with Guy Hogben, i'll make a proposition to him too."

Amos was taken aback. "Why, as for Guy he's a great chap to work with," he said playing for time. "We've really been running a combined operation with him these last few years – sort of dividing the responsibilities. Margie and I have a lot of time for Guy and his wife. They've been very kind to us and taught us a lot. It's possible that one of these days Mrs. Hogben will want 'to up sticks' and join the boy who went off to farm in Australia before the war. Still that's something you'll be able to find out. But what's all this about a company and shareholders?"

"That's right," Philip replied. "A limited company owned by shareholders who won't all be members of my family. Nor are we going to have a bunch of city slickers who want to turn every green acre into a housing estate. Which means that the shareholders will be confined to those who want to see Ockenham remain a farming community – as it always has been. How do you fancy the idea?"

Margie smiled at him. "Marvellous but plumb crazy. It's just one of your high flying stories. Shares cost money and who can you find round here to buy them? Amos and I and the Hogbens are happy to live and work at Ockenham, but I doubt if any of us have cash to spare. I know we haven't, have we Amos?"

"Don't worry about the cash," said Philip. "The point is – would you like to join me in running the company and take a share of the profits?"

"Bet your life I would." Amos had always been positive. "Might even let Margie in on the deal if she promises to behave herself."

Margie looked at Philip, her grey eyes searching for meaning. Then abruptly she went off to round up the children, leaving the men to finish the beer. Later she and Amos watched Philip's tall figure striding off towards the Dower House.

Amos turned to his wife. "You know, Margie, that man means every word he says. I've never known him make a promise he hasn't kept. But I wonder why he's done it."

Margie thought for a moment. "You never know what sparks him," she said. "Only that he's a very generous man. Maybe the war's done something to him, changed his ideas, taught him about other people – the way they think, or something. But I'll tell you this, love. His father and brother aren't the only war casualties in the family. Nor his step-mother either. That man's had a rough ride in Italy, sure as my name's Margie Williams. And what's he got to show for it? If any man needs friends, it's a man who is deaf at forty."

By the time of Penny's second marriage, Martin was able to report to Philip that his father's will was finally out of the way and that estate duties and debts, ranging from Fortnum and Mason and a Savile Row tailor to a firm of Ramsgate boat builders, were all settled. Not without some additional land sales, and not without some diminution of Philip's personal capital. But the sale of some cottages in Ockenham and Little Ockenham greatly eased the cash situation, while money for farming improvements was now available at long-term, low interest rates. Martin could confirm that the Mortimer-Wotton family still owned 1,000 acres of its ancestral property in some of the best farming land in the county.

Moreover, compensation for war damage to the Great House had been successfully negotiated: and its rebuilding on the basis of Philip's Jerusalem plan was going forward under the skilled direction of Canterbury's leading architect. For the first time in history, the Mortimer-Wotton household was to enjoy the benefits (and economies), of running water in all the bedrooms and a modern central heating system. Taken all in all, the ground was clear for the next phase – this common ownership plan which Philip had discussed with Amos and Margie.

In the high summer of 1954 Philip summoned Martin to Ockenham. The two men took tea together, sitting in deck chairs on the croquet lawn in front of the Great House. Martin wondered whether he'd ever seen a more peaceful sight than the view across the park to the lake and the trout stream beyond. What a wonderful inheritance it was. Could Philip really mean to share it out? Where did he begin? What degree of control did he want the family to retain?

But Philip's answers to Martin's hesitant questions were as clear-cut as an army operations order.

"This is how I see it, young Martin. First, the two houses with their gardens remain my freehold property. Secondly, we put a capital value on the property less the houses – let's call it £100,000 at present day values. Thirdly, we ensure the family gets a fair cut off the joint in fixed interest redeemable preference shares, divided equally between Eleanor, Penny and myself.

Next you establish an ordinary share capital – say 20,000 £1 shares, a sizeable fraction of which I give to the people here – to Amos Williams and Guy Hogben and perhaps to Evan Morgan. Finally, since the company remains private, you ensure that further disposal or re-sale of these ordinary shares remains in the hands of the directors: say Amos, Guy, Eleanor and myself for the time being. The shares will, of course, only be given or sold to men and women dedicated to the idea that Ockenham continues as a farming community. Get the general idea?"

"But hey, just a moment, Philip. Do you realise what you are proposing to hand over? This is Don Quixote gone mad. Madder" – and Martin laughed – "madder than that crazy fellow who bought a villa in Ravello with his Uncle Charles's money. Anyway, what about your step-mother and Bobby's widow?"

"For goodness sake, Martin, no 'ifs' and 'buts'. Naturally, I realise what I'm doing when I share the ownership of Ockenham – or rather Ockenham Farms Ltd. – with the men and women who work the land. That's the object of the exercise. I'll square Eleanor and Penny – remember, each of them has considerable private means. One day, I hope that anybody who serves us for five years consecutively can get a stake in the company if he or she wants it.

But we've got to start somewhere, so we'll start with Amos and Guy and see how it goes, eh? Now you go away and worry out the details with your legal and accountancy pals. I've given you the 'intention'. You organise 'the method'. Oh – there's one other point. You'll have to reorganise the garage and the building companies under Evan. Treat them as wholly-owned subsidiaries with Evan as managing director. If you think his position is best established by giving him a share in the parent company, let me know. We shall need him, anyway, when it comes to all this form-filling the government inflicts on us.

O.K.? Got enough to go on with? No more questions? Right, let's draw stumps. It's a bit chilly here compared with Ravello. If you have any more problems, we'll discuss them over dinner."

Philip was still living with Eleanor while the Great House was being rebuilt. He and Martin strolled across the park to the Dower House – Philip monopolising the conversation, pointing out different features of the landscape, recalling the former days: and Martin listening entranced beside him.

The conversation turned to Eleanor. "I just don't know how to help her," Philip confessed. "It was bad enough when the war ended and Penny and the children still filled the place with some sort of life. But with their departure, nobody can get my stepmother out of her depression. The gloom – I can't describe it. It's all-pervasive. I half feel I should take her with me when I go back to the old house next month. Then I see an endless succession of ghastly dinners – night after night – and I go into reverse, trying to persuade myself it's better for her to make her home at the Dower House where she's lived since the old house was bombed."

"Has she no friends who might be willing to join her?" asked Martin. "Or a companion? Or something?" His voice trailed away in doubts.

"Sounds right in theory," Philip said. "But mention a companion to her – and she goes dumb. Penny has done her best to help, but the latest news from that quarter is that she's just off to join her R.A.F. husband on an overseas posting. In fact, I've got Susan and Kate on my hands for the summer holidays and I've promised to show them the villa."

"Lucky girls," laughed Martin. "And a perfect excuse for a second visit to your hide-away. But don't tell me the journey is solely to give Bobby's children an Italian holiday."

"Well, there *is* a second reason," Philip admitted. "The servant problem, you know. Can't run houses without a bit of help. And if I leave Eleanor with the staff at the Dower House, we'll need a few replacements, what? No, seriously, Evan Morgan gave me the idea a few days ago. 'Servants, Major?' he says. 'Nothing simpler. Clap your hands at the Villa della Robbia and take your choice. Giovanni and Maria, perhaps? If they're a bit long in the tooth for export, they'll find somebody, you see.'"

Martin was laughing. "Cannelloni and lasagne at the Great House, eh? Washed down with a little Chianti or perhaps Verdicchio? Really you've got a nerve, *Comandante mio.*"

"You may laugh, you stuffy lawyer, but let me tell you that everybody round here is moaning about running their houses without domestic help. Anyway, I've opened a bottle of claret for this evening. So let's go and enjoy it. No whisky, you understand? I've throttled down on that at the Dower House – *pro bono publico*, as you might say. But I'll be grateful if you can find a few excuses to call on Eleanor while I'm away. As to Ravello, the route's fixed. Off next week overland. Should be fun. Giovanni and Maria have been warned to expect me in a big black Rolls with a couple of young women in the back."

The very thought of escape from Eleanor boosted Il Comandante's morale. He enjoyed his claret that night.

The big, black Rolls was no figure of speech, still less a figure of fun. It was the real thing – 1933 vintage, immensely dignified like its original owner. Evan Morgan had spotted old Mrs. Mortimer-Wotton's chauffeurless car languishing in the Dower House stables – how unbelievably careless this family was, to be sure. Evan's thrifty nature was affronted. Nothing would satisfy him but to get the splendid monster back on the road. He christened it 'Black Beauty'.

"It's just your style, major" the Welshman said, as if he were a tailor selling a slightly daring tweed to a doubting customer. "It will suit you beautifully and you'll feel great when you drive it around. You see."

The twenty-year-old Rolls was now a well known sight in Canterbury and the surrounding country, lording it over the other golfers' cars at Sandwich, and resplendent in Canterbury cricket week, parked behind the Club tents on the St. Lawrence Ground. So when, some three weeks after Martin's visit to Ockenham, the black Rolls completed its faultless journey across Europe with a triumphal entry into Ravello, it produced a mighty sensation.

"*Ecco Il Comandante,*" cried the children in great excitement. "Bravo, bravo." The fathers gazed with awe on the car – "*Qualchuna bellissima machina.*" The mothers waved their welcome to the two girls – "*Due ragazze Inglese – non è vero? blonde, molto elegante.*" And they chattered away, all talking at the same time, while Giovanni and Maria stood at the gates of the Villa della Robbia. Their 'Comandante' was back in style.

As with all his annual visits – and not a year passed without a visit – Philip experienced a growing sense of release as the car negotiated the serpentine bends on the road from Amalfi. It was as if he was re-entering the feudal world into which he'd been born – a world, he supposed, that had gone from England for ever.

But this time it was even more exciting. Here were Susan and Kate and the Rolls making their first visit to his Italian paradise. Big sensation. No constraint. Laughter, young laughter at the villa. The girls looking lovely in their summer clothes. Giovanni showing off the garden and the view from the Belvedere. Maria producing marvellous meals in a spotlessly clean house. And the sunshine and the bathing – perfection.

Together they pottered round the ancient relics of Greece and Rome. They enjoyed a tremendous party with the Tibelli family in Naples. They took a box at the San Carlos opera, entertained dear old Don Pietro, sailed across to Capri . . . it was a fabulous holiday. The younger girl, especially, seemed to fall head over heels in love with the place. "I'm coming again and again," she said, "and I'm going to learn the language so that I really belong here. Just like your Uncle Charles." Kate's enthusiasm was charming.

A month later they took the road north. It was really at Penny's request that Philip stopped to show the two girls their father's grave at Cassino. After his visit with Penny, he'd arranged for an inscription to be added to Bobby's memorial. Now, with Susan and Kate, he stood reading Julian Grenfell's lines at the foot of the headstone.

> The fighting man shall from the sun take warmth,
> And light from the glowing earth.
> Speed with the light-foot winds to run,
> And with the trees to newer birth:
> And find, when fighting shall be done
> Great rest and fullness after death.

Bobby was different. And the words fitted his spirit, as they had fitted the young men of an earlier war.

With a slow dignity the big man led his young nieces back to the car. He drove them up the hill to the Benedictine monastery, now proudly and lovingly restored, a symbol of eternity. They stopped before the Polish Memorial on the hillside. And Susan, the elder girl, said – "I'm glad you brought us here, Uncle Philip. It must have been hard for you to do so. I don't think I understood before how many people died at Cassino, or how many people lost here what they loved most."

Philip was far away in time and space – back on 'Hill 601' and the mud and tempest of the Sangro crossing. These orderly memorials brought back other terrible memories to his mind. He jerked himself back to the present. "Yes," he said slowly, carefully choosing his words. "When people talk about a million dead, it means nothing – just one more statistic. It's only when you isolate the losses to a single battle – or even to a single school like Eton which lost 1100 of her sons in this second war – that numbers acquire meaning. Still, it doesn't do to dwell too long on these things. The finest man I've ever known – he was an old priest who knew you when you were babies – used to tell me that whenever catastrophe strikes a family or a country, the survivors have a positive duty to look to the future. That's what your mother has done, bless her: and that's what Bobby would want us to do. So on we go, up Highway Six to Rome, Florence, Milan and eventually – if Black Beauty behaves properly – to Ockenham.'

219

Neither Susan nor Kate mentioned the war again. After all, when you're seventeen and fifteen and driving across Europe in a big black Rolls, it's the present and future that count.

But as Evan Morgan had foretold, Philip found time in Ravello to solve his servant problem. The Battista's eldest boy confirmed that he longed to learn English. He and his wife would be happy to visit the Comandante's English castle. "She very good cook, Signore: and our Antonio, 'e maka everything grow, *ottima verdura, belliss imi fiori.*"

Maria implied that no better cook and gardener would ever be exported from Campania to Kent.

25

THE people of Ockenham live on a day-to-day basis. During the Fifties they registered joy as Churchill swept away the last of the war-time restrictions and in so doing ended the time-consuming labour of circumventing them. They marked their loyalty to the new queen with a magnificent fireworks display in the park of the Great House – laid on by the major and organised by Evan Morgan – "best show ever seen in these parts yer know." And Hunt's ascent of Everest was a talking point at the school where the climbers' progress took the place of geography lessons for a few weeks. But by and large, the village did not get over-excited by events in the wider world. What mattered to them was the land. And in those years routine farming complaints began to sound a trifle hollow in the mouths of Kentish farmers whose big cars surrounded Ashford market each week like tycoons round a boxing ring.

But they're shrewd observers all the same – these men and women of Ockenham. Increasingly they became aware of revolutionary change at the very centre of their lives: and – surprise, surprise – the source of the revolution was indubitably to be found at the Great House.

"See what that Evan Morgan's done at the garage?" they'd say. "'E's a younger brother of Gwynedd Morgan, yer know – 'er that used to look after the old lady up at Dower House. They say 'e 'ad a lot to do with the major in Italy or summat. Sure 'e took over the garage pretty quick. Soon put an end, 'e did, to Joe Fagg's 'okey-pokey.''

"That's right, Mrs. Evans," a customer confirmed to the village postmistress. "My son, as works there, says Mr. Morgan started ever so friendly by 'aving a little check-up on the spare-parts store. Found a lot missin', they say. So 'e tells Joe, still friendly-like, that

221

'e'd best get them spare parts properly listed and a good stout lock put on the store. Seems like there's some light-fingered type round 'ere, 'e says."

"Yes – and just to be on the safe side – 'e thought 'im and Joe would clock in at eight o'clock every day to set the lads a good example. A few weeks later, 'e introduced a proper work sheet for each job."

"Poor old Joe, the pace was too 'ot and the jumps too 'igh for a fiddler like 'im. Reckon 'e got the message loud and clear. In less than twelve months, 'e found a job up Bromley way. Mind you 'e was a good mechanic, was Joe. But no one was sorry to see 'im go. Just couldn't trust the old so-and-so."

They were equally impressed by the new management at the Wotton Arms. Soon after Evan Morgan's family moved into their refurbished house next to the garage, Philip had received a letter 'out of the blue' from Ted Baker – formerly Sgt. Baker of Hill 601. Remembering his old company commander was the director of a Faversham brewery, he wrote to ask whether the major could find him a job. He rather fancied the life of a publican and so did his Italian wife, acquired somewhere north of Florence after Sgt. Baker and his Battalion had been pulled out of the Gothic Line.

Philip was delighted. "Not a sounder character in the British Army," he told Amos and Margie and Evan Morgan. "And I bet he's found himself a lovely girl for a wife." With Jack Kemsing anxious to retire to his gardening and no member of the Kemsing family keen to follow his calling, the Wotton Arms was crying out loud for Sergeant Baker. A brief training period, a careful assessment of the Italian wife: and Ted Baker and the dark-eyed Luisa became an integral part of Ockenham life. Soon the Wotton Arms acquired a reputation for good food and cleanliness well beyond the village boundaries. And the villagers took a new pride in the 'local'.

Margie Williams who often went down to 'the Wotton' with Amos on Friday evenings had her own reasons for welcoming the change. "It's like this," she explained to Amos one evening. "Alex and Mary – and the other children, with a bit of luck – are set on a new course. Look at the way it's been with Alex. First he won't try for Oxford, though his headmaster thinks he ought to jump at it.

Chooses National Service instead, gets a commission and serves in Germany. When he comes home, he's as restless as a dog with fleas. Must see the world, he says. Takes off for Australia – and now he's a Jackaroo, or whatever he calls himself, rounding up sheep on the Queensland–New South Wales border, close by Guy Hogben's son."

Amos stopped her. "But what's that got to do with you and me and this new bloke at the Wotton Arms? Alex never thought of running a pub, did he? Wouldn't be right for him after King's School and the army. I reckon he was right to set his own course. It's natural for lads like him to get foot-loose, and a bit head-strong, like most of us did at his age." He gave Margie an old-fashioned look. "Still, the land's in his blood however you look at it. I shouldn't be surprised if he comes back to Ockenham one of these fine days. We've got a thing or two here, you know, that the Aussies can't offer."

"O.K. love. We'll leave Alex with his Australian friends for the moment. But what price Mary? She's done us equally proud at the Simon Langton School. Now she's a private secretary in Canterbury and making lots of new friends. I fancy she'd prefer to remember you're a director of Ockenham Farms Ltd. and forget my old home at the local pub."

Mary was very much on her mother's mind. Anybody with half an eye could see that Mary, the schoolgirl, had grown into a stunningly beautiful woman: and a covey of young men were well aware of it – not least among them, Martin Harrison who made the major's business an excuse for more and more visits to Ockenham. "Funny," Margie said to Amos one day, "how often Martin Harrison leaves his office the same time as Mary leaves hers and just happens, would you believe it, to need a consultation with you or Evan Morgan or Mrs. M-W. All I will say is that if that boy's keen on our Mary, he'd better get into top gear quick."

Actually, the affair between Martin and Mary dated back to a summer afternoon when Martin was persuaded by Alex to turn out for the Ockenham cricket side. The village cricket ground was situated in the corner of the park close to the main Lodge gates: and serving teas in the small wooden pavilion was Alex's sixteen-year-old-sister. Though still at the Simon Langton School, she was already good-looking by any standards you liked to name. Five foot seven perhaps, good legs, slim hips, curves showing in all the right places, auburn hair, a hint of laughter in the eyes and mouth . . .

"Who's that girl, Alex?" Martin had asked.

"Which one? You mean my sister, Mary? Good heavens, Martin, she's still at school, half your age." Her brother's off-hand reply could scarcely have been more discouraging.

But while Alex was completing his National Service at Eaton Hall and in Germany, Martin watched Mary grow up from sixth form and 'A' levels to stenography and private secretary.

His visits to Ockenham often necessitated a call at Dark's Place where through Gwynedd and Margie, he incidentally gained a new insight into Philip's background. But Mary was the prize to be won. Half his age, was she? Yes, but wasn't he still young if you subtracted those six fleeting years of war when age groups lost their meaning?

Suddenly, jealousy – angry, green-eyed jealousy – drove him forward. It happened one day in Canterbury when, looking down from the office windows of Dawson & Leadbitter, he saw Mary, his Mary, walking down Castle Street, arm-in-arm with some ghastly long-haired yob she must have met at work. Martin watched her retreating towards a small café, with this spotty kid looking positively proprietorial beside her. He couldn't bear it. He stayed in the office through lunch-time, his eyes scanning the street. He watched Mary return, imagining the sound of her laughter. There and then, he made up his mind.

He found excuses to be alone with Mary in Canterbury; lunching with her and taking her to the Marlowe Theatre. One Sunday he motored with her to see his parents in Beckenham, giving her dinner at a little Italian restaurant where he told her of his first meeting with Philip Mortimer-Wotton in Ravello.

Together they explored the countryside and, at some time in the course of these journeys, Mary made up her mind, too. Martin, she decided, was the man she wanted – a man, not a boy. A strong good-looking man, full of character, who'd seen life away from Ockenham, who knew where he was going. A man whom other men liked and trusted. Did he seem shy compared with all these boys of her own age who, cinema-fed, pawed every girl they met? Then she'd show Martin she wanted him as much as she knew he wanted her. And she edged more closely to him, so that he sensed the warmth of her body, and kissing her knew the excitement of her response . . .

Neither knew who proposed to whom. Their loving was so natural, so real, no make-believe about it. And it was Mary who, with Martin beside her, told her parents they wanted to marry as soon as possible.

A few weeks after Philip's return from Italy, the bells rang for Martin and Mary from the old Norman tower of Ockenham Church. There was a reception at Dark's Place, with Philip providing champagne and proposing the health of the bride and bridegroom.

The honeymoon was spent at the Villa della Robbia just as Philip had promised in 1944, not knowing who Martin's bride would be. And in due course Mary and Martin Harrison returned to a house near Wingham the other side of Canterbury – "just to make sure, Mum, that Martin doesn't feel he's imprisoned for life in Ockenham." Thus Mary to her mother.

And Philip added, "She's just like you, Margie. A mind of her own and lovely to look on. Martin's a very lucky man."

Gwynedd said nothing. But down at the Wotton Arms they noted that "young Mary – grand-daughter of Jack Kemsing yer know – had got 'itched to that pal of the major's. Not a bad bloke, either, though they say 'e comes from t'other side 'o County."

At long last, Philip was back in residence at the Great House. The action was master-minded by Evan Morgan who had been recruited to indoctrinate the newly arrived Antonio and Franca into the major's ways – both as concerns good living and tidiness.

"You know the form, Evan," said Philip. "English breakfast, light lunch, decent dinner. I look after the cellar and you teach 'em English and make sure Antonio really is a good gardener. Any questions?"

"Dozens of them," replied the Welshman, "but we'll take them as they crop up. We'll start by getting Luisa Baker to deal with the language problem and perhaps my sister Gwynedd can educate them in the workings of the Great House. After all, she knows more about you than the rest of us put together."

"I leave the details to you," said Philip grandly. "But here's a thought. You know the Italians. I'll wager 50 to 1 there's a *bambino* on the way before the year is out. So we'd better have an emergency plan, eh?"

Evan was ready for that one too. "You're right, it's an odds-on certainty. That's one reason for having Gwynedd around. And my wife will be happy to help in the house when Franca's confinement comes along as it will do for sure. If you want to place your bet you'll need to find somebody who's seen less of Italy than your old staff-sergeant. And now, can we please get back to England and concentrate on these grants that Amos thinks we can push through with the Ministry." Evan Morgan returned to the desk in the estate office in the old undamaged corner of the original house.

Philip liked it that way. The farming and the control of it – right in the centre of things where his grandmother had once held sway. That was the name of the game. Ockenham Farms Ltd. must be a continuing thing like the land itself.

He was going to live in the new rooms and furnish them with some of the old heirlooms – his grandmother's desk from the morning room for instance, and the family pictures from the library. But most important of all, he must recover the French paintings from the Dower House. Those four paintings – he didn't care a damn whether they were signed or not – were Bertha's most precious visible relic. Eleanor must know that Francis had given them to him. He would tackle her about it right away.

The same evening he walked down to the Dower House to see Eleanor. The contrasting colours of the trees and the pasture, high-lighted by the September sunshine, were just as Bertha must have seen them when she first came to Ockenham. To him, as it had been to her, this stretch of country was the most beautiful place on earth. But how was it with Eleanor? Did she care? Who knew – did his father ever know – where her love lay? Discarding each of her interests, one by one, just as his father had warned him. First the theatre and the ballet and London Society in its Edwardian heyday, all forgotten in that ghastly '14–'18 war when she and his father drifted apart. Then the intense interest in the farming which had given place to the Ockenham Motors project. Extraordinary woman. They said that in the war after Francis's death she'd worked at the garage virtually full time, in mechanics' overalls. Hardly surprising the County couldn't understand her. Then with Bobby dead and Joe Fagg replaced by Evan Morgan, she'd become a recluse as well as an alcoholic. Her latest craze was bird-watching. Day after day she raced off in her Austin Healey to the marshes beyond Fordwich or the flat ground beside Sandwich Bay where the Stour wound its way towards the sea. No bad thing, he supposed, if it kept her off the whisky. But a damned lonely occupation, all the same.

Eleanor was just back from one of these expeditions when Philip reached the Dower House. She seemed almost animated as she told him of the birds she'd spotted that day. Would he stay for a drink? Philip was only too happy to join her in her present mood. Over a glass of sherry he settled about moving the pictures to the Great House. She evinced no desire to keep them in their original Dower House setting. All she said was, "watch the market prices for French impressionists. Those pictures are worth a hell of a lot more than you think. You ought to get them valued and properly insured."

As she swallowed her whisky and poured herself another, her mood changed. She turned on her companion with pathetic irritation. "Stop watching me, Philip. You know I can't help it. And at my time of life, I'm damned if I'll try to do so. I just don't tick without it."

Philip left her slouched dull-eyed, in a chair with the whisky decanter beside her. The problem of Eleanor was beyond him. Yet he couldn't rid his mind of the conviction that the fault was not with her. How solitary she had become. Unwilling to adjust to the County society where she could have found a welcome, unable to harness her ability to any single pursuit, losing Bobby whose achievements had brought her happiness between the wars, preferring the company and talk of the garage to the people of the household who really understood her loneliness – and now, inevitably falling back on the vice and the pastime of the lonely . . . Eleanor who, in her youth, had loved company! It was pathetic.

26

PHILIP turned with relief towards Dark's Place. He wanted a word with Amos: and the Williams children, thank God, presented no problems. Just to hear and see them would raise his spirits and take his mind off Eleanor.

He was greeted by Margie's youngest child, Arthur. "Heard the news, Sir?" he shouted, kicking a football at the outline of a goal chalked on the wall of the barn. "My big brother, Alex, is coming home from Australia. Mum will want to tell you about it. Gwynedd's there already."

Arthur kicked the ball again. From the rebound off the wall Philip headed the neatest of goals. A fabulous fluke, he murmured to himself as the little boy cheered. But what a spirited lot these children are. This kid is as full of 'go' as the rest of the family.

Margie was in a state of great excitement, her eyes sparkling, words tripping over each other.

"Oh Phil," she cried, "you've arrived at just the right moment. Alex is coming home and Amos has opened a bottle of sherry. Returning by ship apparently. Amos says that means he must be packing it up in Australia. What d'you think? Once or twice lately, we've thought he sounded a bit homesick. Wouldn't it be super if he came back for good? And all Gwynedd says is, 'Now Margie, don't count your chickens before they're hatched'."

"That's not what I said at all, Mr. Philip." The old lady, seated in the high-backed chair she always occupied in Margie's sitting room, defended herself with dignity. "Amos will bear me out. But Margie always has been one for jumping to conclusions."

Present and past were increasingly liable to confusion in the old lady's mind. But though babies and adults constantly changed places in her thinking, she coined for each of her children a

Homeric epithet which quantified their characteristics with the exactitude of a chemical analyst.

Each had his label and her brother and his wife knew them by heart. Margie, "impulsive, pretty as a picture." Amos, "hard-working, loyal." Dear Bobby, "Just like his father." Alex, "a very determined young man, knows his own mind." Mary, "Mr. Harrison's a very lucky man." And Philip? "Ah, Mr. Philip, he's different, but there's a lot of his mother in him, God rest her soul." And at the drop of a hat the old lady would recount a hundred incidents from Philip's past or listen with tears in her eyes to the stories which her brother and Ted Baker had to tell of his exploits as a soldier.

Philip was different. The old nurse's judgment was echoed by his pre-war friends, both in London and the County. At this time, Philip still retained contact with an earlier, more circumscribed world which in his case radiated from his London club in St. James's Street. It included a stretch of Piccadilly – Hatchards for books, and Fortnum's for special delicacies (how he had enjoyed sending exotic parcels to surprise and amuse his nieces at boarding school!). He patronised certain shops in Jermyn Street – Paxton's for cheeses and Hodgkinson for ties and shirts. He walked through the Burlington Arcade to visit his tailor and returned to St. James's Street for his hats and his wine merchant. Only on very rare occasions did he go to the City, normally asking his stockbroker to lunch at the Club. This square mile of the West End was, so to speak, his shopping centre.

The habits of his pre-war life died hard and he never pretended he didn't enjoy the luxury and freedom to which he had been brought up. But a marked difference of outlook was beginning to show between Philip and those who had once shared the same privileged world with him.

Brian Melchester noticed it first. "Saw Philip in the Club the other day," he told Guy Venables and Jack Biddulph. "Looked much the same. He's put on a bit of weight, uses a hearing aid and his hair's going grey, but he still enters the club as if he owned the place, just as he always used to do."

"What does he do with himself, alone in that great house?"

"Haven't a clue. There's no wife to cheer him up, but he seems happy enough. Talks a lot about some damn-fool scheme for taking the locals into partnership or something . . . Crazy fellow! What do you say, Jack?"

"Crazy? Or sane? I wouldn't like to say. He works things out for himself, does our Philip. And once he makes up his mind, he's unstoppable. You can bet your boots that, if he's planning some new deal, he'll be mighty choosy about who gets a cut off the joint."

"Funny you should say that," Venables chipped in. "A young solicitor, name of Martin Harrison and one of the best chaps on my staff in Italy, mentioned Philip in a letter he wrote to me only the other day. Seems he's doing a lot of legal work for Philip in Canterbury. Odd the way things work out. The pair of them first met south of Naples after the Sangro crossing. I can still remember Martin's excitement telling me a preposterous story about Philip buying a villa in Ravello. That boy certainly saw something in Philip. I suppose Philip saw something in Martin, too."

Philip's name frequently cropped up in their conversation, though they saw him so rarely. Why did they see so little of him, especially when they all wanted to know what he was up to? They were really very fond of him.

"It's his deafness, I suppose. Can't follow conversation in a crowd. Rotten luck."

"I don't know about that. Others make out well enough with a hearing aid. Perhaps he keeps a girl at his villa in Italy. Who looks after the place, anyway, when he's not there?"

"Grow up, for heaven's sake. In my view, he's a perfectly happy old bachelor – but disillusioned, perhaps? The girls certainly fell for him in the old days. Remember Annie Sherwood in Cairo?"

"Do I not? And Jack Biddulph's mopping up operation too. No wonder he's a major-general. Philip was well clear of that girl."

"Why d'you say that?"

"Good God, didn't you know? She hitched up with a Vichy Frenchman in Ismailia. Never proved anything against her personally, I gather: just too many officers invited in for drinks. 'Walls have ears' – that sort of crap. Anyway, she and the Frenchman got it loud and clear from our Intelligence boys to get out of range quick. You never can tell, can you? Somebody told me they'd been spotted in Cambodia running travel agency tours to the Angkor Temples. Not much of a future there, I shouldn't think. Better leave Philip to till his acres in peace."

The subject of these speculations remained supremely indifferent to his friends' concern. His detachment from their society had its parallel in a similar detachment from his traditional haunts nearer home, where again he seemed to be inching away into a new orbit.

He still enjoyed his golf at Sandwich, but tended to play a round with the professional until he persuaded Martin Harrison to take up the game.

At Canterbury, he was an easily recognised figure, still serving as a director of certain local companies. But he had retired from the Bench because of his deafness – or so he said. And if he watched the County playing at Canterbury or Folkestone or Dover he generally did so, sitting in a deck chair by himself. He never went to the Marlowe theatre – not even for the Old Stagers except on two occasions when his nieces persuaded him to do so.

The long and short of it was that Philip was happiest either among his own people at Ockenham or with his equally devoted Italians at the Villa della Robbia. He knew they wanted to have him around. They – the children especially – understood his hearing problem. If older friends with long memories liked to think of him as one of the great landowners of England, in a class apart from lesser mortals, let them do so. Like many of the Mortimer-Wottons before him, he didn't care a hoot what people thought. His family had always made their own rules which, apart from early Mortimer lapses on the Welsh Marches, normally conformed to the law of the land. If Society mourned the apostasy of Philip Mortimer-Wotton, that was their affair.

For his part, he was happy to be sitting with his old nurse and Margie and Amos, drinking to Alex's safe return from Australia.

A few months later, Alex was back. In his four years away from home he had developed into a very good-looking young man – tall, strongly built, his skin tanned by the sun of the Outback, his features strongly etched but softened by his mother's humorous eyes and easy smile. Margie was very proud of him.

231

Philip, also, found a lot of time for him, and delighted in his company, hardly recognising in the full-grown man the gangling schoolboy he'd met at Paddington.

"Australia's a great country," Alex told Philip, "and the Australians are great guys. But they're growing apart from us as certainly as the Americans did after the War of Independence. It's not a question of friendship – they're as friendly to us as the Americans are and I've got some marvellous friends there. But . . . they are different somehow . . . different outlook . . . different horizons."

"So where do you stand?" Philip asked. "Are you going back to them?"

"No," said Alex. "I'm not going back. There's a good job up country on the Queensland border if I want it and the money is very attractive, like the people I've worked for. But I don't want to be labelled a 'Pommy' for life. And I don't see any escape from it unless I forget all the things I've learnt here. In my view, it's much easier for a lad from the East End – or even a slum child from Naples – to merge his identity in Australia than it is for somebody who's had the luck to be educated at King's and hold a commission in the Rhine Army, if you see what I mean. The last thing I want to do is to be sucked into Sydney or Melbourne like so many of the chaps I've met. Might just as well be 'something in the City' over here.

"But you're sticking to the land, are you?" asked Philip.

"Oh yes, I think so," Alex replied. "It's in the blood, isn't it? I'd be miserable away from farming. It's just a case of getting started. Can you use me here, d'you think?"

"It's a good question," Philip replied. "As far as I'm concerned, the answer is 'Yes'. But you've heard about our new set-up. I'll have to consult the Board, as your City slickers say." Philip laughed. "Leave it with me for the moment, Alex. Come and have a drink and take a look at the way we've rebuilt the house."

The older man and his young companion strolled across to the new wing. "Beer, sherry, gin, whisky?" Philip was bending over a cupboard talking away with his back to the boy. "D'you remember the pictures at the Dower House? Look rather good here, don't you think? I've kept the two small ones in the hall – some fellow who was here the other day believes they're unsigned Cézannes from his early hard-up days. But I expect the man only said it to put up the insurance premium."

There was no answer from Alex. Philip continued his monologue. "Got my niece, Susan, staying here for a week or two. She'll be down any moment. The other one – her sister Kate you know – she's staying in Rome with a school friend who is an archaeologist's daughter. Works at a British School of something or other. Anyway, they dig like mad all day, unearthing the occasional spoon or drinking bowl to keep their spirits up. Not Susan's line at all, I'd say. She's no good with a spade. It's a good thing girls aren't all made the same way."

There was a burst of laughter from the other end of the room. Susan stood in the doorway contemplating her Uncle's backside with undisguised amusement. "For heaven's sake stop talking such nonsense, Uncle Philip. What we need is a drink – not a series of character assassinations. Come, you get into your usual chair and Alex and I will fix the drinks."

She moved across to the cupboard with a mature grace which took Alex by surprise. Learnt at school or born and bred in her? The young man could not believe that Susan whom he'd last seen as a schoolgirl was his junior by six years. He was fascinated by her self-assurance and the charming way she handled her Uncle Philip to whom she was clearly devoted. He'd never met a girl with such style. The drinks – Susan gave herself a tomato juice – merged into supper with Franca producing a typical Italian meal of cannelloni, fruit and cheese, accompanied by a bottle of Verdicchio. Philip was entranced with his youthful company. The conversation was so easy and natural – Philip bringing them up to date with Ockenham activities: Susan laughing over her Uncle's pidgin Italian which he employed successfully both at the Villa della Robbia and the Great House: and Alex recounting his Australian adventures in a grossly exaggerated 'Strine' accent. It was an hilarious evening and the host was in his best form as though he had no cares in the world. Perhaps if Martin or Evan Morgan or Ted Baker had been present they would have noticed that the major was assessing the character and quality of young Alex with a professional skill with which they had long been familiar.

The next day Philip saw Martin. "Now then, young Martin," he said. "Think hard. Where can we use Margie's boy, Alex, to best advantage and at the same time give him some sort of independent command of his own?"

A few weeks later Martin who had always been Philip's chief 'ideas' man, was back with an answer. A neighbour of his in the Wingham area was anxious to sell out in the next twelve months. Like most of the farmers and small-holders east of Canterbury, he concentrated largely on vegetables and potatoes for the London market. If he had a firm promise at a fair price, he might easily be persuaded to employ Alex as an assistant and teach him the ways of the market with a view to taking over in twelve months time.

Philip and Martin talked it over with Amos and Guy Hogben: and Amos, conservative steady Amos, came down firmly in favour of purchase. "I'm not thinking specially of Alex," he said, "but of something my old father said to me years ago. 'Amos,' he told me, 'those chaps who farm the light soil towards Thanet have got the London market in their pockets. If you ever want to start up on your own, that's the place to go.' I reckon the old man knew what he was talking about. So Martin's idea gets my vote, if Alex likes the scheme and we can raise the cash."

Philip had heard all he wanted. "Right Amos, you fix Alex. If that's O.K., Martin fixes the deal and I find the money." Eighteen months later Alex was managing a hundred acres of good land in East Kent on behalf of Ockenham Farms Ltd.

27

IN THE years that followed Alex's return from Australia, two events changed the shape and sum of things at Ockenham. The first was the death of Eleanor. The second was the marriage of Alex to Susan Mortimer-Wotton.

Philip was on one of his Italian visits when Eleanor died. The facts were not easily established, but it was certain that on a September day in 1956 Eleanor parked her car on the quay at Sandwich, hard by the Barbican and the bridge over the Stour. She was seen in the late afternoon walking along the river bank and across the golf course to the bird sanctuary at Worth. That was the last time Eleanor was seen alive. It could only be assumed that in the late evening she returned to the car and in a state of physical fatigue or mental aberration engaged the forward gear of her car instead of reverse. The Austin Healey plunged over the quayside. The Stour estuary was at high water. And Eleanor met her death by drowning before a rescue operation could be mounted.

Philip returned to find that an inquest had been held and the Coroner had returned a verdict of accidental death. The post mortem revealed no evidence of barbiturate poisoning or excessive alcohol in the blood: and it was held that tiredness must have caused the fatal accident.

It was only after Eleanor's funeral, when Penny was sorting through her mother-in-law's clothes and possessions, that a horrible discovery turned the accident into a more intimate, personal tragedy.

In turning out the bottom drawer of a wardrobe, Penny uncovered a painting slashed through and through with a knife or some sharp instrument. Such an act could only have been committed in a frenzy of anger. It suggested a streak of madness in the mind of anybody who chose to do such a thing and then retain among her own possessions the pitiful evidence of the deed.

Penny, greatly distressed, rang Philip at the Great House: and from her brief description he knew she could only be referring to the sketch which his father and mother had brought back from their Paris honeymoon. He had last seen it before the war in his father's London flat. How or when Eleanor had come to possess it remained a mystery. Presumably, at some stage towards the end of her frustrated life, her hatred for Bertha had erupted in the destruction of this picture which meant so much to Francis and his first wife.

Philip and Penny told nobody of their discovery. Together they burnt the picture with a lot of other rubbish which Eleanor had accumulated. That was the end of the matter until a day some three months later, when Philip opened a letter addressed to him by an attorney writing from Cleveland, U.S.A. Very formally, a covering note stated that the enclosed sealed letter was forwarded at the request of Mrs. Francis Mortimer-Wotton and would the recipient please acknowledge its receipt.

Philip broke the seal and read:

Dear Philip,

You will receive this letter after I am dead. How the accident of death will occur, I do not yet know. But I am tired of living. I have no pride left. I have lost all that I once valued – even my self-respect.

I had thought of leaving this world without a word to anybody – certainly not to Penny, now happily remarried; nor yet to the two girls. For them my death will, I hope, remain an accident. But since I have named you my executor, I want to ask your forgiveness. You have been a wonderful step-son to me. You were Bobby's greatest friend. Nobody could have done more for his children. And nobody could have done more to save me from myself.

It is I who have failed. I want no pity or sympathy for a useless life. But please in your goodness remember Penny and Susan and Kate. They are more deserving of your love.

Goodbye, dear Philip,
   as always, affectionately,
   Eleanor.

Philip read the letter again, and then very deliberately for the third time. He stared at the firm hand-writing. So much ability under-employed. So much passion thwarted. And yet, like every suicide, Eleanor had to tell somebody 'the reason why'. Well, her secret could rest secure with him. He tore the letter into small pieces and watched each bit turn to nothingness in the log fire before him. It was the second time in his life that he had destroyed the last testament of a member of his family. But this time not even Martin knew what he had done.

There was nothing unhappy, thank God, about the engagement of Alex and Susan. Philip watched with the most lively interest the development of their romance. After the announcement of the engagement he was wont to tell his friends that it all began on the evening that his niece met Alex at the Great House after the boy's return from Australia. But it wasn't as simple as that.

Alex was indeed delighted with Susan's slim grace and calm assurance: and when she visited Ockenham he loved to watch her skill in wangling anything she wanted out of the old man. Everybody knew that the major had a very soft place in his heart for his brother's elder daughter. But laughing with Susan on her occasional weekends was no more than a lighthearted diversion at a time when Alex's main objective was to make a success of the small-holding at Wingham. It was the profit he made as a farmer that led to a gift of shares in Ockenham Farms Ltd.: and with it the conviction that his future lay in Kent.

Susan, for her part, was thoroughly enjoying a life of independence in London, with a far-from-overwork job in the City and a shared flat in Kensington. 'Hard to get' was a good game when there was no shortage of boy friends for company. But like other games played for fun, it becomes serious for no very clear reason.

One day the most persistent of her current admirers was persuaded to drive Susan to Ockenham for the weekend. It proved to be the moment of truth. Uncle Philip received them kindly enough though the pair arrived late for lunch having stopped for a drink at

Chilham. After this unpropitious start, he didn't see the young man again until dinner to which he'd also invited Martin and Mary Harrison to keep him company.

At the end of the evening only Martin appreciated that the major's occasional staccato questions were being directed at Susan's boy friend with pin-point accuracy. Driving home to Wingham, Martin said to his wife, "That lad's failed his 'viva voce' exam, my love. You'll see."

"What on earth are you talking about?"

"Why, didn't you notice? The major was giving him the once-over from the moment the drinks were served before dinner. All under the guise of being a good host but slightly deaf. It's a very neat bit of camouflage."

"The cunning old devil. So what's the verdict?"

"Something like this, I'd say. Self-satisfied, over-ambitious, won't fit here, not good enough for Susan. How's that?" Martin laughed.

"I'd be furious if I were Susan," said Mary.

"Oh, but Susan won't know. Philip won't say a word. He's much more subtle than people realise. I'm only saying that, in my view, the odds on that boy marrying the major's favourite niece have lengthened considerably."

The odds lengthened still further the following morning when Susan and her escort happened to meet Alex who was lunching with his mother at Dark's Place. The contrast was unmistakable. The tall, tough, athletic Alex fitted the scene. The city dweller did not. After that encounter, it became a one-horse race.

Susan met Alex with increasing frequency in Canterbury and London. She was a high spirited girl who knew what she wanted, and she may have made the running. At one point her uncle certainly made a private date with Penny and her R.A.F. husband just returned from overseas to take up a home appointment. But Alex, completely bowled over, also made it transparently clear to his mother that he meant to marry Susan Mortimer-Wotton. It's doubtful if, on these occasions, any mother – and certainly not Margie Williams – fails to read the light in her son's eye.

The engagement was announced in *The Times* in the spring of 1960 and the wedding followed in July of the same year. By her own choice, Susan was married from the Great House. She was given away by her step-father, recently promoted air vice-marshal. Kate, and Alex's younger sister attended the bride. The headmaster of the King's School conducted the service. The little church of St. Dunstan, Ockenham was packed to overflowing. The County was present in force. Special cars met London guests at Ashford station.

The village people were everywhere, weaving in and out. What a moment for them! Young Alex, Amos and Margie's eldest yer know, marrying into the family up at the house. Makes you think, don't it? Could anybody ever remember such a wedding? Such sweet children . . . such a lovely bride . . . Alex so handsome and self-possessed. And the major – Mr. Philip – you simply couldn't miss him in his grey cut-away morning dress . . . nobody had seen him looking so happy for many a day . . . old Gwynedd, god-mother to the bridegroom and sitting in the front of the church with his parents, was literally crying for joy.

The bells rang out across the countryside as Alex and Susan emerged from the West door to drive to the Great House in Black Beauty, with Ted Baker's handsome son at the wheel and cheered by the crowd along the village street, past the Lodge gates and up the Beech Drive to a reception on the lawn before the house. What a day in the life of the village . . . what a setting . . . what a party – catering by Searcy . . . champagne by the bucket, but a very nice man, said Gwynedd, found her a table and chair and a good strong cup of tea . . . and didn't Mr. Philip look splendid as he proposed the health of the bride and bridegroom . . . no, dear, she hadn't heard what he said but she'd seen his head above all the other guests and was sure he was very pleased and happy . . . she only wished his dear grandmother could have been present . . . she did so love the big occasion. And the old lady rambled on until Alex and Susan left for their honeymoon and Margie and Amos took Gwynedd and the younger children back to Dark's Place.

Only two people among the wedding guests knew of the urgent conversation which preceded the announcement of Alex's engagement.

"Phil," Margie had sounded most anxious on the phone, "I

must see you alone. Where can we meet? Can you hear? It's about Alex. It's serious, I tell you."

"About Alex, you say?" Philip had replied. "About Alex and Susan? Yes, yes, I understand. I tell you what. Meet me by the footbridge over the trout stream. I'm just going to take this lazy dog of mine for a walk. Join me there."

The moment they met, Margie started again. "You know what I'm worried about, don't you Phil? Alex, he's out with your niece all the time ... sees her in Wingham as well as in London ... they're inseparable. I'm sure they're in love. What are we going to do, Phil? We've got to face up to it. It's *our* son we're talking about – your son and mine. I don't know whether he's doing the right thing or whether we ought to tell him who his true father is."

Philip looked down at her from his great height. Then he slowly stretched out his arms towards her, held her shoulders, drew her close to him. His eyes looked into hers. He kissed her lightly on the forehead and said, "This is where we sit down. Don't worry, Margie, don't worry. I may be a bit hard of hearing but I've got good eyesight, you know."

Then he said, "I've seen this thing happening for months past and I've had a doctor confirm to me that there's nothing to worry about so far as children are concerned. There's no need to worry, Margie, about their relationship."

"But you and me and Alex?" She was so full of doubt.

"My dear, he's not an adopted child. He remains your son as he has always been. If Susan accepts him, she accepts him as Alexander Williams – just like that. I know Susan. She's got no side to her. She's never wanted to marry a duke."

"But Phil ... what about you?" There were tears in Margie's eyes, tears for Philip. He looked away from her across the open, tidy fields, as if he were searching the future.

"Dear Margie, I understand, but we can't change things now. I would love to tell the world that Alex is your son and mine. But we're thinking of his future – not mine. As Arthur Waddilove warned me long ago, lovers often have to make some sacrifice. I think it's better if only one of us takes the strain. Arthur knew the truth about Alex: but our secret was always safe with him." And Phil drew Margie closer to him. He gave her a quizzical look. Then

240

he added softly, "I'm sure you must have told Amos. You're too honest not to have done so."

"Yes," she said and he sensed the relief in her voice. "I did so at Canon Waddilove's own suggestion, before he christened Alex. He thought we should be happier if I did so. Thank God we both know we can trust Amos to the end of the world."

"So that's where our secret rests – with you, me and Amos." Philip's hands ran through Margie's hair. He kissed her again. Then he got up briskly and pulled her to her feet. "Lucky old Amos," he said, and called to his dog. "Come on, you old fool. Time to move. And remember, you haven't heard a word, have you?"

The Labrador gave him a look of utter devotion. And the three of them – Margie, Philip and the dog – returned along the path beside the river.

28

THE SIXTIES merged imperceptibly into the Seventies. Philip was depressed by the way of the world as he saw it through the eyes of *The Times*, the Sunday papers and the B.B.C. It seemed to him that, with the break-up of the Empire which so many of his family had served, people had lost their sense of purpose: and were still searching for a new destiny in the fog of ugliness, selfishness and violence which had enveloped their country. It was an unkind, unlovely world.

But life must go on, and in well-favoured places it continued to flourish. In Ockenham each spring brought its individual promise to a stretch of land where farming was vital business. Children were born to Mary and Martin and to Susan and Alex. Kate Mortimer-Wotton married an Italian lawyer she met in Rome and started another family. Other children grew up. One of Evan Morgan's boys joined the regular army and the other two were working on the farms. Ted Baker's boy was virtually in charge of Ockenham Motors: he had inherited not only Luisa's good looks but also the engineering skill of his North Italian stock. Nowhere in Kent was farming machinery better serviced. Ockenham Farms flourished.

Philip, restricted by the all-too-even tenor of a deaf man's world, was well content to survey the success of the farming which he had transformed by his own decision from a feudal to a co-partnership operation. Only rarely now did he visit London. And Canterbury and the County saw less of him than they saw of Alex and Martin. But in Ockenham everybody knew the tall man in the long-cut tweed with the slanted pockets, as he moved around his acres accompanied by his Labrador bitch. And he knew everybody too. He was happy with his partners and happiest of all with the children he watched growing up.

In October, 1973, he felt free to make another of his regular trips to his Italian villa. At the age of sixty-eight, he was a bit overweight and beginning to feel his years, but he hadn't a care in the world as he left Heathrow that autumn. He always enjoyed the flight, savouring in advance the welcome he would get at Ravello. Suddenly, high above the Alps, he felt a recurring pain across his chest. Short of breath ... must be out of training ... indigestion perhaps. The stewardess noticed his discomfort and had an airport doctor to meet the plane at Rome. Philip loathed this sort of fuss and insisted on having a call put through to Kate. The result was some fluent and decisive Italian, as a result of which he found himself, willy-nilly, under observation in a British nursing home on the outskirts of Rome. His younger niece was a very decisive person: and it was seven days before he was allowed to leave hospital and travel south in Kate's car. He was under the strictest orders to take things quietly. So he found himself sitting on the ornamental seat in the Belvedere at the far end of his Italian garden. In the cool of the evening he gazed across the Mediterranean towards Salerno, sipping the local wine of Campagna.

He had just made up his mind to sell the Villa della Robbia. "It's not the expense, my dear Tibelli," he'd told his old friend who had come out from Naples to visit him the previous evening. "And it isn't the worry, for who could look after the place and its guests more charmingly and cheaply than the Battista family? No, it's just a matter of age – a feeling that, for me, the Italian adventure is over. I never want to feel that my annual visits have become a duty."

As he reflected on his decision, logic – or maybe the new wine – brought further inspiration. A succession of new ideas flooded his mind. No, damn it, he wouldn't sell the villa: he'd give it to Kate and her husband. No strings attached. But hopefully, since Roberto practised in Naples – he and Kate would make it their family home.

And Susan? In that case, Susan must have The Great House. Simple division. Problem solved. Kate and her Italian family here. Susan and Alex's children there.

"Alex, Alex ..." As he repeated the name, the full significance of his plan struck him. Margie's son, his son, possessing the Great House? Who'd have thought it possible? Who, if it comes to that, would ever know except him and Margie and Amos? Williams? Mortimer-Wotton? What's in a name? "It's the breeding that counts," were almost the last words Gran had said to him before she died.

There was a look of happiness, almost of triumph, on Philip's face as he returned through the garden to the villa. Not a moment to lose, he said to himself, and to think that I haven't looked at my will since I made one in a hurry before leaving for Egypt in '39.

Nevertheless, he hastened slowly. He stayed at the villa for as long as he had originally intended. He toured the local farms. He greeted Don Pietro's successor and was in turn greeted by numerous nameless children.

He entertained Kate and Roberto and their young family and arranged for a new Italian couple to take over from the present incumbents at the Great House. Apart from Kate and her husband, he told nobody except Tibelli of his intentions, and finally returned to England over-land – just to see what European railways are like, he pretended to himself by way of justification.

Before leaving he took a last tour of the house, now beautifully furnished, its walls hung with a selection of his Uncle Charles's Calabrian paintings. He strolled round the formal Italian garden, weedless and carefully tended – but how can you see flowers at their best except against the background of an English lawn? He walked again to the Belvedere and looked down at the men and women working on the slopes in preparation for the olive harvest in November. Yes, he thought, looking at those sturdy Italian peasants, he must remember the Battistas, too, in his will. But for the moment he'd ride light on sentiment. Who could say? He might be back next year as a guest. Meanwhile – and for so long as he lived – he'd remember the happiness he and his friends had enjoyed in this private paradise created out of the grief and boredom of war.

He returned to Ockenham to find the village full of a cock-and-bull story about some young men who had visited the Wotton Arms the previous weekend. The Italians up at the house were laughing their heads off. Steady old Amos said you could get most of the truth from Ted Baker and the rest from the police constable who lived in the village: and he hoped there'd be no repercussions. But it was Evan Morgan with his Welsh story-telling gifts who really put it together for Philip.

"It was like this, you see, Sir," he started. "Me and the missus were spending Saturday evening at the Wotton when in come these fifteen young bruisers. Not their first port of call, I'd say. Anyway, they take over the dart board without so much as by-your-leave. They make a lot of noise and I see Ted Baker watching 'em. They're not too popular, you see, barging into the regulars and one of 'em whistling at Luisa. But it was you that caused the trouble, Sir."

"Come off it, Evan. I was miles away in Italy."

"Ay, but your name was on the pub, see? One of these boys asks who Wotton is. Another says it's a misprint for Rotten. Ted says – he's icy-calm, which is when you want to watch Ted – 'Actually the family pronounces it Wooton.'

And then another of 'em says: 'And who's the family, for Gawd's sake? Been here for centuries, I suppose, grinding the faces of the peasants.'

Well, his chums try to shut him up: but this chap – George his name was – is one of these political blokes. You know what I mean, Sir? Anybody owning land must be rich and therefore he's the reason why the rest are poor – silly young bastard."

"Seem to have heard that story once or twice before, Evan. But go on."

"Why, our lads don't like that sort of talk round here and we all looks to see what Ted's going to do next. It seems there'll be one hell of a punch-up, when Ted sees his son slip out, accompanied by your Antonio from the house. Then Ted winks at me – as much as to say – 'You leave this to me, Evan bach and keep the rest of the troops under control.'

And what do you think that black-haired boy of his did? Unlocked these blokes' minibus and drove it away. How's that for an answer?

When they eventually leave the pub they can't find their bus – it was hired by the way and they don't know its number. So they make a hell of a fuss. But Ted's very masterful and calls in the law."

Evan was laughing with tears pouring from his eyes. "You

should have seen Constable Buckley come on the troubled scene, Sir. A real pantomime, he was. Notebook in hand. Taking their names one by one, tut-tutting over their failure to give him the registration number of the bus. Never seen anyone move so slow in my life. And then somebody says the last bus for Canterbury's coming up the Street. Ted, still very courteous, manages to get these lads on board. And then, by heaven, he opens up in the back parlour. That Luisa produces food from nowhere and we drink the health of you and your family into the small hours. It was a great party – and all on the house. Great man, Ted Baker."

"Of course," Evan graciously added. "Fair's fair. It was these Italian laddies that did the trick. And to think we were chasing them all over the desert only thirty years ago."

Every version of the story added to Philip's amusement. Later that week Constable Buckley cycled up to the house to complete the saga. Evidently, the bus was discovered the following day over at Waltham, neatly parked on the verge of the road and resting on deflated rear wheels and its front axle. The two front wheels – and the spare wheel for good measure – had been rolled to the bottom of a nearby hill. No sign of a key or mark on the car. No suspects. The bus duly recovered and returned to its owner. No case for police prosecution. And the silly young men had all reached the coastal town from which they'd started, after long walks and thumbed lifts from Canterbury.

Philip tried to draw out Ted Baker. But the latter was impressively silent about his son's skill in unlocking car doors with a stretch of wire. All he would concede was that the evening ended happily: and that the whole operation was as pretty a defence of a strong-point as the major could ask for.

But later in Ravello, when the Italian staff returned home, the story lost nothing in the telling. Those who gathered in the Trattoria in the corner of the piazza were left in no doubt that Italy had won a sensational victory at Ockenham and all the heroes were Italian.

Philip saw Martin in Canterbury, and changed his will as he had intended. He added four cash gifts to the Living at Ockenham Parish Church, the Salvation Army, the Army Benevolent Fund and the Restoration Fund for Canterbury Cathedral: and made ample provision for those who served him.

Then he turned to Martin. "Now look here, young Martin" – somehow the name from the early days had stuck. "I haven't forgotten you and Evan. For one thing I want you to be my executors. For another I want to show my gratitude to you both, and Amos too, for seeing through the changes of the last twenty years. Amos and Evan will receive my shares in Ockenham farms and I'd like you to have some of my preference shares. But what about you and Mary taking on the Dower House on a 99 year lease? That would last your time, eh? And still remain part of the estate. What do you say?"

Martin was speechless. At last he stammered his gratitude. "Sorry to seem so dumb but . . . what the hell can I say? Mary and I are never likely to see a more lovely house – so if it comes our way, you can be sure we shall treat it well. Perhaps that's the best way I can thank you, except to promise to keep Ockenham going at full belt. And I'll do that, whatever government's in power and wherever we live."

"That's a long speech, young Martin – and I'm just as grateful to you. So let us cut out on the speeches, get the will drawn up for me to sign, and then bring Mary over to celebrate the occasion."

Martin never forgot the evening the will was signed. Philip had made his arrangements with great care. "Half an hour to ourselves, Martin, so as to get the will out of the way. Leave Mary at Dark's and let her join us later for champagne and dinner."

That was the way it went. Champagne by way of aperitif. Cannelloni, followed by vitello in the Italian style and fresh vegetables from Antonio's garden. Afterwards fresh fruit and a selection of cheeses ("chose them myself, Mary, in Jermyn Street"). The meal washed down with a dry Soave, as once enjoyed at the Excelsior in Naples.

Afterwards, with a Havana cigar and a bottle of Hine from which, from time to time, he replenished a brandy balloon snifter, Philip began to talk about the changes from the old order at Ockenham.

"You'll soon discover," he said "if you haven't done so already, that half the people round here think I'm crackers. Not just because I've turned the farming into a limited company – many of them are doing the same thing for taxation purposes. But because of the way I've shared out the property, letting down the family and all that sort of thing. They'll get their answer in the success of Ockenham Farms Ltd. which you and Alex and the Old Guard like Amos, Guy Hogben and Evan Morgan will certainly achieve.

But Martin – and even you, Mary – may still be wondering what's possessed me. That's true, eh?"

He paused to swirl the brandy in his glass and contemplate the length of his cigar ash.

"Well, here's my story and I hope you won't be bored. When I was a small boy, convention separated me from all the children who lived in the village – your father and mother, Mary, in particular. It was considered right in those days and nobody realised there was something horribly wrong about it.

The chance of life brought me into touch with a marvellous parson. This chap, Arthur Waddilove – he knew Amos and Margie well – was killed, as I think you know, in the 1942 air raid on Canterbury. But in those years before the war he taught me more than all my other teachers put together. We remained close friends after I left school.

Now Arthur had formed a clear pattern of life – and indeed history – which he saw as a constant interplay between change and tradition. His own career exemplified his beliefs. As a young man of brilliant accomplishments everybody believed he would go to the top – prime minister, viceroy of India, Archbishop of Canterbury – you name it. Instead, he lived unmarried, serving the poorest of the poor in the villages of India. He wanted to be a mediator of change. He was a very old man when he was killed, but I've been told that he died saving a baby's life."

"Of course, I remember him," Mary said. "A tall, thin man with deepset eyes. He used to take the services at St. Dunstan's and often called at Dark's Place. We all loved his visits. Actually, my youngest brother was named after him."

"That's the man," Philip continued. "Well, we often talked about his theories of history. One day he used a strange phrase. We are all prisoners of destiny, he said. Outside events – the war,

248

for instance, which caused Martin and me to meet – these outside events which we can't control dictate the pattern of our lives."

But then Philip hesitated and continued in a speculative voice, as if posing a question. "But we're not all prisoners," he said. "In a war it's the duty of every prisoner to try to escape. In peace, it's not a duty, so much as a matter of choice. See what I mean? Martin's prison walls might have been the suburbs of London or Lincoln's Inn. But war gave him the chance to escape. And he's chosen to change the pattern of his life by coming down here."

"Don't over-state the case, Philip. You blooming well persuaded me. Still I'm glad you did," and he looked at his wife.

"Oh well, have it your own way. But my prison was not so much a place as a tradition – a past that put chains on me. So I planned my escape, but it took a war to break the chains. It was then I discovered for myself what Arthur had so often hinted. Not only was change inevitable in the English countryside. The means of change were close to my hand in the form of people. The top brass, I found, was not the monopoly of one section of society any more. It was the present quality of a man, not his past pedigree, that counted."

Philip swallowed the rest of his brandy and a few minutes later saw the Harrisons into their car. As they returned to their home in Wingham, Mary said to her husband, "I've never known the major so wound up. Was it the brandy? I was rather sad for him. He told us so much and yet I had a feeling he was holding back on something. All that stuff about tradition and change. D'you think that's why he never married?"

"Search me," said Martin. "I've found he only tells us what he wants us to know."

29

PHILIP spent the following Easter in England. Cold it might be compared with Southern Italy. But how lovely the English colouring was. The blaze of daffodils, the pear blossom in bridal white, the scent of the wallflowers, the budding tulips standing ram-rod straight among the forget-me-nots. He looked across the garden and counted his blessings.

With the farming well forward, the village would be making the most of the holiday. He expected to spend the day alone, but this did not worry him. There were his books – he had just re-read *The Reason Why* and was now retracing the Italian campaign in Jackson's *Battle for Italy*. He could still enjoy music though he needed to turn up the sound volume for Radio 3 and the radiogram to an extent that made listening a solitary occupation. He had a television set and enjoyed the sport and nature programmes. If he needed company there was always the dog beside him. Carla was the latest in a long succession of Labradors each of whom answered, somewhat incongruously, to Italian names: as Philip readily admitted, nothing could be less Italian than an English bred Labrador. But Carla she was and Carla, like her predecessors, accompanied him everywhere; placid, perfectly trained, riding beside him in the car, padding alongside when he walked the estate.

Since it was Easter Sunday, the Italian staff were taking the day off: and had prepared a cold lunch for him before departing for their Easter Mass.

He woke up, uncertain how to spend Easter. In the old days he would have gone to the parish church morning service with his grandmother as a matter of course. His father was automatically one of the church wardens though he was rarely in church, and even at the end of the war the office was still widely regarded as hereditary. But he'd stopped that nonsense. The whole idea was outdated, he told the young vicar who was building up quite a congregation among the new house owners in the Ockenham neighbourhood. He had persuaded the young man that this sort of survival custom from a pre-war world would prove a positive deterrent to his developing a family spirit in the congregation.

But it had a curious consequence. Some people in the village still expected Philip to take on these special responsibilities as of right – to read the lessons and take the collection on the big Feast days of the Church, if not every Sunday. As a result, he found it embarrassing to worship as an ordinary member of St. Dunstan's congregation. It was, he supposed, a transitional situation.

So why not go to the Easter Service in the Cathedral? His mind made up, he dressed carefully – choosing the chalk and black stripe tie of the Band of Brothers which looked well with his light country tweed as well as heralding the cricket season. At ten o'clock on Easter morning he set off for Canterbury in the immaculate Black Beauty, with Carla riding beside him.

He was a bit late starting, but why worry? He had a special place for parking at the Poor Priests Hospital and from there it was only a short walk across the High Street, down Mercery Lane and through the Butter market to the Christ Church Gate. He'd make it easily. But he had not visited the Cathedral on an Easter Sunday for many years. As he entered the Precincts, he found himself at the tail of a huge crowd – made up of young and old and very young – pouring into the Cathedral. He had to wait for the Mayor and City Councillors to take their places. The Dean and choir were already moving towards the great West Door to await the Archbishop's arrival. Luckily a cathedral sidesman recognised him towering above the late arrivals.

"Quick, Sir, come this way," he hurried forward. "We've never had a bigger congregation. No seats I'm afraid, but we'll find you a place on the Chancel steps." And it was from this point of vantage that Philip watched the choir and the Cathedral clergy preceding their new Archbishop up the full length of the nave.

He was fascinated by the colour and the dignity of the pageant – almost medieval in its splendour. Then in contrast he watched the Archbishop moving to his place – medium height, moving well,

251

strong face, sense of humour behind his glasses, humble, the very antithesis of the proud prelates who had once dictated to kings from the See of Canterbury. Philip was carried back in spirit to his own boyhood, standing beside Arthur Waddilove and looking up to the high pillars of the Nave, remembering Arthur's words about William of Sens and William the Englishman. Then as the Cathedral echoed to the boys' voices, he returned to the present, just one man among three thousand pilgrims.

He was close to one of the amplifiers and heard every word of the sermon. An Easter text from Mark – 'no nonsense' Mark, Arthur used to call him. Philip listened, spell-bound. The Archbishop's simple language, so concise, so perfectly enunciated, completely held the great congregation. No coughing, no shuffling – you could have heard a pin drop. "Remember always, good Christian people, for all of us the message of Easter concerns the present and the future, not the past."

After the service Philip left by the small door at the south transept, passing on his left the battle honours and the Book of Memory in the Warriors chapel. In a curious way he did not feel alone. For a moment, it was as if he was in the presence of his ancestors. But as he emerged into the sunshine and moved slowly to his car through the crowd of sightseers and worshippers, it was the Archbishop's words that were ringing in his ears – "the present and the future, not the past."

He returned to the Great House in a mood of high elation. He addressed his companion, "Carla, my beautiful girl, Easter is a day for celebration. As a special treat I shall invite you to share my cold beef with me, but not the imperial pint of champagne which I have just opened. I would not like the bubbles to tickle your sensitive nose – I hope you understand." He patted the Labrador, who gracefully caught a slice of cold beef which her master flicked off his knife.

After so ample a lunch he might have slept for a spell. But the sunshine beckoned. With Carla by his side and a stick in his hand he walked across the lawn to the gate opening from the walled kitchen garden, and joined the path leading to the Dower House. Unconsciously, his steps took him along the path he had trodden long ago in his vain quest for Margie.

Across the park to the water-meadows beside the Stour, westwards up-river towards Hogben's farm, then back by the high ground to the south – the past flashed through his mind with its humiliations and disappointments and tragedies. But dominating all his thoughts was the memory of the people who had watched over him as he grew up. His grandmother, Arthur, Gwynedd . . . He was so glad that the little old lady, growing ever smaller in stature as her years advanced, was happy in the cottage where Amos and Margie could keep an eye on her and give her a lift to the Baptist chapel.

His thoughts returned to the present, to the people who had put their trust in him – to Martin, Evan Morgan, Ted Baker (where now was the Shropshire Lad of Hill 601?), to Amos, to Margie, to Susan and Alex . . . Pray God they had chosen the right way into the future.

The climb to the woods tired him – out of training, you know . . . must watch my weight . . . ought to eat less, drink less . . . He was half talking to himself, half talking to Carla as he came out of the woods at the very point from which, forty-five years earlier, he had seen Margie kissing Amos outside the Home Farm.

He sank back exhausted on the slope of the hill, the Labrador slumping down beside him. Slowly, sleepily, his eyes took in the scene. He saw the panorama of spring everywhere; the primroses under the trees on the edge of the wood: below to his right the pear blossom and the well-kept gardens of the Great House (those Italians were one of Evan's greatest ideas): straight before him the park with its clumps of trees bursting into new leaf, and the lake alive with the mating of birds and animals: to his left, Dark's Place and the coronet of wild daffodils that had, since his earliest memories, surrounded the outhouses down there.

His eyes closed. His heavy breathing became uneven, but he slept on. He altered position so that he was sleeping on his back. A strange spasm seized his body and his mouth went slack.

The sleeping Labrador stirred, roused herself and looked at her master. Suddenly, in desperate agitation, she licked his hands and his face. There was no response.

To a dog death is no great mystery. It is something to be understood and accepted. Carla who had been trained to silence, lifted

253

her head in a cry of grief which echoed and re-echoed down the valley, the Last Post sounding for her master. Then with a series of panting staccato barks, she ran in panic down the hill to seek the love and protection of Margie and Amos Williams.